MW01136627

Beyond & Within

FOLK HORROR

Short Stories Edited by
Paul Kane & Marie O'Regan

Beyond & Within

FOLK HORROR

Short Stories Edited by
Paul Kane & Marie O'Regan

FLAME TREE
PUBLISHING

Publisher & Creative Director: Nick Wells
Senior Project Editor: Gillian Whitaker

FLAME TREE PUBLISHING
6 Melbray Mews, Fulham,
London SW6 3NS, United Kingdom
www.flametreepublishing.com

First published 2024
Copyright in each story is held by the individual authors.
Volume copyright © 2024 Flame Tree Publishing Ltd

24 26 28 29 27 25
1 3 5 7 9 10 8 6 4 2

Hardback ISBN: 978-1-80417-732-7
ebook ISBN: 978-1-80417-733-4

The cover image is created by Flame Tree Studio. Frontispiece and detail
on cover is *The Ace of Ivy* © Oliver Hurst 2024.
All other images © 2024 Flame Tree Publishing Ltd.

A copy of the CIP data for this book is available from the British Library.

Printed and bound in China

Table of Contents

Introduction: Folk Horror

Paul Kane & Marie O'Regan

IT'S HARD to remember a time when the term Folk Horror wasn't around.

At least for us, anyway. It's certainly been a part of our lives since we were kids, and anyone who can remember those '70s public information films like Jeff Grant's *The Spirit of Dark and Lonely Water*, or the one-off Nigel Kneale-penned show *The Stone Tape*, or even those *A Ghost Story for Christmas* adaptations of M.R. James classics by Lawrence Gordon Clark, will undoubtedly have been scarred by the phenomenon while they were growing up.

Its use, at least as far as cinema is concerned, can be traced back to a trio of famous – or perhaps that should be *infamous* – movies from the late '60s/early '70s known now as 'The Unholy Trinity': Michael

Reeves' *Witchfinder General*, starring Vincent Price as the notorious witch-hunter Matthew Hopkins; *The Wicker Man* directed by Robin Hardy, starring Christopher Lee and Edward Woodward; and *Blood on Satan's Claw* starring Linda Hayden and Patrick Wymark. In actual fact, it was during production on the latter that a piece appeared in *Kinematograph Weekly* where Rod Cooper referred to the film as a 'study in Folk Horror'; a description director Piers Haggard liked and ran with.

Years later, the term gained a new lease of life when people like Jonathan Rigby and then Mark Gatiss began grouping film and television together under this umbrella – most notably in the 2010 documentary *A History of Horror*. But the origins of all this go back much further in the literary world, to well over a century earlier when the work of anthropologists such as Sir Edward Burnett Tylor and Sir James Frazer, and the Folklorist Margaret Murray, influenced a whole raft of writers to introduce paganism into their fiction. Grant Allen's 'Pallinghurst Barrow' (1892), for example, originally published in the *Illustrated London News* and revolved around something weird or strange buried underneath

Old Long Barrow on Pallinghurst Common. John Buchan's *Witch Wood* (1927) reportedly draws on Murray's Witch-cult hypothesis and features a local woman being accused by a pricker of being a witch, then eventually tortured and killed. And Eleanor Scott's *Randalls Round* (1929) sees a university student taking a holiday in the country and coming across a terrifying pagan ritual at Halloween.

To these we can also add exponents such as the aforementioned M.R. James, Arthur Machen, H.P. Lovecraft, Robert W. Chambers, Shirley Jackson (her short 'The Lottery' is a classic of the sub-genre), right up to people such as Robert Aickman, Thomas Tryon, Andrew Michael Hurley and Francine Toon…

Obviously, different legends stretch back even further depending on which part of the world you're talking about. The famous vengeful La Llorona of Mexican descent, the Slavic Boginka or the mischievous Kitsune of Japan have all been used as jumping-off points for excellent Folk Horror tales.

But what *is* Folk Horror exactly? Is it witches, is it pagan rituals or maniacal cults, folklore, or is it supernatural? Or all of these and more? It's safe to say it means different things to different people, but one aspect much of it has in common is the intrusion of the old into the new world, or more accurately rural into the urban. The veneer of civilisation being stripped away by something ancient and possibly dangerous or threatening; or perhaps it is being replaced by something more reliable, depending on your point of view. It's one of the reasons why Folk Horror crops up in times of high anxiety, usually after a period of celebration – as it did back there in the late '60s and '70s. It's no surprise that there's a resurgence at the moment then, given the turmoil in the world. No wonder movies like *Midsommar* (Ari Aster, 2019), *In the Earth* (Ben Wheatley, 2021) and *Matriarch* (Ben Steiner, 2022), or books like *Hex* by Thomas Olde Heuvelt (2013/16), *The Only Good Indians* by Stephen Graham Jones (2020) and *The Lost Village* by Camilla Sten (2021), seem to have so much resonance at the moment…

And probably why we decided the time was right to gather together a truly unique set of Folk Horror tales ourselves, hopefully reflecting some of the range and diversity that the genre has to offer.

So, author of *American Gods*, Neil Gaiman, gives us a chilling prose poem about the dangers of trust, while erstwhile Charlie Parker scribe John Connolly presents us with a nightmarish story about a horrifying well. Adam L.G. Nevill's tale is set in Sweden, foreshadowing his popular novel (and the superb film based on it), *The Ritual*, and author of *The Cottingley Cuckoo* (as A.J. Elwood), Alison Littlewood gives us a new spin on an old legend with bite. Lee Murray (*Despatches*), Stephen Volk (*The Good Unknown*) and Helen Grant (*Jump Cut*) give us Folk Horror stories connected to their native New Zealand, Wales and Scotland respectively. V. Castro and Christina Sng turn to Mexico and Asia for their inspirations, while *Dog Rose Dirt* author Jen Williams focuses on an unusual aspect of Folk Horror, and the author of *Anchor's Heart* Cavan Scott reworks the idea of the mythical Grim. Finally, Linda D. Addison (*How To Recognize A Demon Has Become Your Friend*) presents us with a chilling and thought-provoking poem to round off the book.

We're also delighted to present stories from new (to us, at least) authors, an exciting part of this particular anthology. So we have Katie Young with 'The Druid Stone', Benjamin Spada with 'The Great White', Kathryn Healy with 'The Lights Under Rachel',

B. Zelkovich with 'The Finest Creation of an Artful God' and H.R. Laurence with 'The Marsh-Widow's Bargain'. We hope you enjoy their contributions as much as we did!

All that remains is to give you a warning. Keeping to well-lit paths won't save you, nor will reliance on the trappings of the modern world. Be careful what you believe in and, above all else...

Beware the woods!

Paul Kane & Marie O'Regan
Derbyshire, January 2024

The White Road

Neil Gaiman

"…I wish that you would visit me one day,
in my house.
There are such sights I would show you."

My intended lowers her eyes, and, yes, she shivers.
Her father and his friends all hoot and cheer.

"*That's* never a story, Mister Fox," chides a pale woman
in the corner of the room, her hair corn-fair,
her eyes the grey of cloud, meat on her bones,
she curves, and smiles crooked and amused.

"Madam, I am no storyteller," and I bow, and ask,
"Perhaps, you have a story for us?" I raise an eyebrow.
Her smile remains.

She nods, then stands, her lips move:

"A girl from the town, a plain girl, was betrayed by her lover,
a scholar. So when her blood stopped flowing,
and her belly swole beyond disguising,
she went to him, and wept hot tears. He stroked her hair,
swore that they would marry, that they would run,
in the night,
together,
to his aunt. She believed him;
even though she had seen the glances in the hall
he gave to his master's daughter,
who was fair, and rich, she believed him.
Or she believed that she believed.

"There was something sly about his smile,
his eyes so black and sharp, his rufous hair. Something
that sent her early to their trysting place,
beneath the oak, beside the thorn bush,
something that made her climb the tree and wait.
Climb a tree, and in her condition.
Her love arrived at dusk, skulking by owl-light,
carrying a bag,
from which he took a mattock, shovel, knife.

He worked with a will, beside the thorn bush,
beneath the oaken tree,
he whistled gently, and he sang, as he dug her grave,
that old song...
shall I sing it for you, now, good folk?"

She pauses, and as a one we clap and we holloa
—or almost as a one:
my intended, her hair so dark, her cheeks so pink,
her lips so red,
seems distracted.

The fair girl (who is she? A guest of the inn, I hazard) sings:

"A fox went out on a shiny night
And he begged for the moon to give him light
For he'd many miles to go that night
Afore he'd reach his den-O!
den-O! den-O!
He'd many miles to go that night, before he'd reach
   his den-O."

Her voice is sweet and fine, but the voice of my
   intended is finer.

"And when her grave was dug –
a small hole it was, for she was a little thing,
even big with child she was a little thing –
he walked below her, back and a forth,
rehearsing her hearsing, thus:
—*Good evening, my pigsnie, my love,*
my, but you look a treat in the moon's light,
mother of my child-to-be. Come, let me hold you.
And he'd embrace the midnight air with one hand,
and with the other, holding his short but wicked knife,
he'd stab and stab the dark.

"She trembled in her oak above him. Breathed so softly,
but still she shook. And once he looked up, and said,
—*Owls, I'll wager*, and another time, *Fie! Is that a cat*
up there? Here puss… But she was still,
bethought herself a branch, a leaf, a twig. At dawn
he took his mattock, spade and knife, and left
all grumbling and gudgeoned of his prey.

"They found her later wandering, her wits
had left her. There were oak leaves in her hair, and she sang,

The bough did bend
The bough did break

18

I saw the hole
The fox did make

We swore to love
We swore to marry
I saw the blade
The fox did carry

"They say that her babe, when it was born,
had a fox's paw on her and not a hand.
Fear is the sculptress, midwives claim. The scholar fled."

And she sits down, to general applause.
The smile twitches, hides about her lips: I know it's there,
it waits in her grey eyes. She stares at me, amused.

"I read that in the Orient foxes follow priests and scholars,
in disguise as women, houses, mountains, gods, processions,
always discovered by their tails—" so I begin,
but my intended's father intercedes.
"Speaking of tales – my dear, you said you had a tale?"

My intended flushes. There are no rose petals,
save for her cheeks. She nods, and says:

"My story, father? My story is the story of a dream I dreamed."

Her voice is so quiet and soft, we hush ourselves to hear,
outside the Inn just the night sounds: An owl hoots,
but, as the old folk say, I live too near the wood
to be frightened by an owl.

She looks at me.

"You, sir. In my dream you rode to me, and called,
—*Come to my house, my sweet, away down the white road.*
There are such sights I would show you.
I asked how I would find your house, down the white
    chalk road,
for it's a long road, and a dark one, under trees
that make the light all green and gold when the sun is high,
but shade the road at other times. At night
it's pitch-black; there is no moonlight on the white road…

"And you said, Mister Fox – and this is most curious,
    but dreams
are treacherous and curious and dark –
that you would cut the throat of a sow pig,
and you would walk her home behind your fine
    black stallion.
You smiled,
smiled, Mister Fox, with your red lips and your green eyes,

eyes that could snare a maiden's soul, and your yellow teeth,
which could eat her heart—"

"God forbid," I smiled. All eyes were on me then, not her,
though hers was the story. Eyes, such eyes.

"So, in my dream, it became my fancy to visit your
    great house,
as you had so often entreated me to do,
to walk its glades and paths, to see the pools,
the statues you had brought from Greece, the yews,
the poplar walk, the grotto, and the bower.
And, as this was but a dream, I did not wish
to take a chaperone
—some withered, juiceless prune
who would not appreciate your house, Mister Fox; who
would not appreciate your pale skin,
nor your green eyes,
nor your engaging ways.

"So I rode the white chalk road, following the red blood path,
on Betsy, my filly. The trees above were green.
A dozen miles straight, and then the blood
led me off across meadows, over ditches, down a gravel path,
(but now I needed sharp eyes to catch the blood –

a drip, a drop: the pig must have been dead as anything)
and I reined my filly in front of a house.
And such a house. A palladian delight, immense,
a landscape of its own, windows, columns,
a white stone monument to verticality, expansive.

"There was a sculpture in the garden, before the house,
a Spartan child, stolen fox half-concealed in its robe,
the fox biting the child's stomach, gnawing the vitals away,
the stoic child bravely saying nothing –
what could it say, cold marble that it was?
There was pain in its eyes, and it stood,
upon a plinth upon which were carved eight words.
I walked around it and I read:
Be bold,
Be bold,
but not too bold.

"I tethered little Betsy in the stables,
between a dozen night black stallions
each with blood and madness in his eyes.
I saw no-one.
I walked to the front of the house, and up the great steps.
The huge doors were locked fast,
no servants came to greet me when I knocked.

In my dream (for do not forget, Mister Fox, that this was
my dream. You look so pale) the house fascinated me,
the kind of curiosity (you know this,
Mister Fox, I see it in your eyes) that kills
cats.

"I found a door, a small door, off the latch,
and pushed my way inside.
Walked corridors, lined with oak, with shelves,
with busts, with trinkets,
I walked, my feet silent on the scarlet carpet,
until I reached the great hall.
It was there again, in red stones that glittered,
set into the white marble of the floor,
it said:
Be bold,
be bold,
but not too bold.
Or else your life's blood
shall run cold.

"There were stairs, wide, carpeted in scarlet,
off the great hall,
and I walked up them, silently, silently.
Oak doors: and now

I was in the dining room, or so I am convinced,
for the remnants of a grisly supper
were abandoned, cold and fly-buzzed.
Here was a half-chewed hand, there, crisped and picked,
a face, a woman's face, who must in life, I fear,
have looked like me."

"Heavens defend us all from such dark dreams," her
      father cried.
"Can such things be?"

"It is not so," I assured him. The fair woman's smile
glittered behind her grey eyes. People
need assurances.

"Beyond the supper room was a room,
a huge room, this Inn would fit in that room,
piled promiscuously with rings and bracelets,
necklaces, pearl drops, ball gowns, fur wraps,
lace petticoats, silks and satins. Ladies' boots,
and muffs, and bonnets: a treasure cave and dressing room –
diamonds and rubies underneath my feet.

"Beyond that room I knew myself in Hell.
In my dream...

I saw many heads. The heads of young women. I saw a wall
on which dismembered limbs were nailed.
A heap of breasts. The piles of guts, of livers, lights,
the eyes, the…
No. I cannot say. And all around the flies were buzzing,
one low droning buzz.
—*Bëelzebubzebubzebub* they buzzed. I could not breathe,
I ran from there and sobbed against a wall."

"A fox's lair indeed," says the fair woman.
("It was not so," I mutter.)
"They are untidy creatures, so to litter
about their dens the bones and skins and feathers
of their prey. The French call him *Renard*,
the Scottish, *Tod.*"

"One cannot help one's name," says my intended's father.
He is almost panting now, they all are:
in the firelight, the fire's heat, lapping their ale.
The wall of the Inn was hung with sporting prints.

She continues:
"From outside I heard a crash and a commotion.
I ran back the way I had come, along the red carpet,

down the wide staircase – too late! – the main door
   was opening!
I threw myself down the stairs – rolling, tumbling –
fetched up hopelessly beneath a table,
where I waited, shivered, prayed."

She points at me. "Yes, you, sir. You came in,
crashed open the door, staggered in, you sir,
dragging a young woman
by her red hair and by her throat.
Her hair was long and unconfined, she screamed and strove
to free herself. You laughed, deep in your throat,
were all a-sweat, and grinned from ear to ear."

She glares at me. The colour's in her cheeks.
"You pulled a short old broadsword, Mr Fox,
and as she screamed,
you slit her throat, again from ear to ear,
I listened to her bubbling, sighing, shriek
and closed my eyes and prayed until she stopped.
And after much, much, much too long, she stopped.

"And I looked out. You smiled, held up your sword,
your hands agore-blood—"

"In your dream," I tell her.

26

"In my dream.
She lay there on the marble, as you sliced
you hacked, you wrenched, you panted and you stabbed.
You took her head from her shoulders,
thrust your tongue between her red wet lips.
You cut off her hands. Her pale white hands.
You sliced open her bodice, you removed each breast.
Then you began to sob and howl.
Of a sudden,
clutching her head, which you carried by the hair,
the flame-red hair,
you ran up the stairs.

"As soon as you were out of sight,
I fled through the open door.
I rode my Betsy home, down the white road."

All eyes upon me now. I put down my ale
on the old wood of the table.
"It is not so,"
I told her,
told all of them.
"It was not so, and
God forbid
it should be so. It was

27

an evil dream. I wish such dreams
on no one."

"Before I fled the charnel-house,
before I rode poor Betsy into a lather,
before we fled down the white road,
the blood still red
(And was it a pig whose throat you slit, Mister Fox?)
before I came to my father's Inn,
before I fell before them speechless,
My father, brothers, friends—"

All honest farmers, fox-hunting men.
They are stamping their boots, their black boots.

"—before that, Mister Fox,
I seized, from the floor, from the bloody floor,
her hand, Mister Fox. The hand of the woman
you hacked apart before my eyes."

"It is not so—"

"It was no dream. You creature. You Bluebeard."

"It was not so—"

"You Gilles-De-Rais. You monster."

"And God forbid it should be so!"

She smiles now, lacking mirth or warmth.
The brown hair curls around her face,
roses twining about a bower.
Two spots of red are burning on her cheeks.

"Behold, Mister Fox! Her hand! Her poor pale hand!"
She pulls it from her breasts (gently freckled,
I had dreamed of those breasts),
tosses it down upon the table.
It lays in front of me.
Her father, brothers, friends,
they stare at me hungrily,
and I pick up the small thing.

The hair was red indeed and rank. The pads and claws
were rough. One end was bloody,
but the blood had dried.

"This is no hand," I tell them. But the first
fist knocks the wind from out of me,
an oaken cudgel hits my shoulder,

as I stagger,
the first black boot kicks me down onto the floor.
And then a rain of blows beats down on me,
I curl and mewl and pray and grip the paw
so tightly.

Perhaps I weep.

I see her then,
the pale fair girl, the smile has reached her lips,
her skirts so long as she slips, grey-eyed,
amused beyond all bearing, from the room.
She'd many a mile to go that night.
And as she leaves,
from my vantage place upon the floor,
I see the brush, the tail between her legs;
I would have called,
but I could speak no more. Tonight she'll be running
four-footed, sure-footed, down the white road.

What if the hunters come?
What if they come?

Be bold, I whisper once, before I die. *But not too bold...*

And then my tale is done.

The Well

John Connolly

THE HISTORY of British archaeology is a curious one. It probably begins with the monks at Glastonbury Abbey, who, upon uncovering some old bones while rebuilding their church after a fire, concluded, somewhat erroneously, that they had discovered the remains of King Arthur. They were followed – rather more successfully – over the centuries by men such as John Leland, the favored antiquary of Henry VIII, and William Camden, the author of the *Britannia* of 1586, and founder of the first society of British antiquaries in 1586. This institution became popular with lawyers, who used it as a front to debate the flaws of the legal system, until James I became aware of its potential for sedition and shut it down. It was long rumored that one Josias Quayle, a minor figure in legal circles of the time, was the man responsible for informing on the activities of his colleagues, although this has never been proved.

After Camden came Robert Plot, the first Keeper of Oxford's Ashmolean Museum in the seventeenth century; John Aubrey, who credited druids with the creation of the kingdom's stone circles; and, in the eighteenth century, William Stukeley, who pioneered the use of excavation to study ancient sites – which earned archaeologists the soubriquet 'barrow diggers' – and was a founder of a new Society of Antiquaries in 1707. Finally, in the nineteenth century, figures such as John Lubbock and Herbert Spencer helped to place the study of the past on a more respectable and professional footing, leading to the establishment of the first chairs of archaeology in British universities.

But the greatest of them all – at least in my opinion, for I knew him well – was Augustus Pitt Rivers, the first Inspector of Ancient Monuments, and it was at his instigation that, in 1884, I led a field club, a mix of amateurs and students of archaeology, to investigate the site of the Familist settlement on the Hexhamshire Moors of Northumberland. What follows is a truthful account of that dig, and the disappearance of Walter Hodges, a student.

May God have mercy on him, wherever he may rest.

* * *

It should be noted that archaeological digs are not without their complexities, and these are not limited to the technical or physical. Quite often, local superstitions attach themselves to ancient sites, leading to a reluctance among the populace to facilitate any examination or excavation. In truth, this kind of objection tends to be more common in the investigation of druidic constructs – and barrows, of course, due to a fear of disturbing the dead.

But in Hexhamshire we were surprised to find this antagonism extended to the foundational site of the *Familia Caritatis*, the Familists, given that they had only come into being in the 1580s, and had largely ceased to exist by the early part of the nineteenth century. We could only attribute such ill feeling to a misplaced conception of the sect that had become ingrained in the locals over the years, including a belief that the Familists had murdered to protect themselves from scrutiny or persecution. Northumberland lore held that among their victims were men and women from the surrounding villages of Corbridge, Bardon Mill, Haltwhistle, and Wylam. Suggestions that these unfortunate individuals might merely have gone astray on the moors, or been taken by some general class of blackguard, were met with skepticism, at best.

The result of this ill feeling was that our little group of five found it impossible to secure accommodations in any of the nearby communities, and resigned ourselves to spending our nights under canvas. Still, I regarded this as no great imposition, because I have always preferred to situate myself in the vicinity of a dig; or this was formerly my penchant, before Hexhamshire.

Pitt Rivers' curiosity about the Familist site was linked to his belief that the sect's presence there had been but the latest in a series of settlements, and excavation might reveal evidence of earlier Roman and pre-Roman communities. I admit it was curious that Familists should have chosen such a remote, harsh location for their church, one that would have left them vulnerable to the predations of border reivers and other outlaws, but it might well have been a consequence of their desire to worship their god of wood and leaf in secret, and without fear of being tortured or killed for their idolatry. Of course, the church they built is now in Maine, in the United States, and the town they founded there, called Prosperous, has apparently been as successful as its name suggests. Its inhabitants, though, are unwelcoming to outsiders, or so I have been informed, and prefer to leave their Familist roots unexplored.

Of the members of our group, Walter Hodges was the youngest, yet also potentially the most gifted. Pitt Rivers had virtually guaranteed Hodges a post as one of his assistants should he achieve a First in his finals, which seemed a foregone conclusion to most. I was a little less enamored of Hodges. I felt his work was sometimes hurried, and he lacked the necessary patience to be a great archaeologist. Perhaps it would have come in time, but we shall never know. Goetz, the other student on what was intended to be this first dig of three, was one year behind Hodges, but one year older, and seemed to bear him some undefined ill will. Goetz was of Prussian descent, and distantly related to Bismarck himself, or so he claimed. Clement and Morgan, meanwhile, were banker and accountant respectively, and enthusiastic members of the fledgling Northumberland Geological, Archaeological, Botanical and Zoological Society, a range of interests which promised more breadth than depth to their scholarship.

We reached the Familist site shortly before noon on the first day, and set up our camp amid the ruins of the settlement. Although it was early April, and growing milder by the day, much of the Hexhamshire Moors are dreadfully exposed, and we believed we might be glad of the shelter provided by the walls. We were not mistaken, for barely had we raised canvas before a wind rose from the east, blowing in off the North Sea, and had we not enjoyed the protection of the ruins our tents might well have been on their way to Wales before too long. We lit a fire, and made a pot of tea to warm ourselves before commencing our preliminary examination.

* * *

It was Hodges who discovered the well, much to Goetz's displeasure.

It lay beneath the floor of the largest structure on the site, which had probably once been home to the sect's leader, one Deakin Carr, a descendant of Christopher Vitell, the head of the principal Familist group in England, based in Balsham, Cambridgeshire. Carr had enjoyed a reputation for violence in his youth, and was briefly ostracized by his own people, who generally favored a lifestyle of tolerance and reflection, and objected to the bearing of arms. He returned to the embrace of the Familists after two or three years, and was adjudged to be a reformed character, yet it may be that something of the sect's unfavorable reputation in Northumberland may be attributed to Carr's earlier failings.

(But I digress, which is a flaw in my character, one that I have struggled, and failed, to address. It may be forgivable under these circumstances, representing a form of prevarication. I leave it for you to decide.)

The mouth of the well was approximately three feet in diameter, and had been disguised with scree and larger stones, including a single slab of slate wide enough to cover the hole entirely. Over this a thick layer of earth had been placed, one that had, by this time, grown a canopy of grass and weeds. How Hodges was alerted to the well's presence, I cannot say. Whatever my concerns about his temperament, he had an almost uncanny eye for a dig, and some small topographical or taxonomical distinction had clearly drawn his attention while Goetz and I were otherwise engaged in visiting the former location of the Familist chapel. Once he had revealed a section of the original floor, Hodges became convinced that other material had been added for the purposes of concealment, and managed to bring Clement and Morgan around to his way of thinking, for amateurs of their particular stripe are always seeking fame by uncovering something that serious archaeologists may have missed. By the time Goetz and I returned, half of the scree had been removed, and part of the well already lay revealed.

I was angry with Hodges; I am not afraid to admit it. His actions only served to confirm for me that Pitt Rivers' indulgence had exacerbated rather than curbed Hodges' worst instincts. Yet once I had recovered my temper, I found myself intrigued by the well. There was no mention of it in the existing records of the site; in fact, another well had been dug to the west of the settlement, one that was still in existence. It was unclear what reason the Familists might have had for digging a second, particularly inside a house.

The answer to this conundrum was provided by a closer perusal of the stones of the well itself, for they were older than those of the dwelling that surrounded them. Goetz speculated that the well might be of Roman origin, at which Hodges resorted to scoffing – not without some justification, it must be said, but it was still unbecoming to see him belittle Goetz in such a fashion. Nevertheless, Goetz should have known better: the stonework was too crude, and bore none of the precision of a Roman hand. No, this well had been dug long before the Romans came. Clement dropped a pebble into its depths, but we heard no sound, no splash. It was as though a hole had been bored to the center of the earth.

But by then it was growing dark, and any further consideration of the well would require daylight. We lit a fire for cooking, and ate ham tossed in the pan with hot jacket potatoes, followed by coffee and brandy. The food and drink eased some of the tensions between Hodges and Goetz, with the former apologizing for his earlier remarks, and Goetz appearing to accept. I had a quiet word with Hodges before we turned in for the night, admonishing him for his haste in acting without my consent, and reminding him of Pitt Rivers' likely displeasure should any damage be done to the site before its examination had even begun in earnest. The mention of Pitt Rivers in such a context seemed to have the desired effect, and brought the second apology of the night from Hodges. I retired to my tent believing a valuable lesson might have been learned.

The disposition of our encampment meant that we were situated in what was formerly the heart of the Familist settlement, and probably a communal meeting place. The walls of the old buildings provided perfect shelter from the wind, and, as stated earlier, I have a fondness for sleeping outdoors, even when my shelter is being tested by the elements, and tend to rest soundly outdoors as a consequence. I was surprised, therefore, to find myself coming awake during the night, and irritated to realize I had been roused from my slumbers by footsteps. I assumed it was one of our party attending to a call of nature, until I heard someone enter the building immediately to my right, the one housing the well. Whoever it was had no business stumbling around there in the dark, even if we had taken the precaution of replacing the flat stone over the mouth, just in case.

The moon shone brightly through the flap of my tent, but still I didn't care to investigate without the benefit of my lamp. Once I had lighted it, I crawled outside to establish the source of the disturbance, and was more disappointed than shocked to find it was Hodges who had woken me. He was standing by the well, his own lamp raised high before him.

"What are you doing?" I said, and was pleased to see him fairly leap into the air with shock.

"I heard noises," he said, once he had recovered himself.

"Noises? What kind of noises?"

"From inside the well."

I listened, but the only sound was the wind on the moors.

"You're imagining things."

"No, I tell you I heard something."

"It might have been an animal. A rat, perhaps."

He looked at me, and I saw on his face the same expression that had accompanied his belittling of Goetz.

"How could a rat climb up the inside of that well?" he said. "And from where might it have climbed?"

He had a point: the interior of the well was not smooth, exactly, but even a rat would have struggled to find purchase. Anyway, that wasn't what I had meant; or at least, I don't believe it was.

"Not *in* the well, man – outside it, among the ruins."

For the first time, Hodges appeared doubtful.

"But I could have sworn it was coming from under the slab," he added.

"It's the wind. It plays tricks with sound." I decided it was time to be conciliatory, not least because it was one thing to be wrapped up warm in my tent, and quite another to be standing in a roofless ruin on a northern night that had not yet fully shaken off the hand of winter. "Come on, now, back to your tent. We'll take another look in the morning."

I placed a hand on Hodges' elbow, and guided him from the ruin. I reminded myself that he was still barely more than a boy, one that might, with the correct tutelage, and some adjustment to his mettle, make a fine archaeologist. Once I was satisfied that he was safely back in his tent, and had advised him against any further nocturnal perambulations, I returned to my own Euklisia Rug, and my rest.

Did I hear a sound before I slept, as of claws scratching against stone?

No, I did not.

I swear it.

* * *

The next day we commenced a full and proper mapping of the two sites: the settlement itself, and the former setting of the Familist chapel. It was a fractious business, not helped by a soft, steady rain that began shortly before 10 a.m. and continued throughout the day. Goetz's previous rapprochement with Hodges fell by the wayside, and the two young men bickered and fought until lunch, after which I deemed it expedient to separate them. Hodges I sent with Clement to secure milk and bread from one of the nearby farms. Curiously, our own supply had spoiled during the night, the milk turning to sour-smelling curds, and the bread becoming entirely moldy, even though both had been purchased fresh the previous day. Meanwhile Goetz and Morgan remained with me, and we made good progress in Hodges' absence, although Goetz's mood showed no signs of improvement, not even when he discovered an inscription carved on one of the stones cast aside during Hodges' attempted excavation of the well. It read 'Cave Veteris'.

"What does it mean?" said Morgan.

"'Beware Veteris,'" said Goetz, which was probably about right. "Who is Veteris?"

"A Celtic god," I told him, "but one mentioned only by the Romans garrisoned by this section of Hadrian's Wall. Sometimes it's written as 'Veteris,' at other times 'Veteres,' suggesting a god of multiple aspects – not unlike our own tripartite deity, one might say."

Morgan blanched a little at the potential blasphemy, but did not voice an objection.

"They raised altars to it," I continued. "It was a cult."

"I thought they had their own gods," said Morgan.

"They did," I replied. "But that doesn't mean they couldn't accept the existence of others."

"And they worshipped this Veteris?"

"They made offerings to it, yes."

"Why?"

I shrugged.

"Because," I said, "one can't be too careful..."

Clement and Hodges eventually returned with some milk, bread, and fresh eggs, although they'd been made to pay handsomely for their acquisitions, and even then were reduced almost to pleading before their money was accepted by the farmer, one Edwyn Hood, and his wife. We stored away the supplies, and I set Clement and Hodges to measuring the little cemetery to the north of the settlement, and taking what rubbings they could from the stones, most of which were now concealed by grass. I estimated that we still had a couple of hours of daylight left, and the earlier absence of Hodges, and to a lesser degree Clement, had cost us valuable time. We would make up some of it while we could.

I was in the process of examining the brickwork of one of the houses, which bore more Roman lettering and was therefore either part of an older, pre-existing structure, or had been scavenged from elsewhere, when I heard a shout from the cemetery, and my name being called. Fearing some accident, I ran in that direction, Goetz and Morgan at my heels, only to find Hodges and Clement upright and apparently unharmed.

"What is it?" I asked.

I joined them, and saw what had occasioned the cry. Before me lay a partially open grave, with two halves of a flat stone, not dissimilar to that which now blocked the well, protruding from the hole, earth and grass still clinging to its surface.

"I felt it give beneath my step," said Clement. "I almost ended up in that hole."

"Probably a fault in the stone," said Morgan, who knew something of geology, as he peered at the exposed edges. "Over the years water gets in. It freezes, thaws, and the flaw deepens."

"Look inside the grave," said Hodges.

I did. I could see bones, of course, because what else would one expect to see in a grave, but they were obscured by some dark cladding, almost like a web.

"What is that?" I asked.

Hodges had a lamp with him as part of his kit. He put a match to it, lay by the graveside, and lowered the lamp. By its glow we could see that the remains were entirely covered by a system of roots, yet they had not grown through the body but had instead wrapped themselves around it, as though swaddling the bones. Beneath the skeleton could be seen fragments of old wood, and another carcass, although this one was not similarly encumbered by nature's embrace.

"It's a woman," said Hodges, pointing at the first corpse. "See the rounded pelvis?"

I could, although it was barely visible through the roots.

"But where did the roots come from?" said Morgan. "I can see no tree, no shrubs."

He was correct. This part of the moors was bare of all but grass.

"Perhaps she was wrapped in them after she died," said Clement.

"No," said Hodges, who remained lying on the ground. "They've definitely grown around her. No human hand did this."

"And why put a stone over it?" said Goetz. "Why not fill in the grave after the body was interred?"

"My God," said Hodges.

He had dipped the light as low as he could reach, until the base of the lamp was almost touching the woman's bones, and we all saw them: the remnants of the bonds used to secure her hands and feet, and the thin leather strap between her teeth.

"She was restrained," said Hodges. "They buried her alive."

* * *

Our meal that evening was a somber one, with little conversation and less bonhomie. We were all thinking

47

of the dead woman and the terrible manner of her passing. Not only had she been interred alive, but also those responsible had wanted her to die slowly. Had earth been piled on top of her, she would have suffocated; still an appalling death, but one that would have taken minutes at most, not days or weeks. And there was the issue of the roots or branches that enveloped her: they had grown around her, but appeared to have no source, unless the parent tree had died so long ago that these roots were the only evidence of its former existence. Even so, one might have expected to see a vestige of their connection to the soil, but there was none. Also, we could find no evidence of decay upon them. The fibers were strong, and a rich brown. Hodges had struggled to cut one with his knife.

Shortly before we retired to our tents, some passing remark of Hodges' caused Goetz to leap at him, and the latter landed a blow before Morgan and Clement managed to separate them. By now I had endured enough, for I could see no sign of relations between the two students improving under the present circumstances. I ordered both of them to return to Oxford first thing the next morning, where they would eventually be given ample opportunity to explain their behavior to Pitt Rivers. In the meantime, Clement, Morgan, and I would remain on the moors to conclude our observations, as an example of how gentlemen and scientists – even those of the amateur persuasion – should behave themselves. We all repaired to our rest in varying degrees of ill temper, and after a time the night was still.

* * *

I opened my eyes. The noise, when it came, was unmistakably human. It was the sound of sobbing.

I ignited my lamp, and for the second night in a row departed my tent in darkness to investigate a disturbance. As before, it came from the ruin that housed the well. I stopped in the doorway. By the light of moon and lamp, I could see that the slab had been removed from the mouth of the well, and to my right a figure was crouched against the wall. It was Goetz.

"What are you doing out here?" I asked, but Goetz did not reply, and only continued to produce low, regular sobs, while his whole body shook. His gaze never left the well.

I moved closer to the hole, and saw a man's boot lying by the edge. It was dark brown, and made by Tricker's of London. Only one of our group wore such a boot: Hodges. Beside the boot was a broken lamp.

I rushed to Hodges' tent, calling his name, but just Clement and Morgan answered my call. Hodges' tent was empty. Together, all three of us returned to the well, and Goetz. I knelt before him.

"What happened? Goetz, where is Hodges?"

Goetz pointed at the well.

"Die Wurzeln," he said. *"Die Wurzeln nahmen ihn."*

"What's he saying?" asked Morgan.

I looked back at the well.

"He says the roots took him."

* * *

I sent Morgan for the police at first light. We were all questioned, although Goetz would speak only German – I could not tell if this was a deliberate attempt at obstruction on his part, or a genuine result of shock; the police suspected it was the former, and I the latter – and so I was forced to translate as best I could. He stuck to his story, which was that he had heard Hodges get up during the night. Some instinct, perhaps the lingering bad blood between them, had caused Goetz to go after him. When he arrived at the well, he found Hodges standing before it, the slab already removed from the hole and lying some three or four feet away, although it would have been too heavy for Hodges to have shifted it so far alone.

"I heard something," Hodges said to him, and then Goetz heard it too, or so he told us. It was a scratching, like nails or claws on a wall. It was coming from the well. He watched Hodges approach the hole, and lift his lamp. Hodges peered over the edge, and Goetz saw a dark tuberous length wrap itself around his right foot. Hodges tried to pull back, which was when his unlaced boot came off, and he fell to the ground. Before he could cry out, a second root coiled around his head, gagging him.

And then Hodges was gone.

They tried Manfred Goetz for the murder of Walter Hodges. He was found guilty, but avoided the gallows due to the intervention of some senior figures in the German government – it appeared he had not been lying about the Bismarck connection after all – aided by the fact that there was no body, and hence only circumstantial evidence of his guilt. He was sentenced to life imprisonment in Pentonville, but in the end lasted only a year before killing himself with a noose fashioned from bootlaces.

Did Goetz murder Walter Hodges? I do not know. All I can say is that I hope he did, pushing the younger man into the well, and Walter Hodges broke his neck when he eventually hit the bottom, or fractured his skull against the walls on the way down. I do not care to think about the other possibility. I do not want to believe that Goetz was telling the truth. I think of that woman's remains, bound by tree roots. I think of the warning on the stone.

I think of it all the time.

These impressions I shared only with Pitt Rivers in his study one night over brandy, not long after Goetz's death, and now I am committing this account to paper. What Pitt Rivers made of my version of the tale I cannot say, for he could be most taciturn when he chose, except that he suspended all further investigation of the Familist site on the Hexhamshire moors, a decision that has remained in force even after his passing. For many years, the Hodges family made a pilgrimage to the settlement on the anniversary of the boy's disappearance, and placed flowers by the well. I came to know Hodges' younger brother a little, after he went up to Cambridge. He told me the flowers would begin to die as soon as they were laid down, and were withered entirely before the last of the prayers were said. Make of that what you will. As for me, I have lived for many years on a top floor flat off Church Street, close to the university that I love. I chose the house because it has no garden.

Make of that, also, what you will.

Rabbitheart

Jen Williams

MIRABELLE didn't know what she'd find in the snare that day, but she knew she would find something.

It had to do with the rain. They often had rain on the farm, even big rain, storms, walls of water that would crash against their house hard enough she half-thought they would be washed away. That day, standing under the lean-to listening to water drum against the corrugated iron roof, Mirabelle had found the rain strange. It fell in a solid curtain across the wheat field, kicking up a seething cloud of dust that rose about knee-high, turning the crops themselves into a muddy yellow haze. Perhaps the rain would wash the wheat away, which would actually be much worse than losing the rickety little house.

As she stood and watched, waiting for it to stop so she could go and check the snares around the cabbages, she began to get the idea that the rain was hiding something. This grey curtain was a hiding place; things were moving, perhaps, that she could not see. That didn't want to be seen.

It made her afraid, and she was just about to turn and go back indoors – the rain clearly wasn't stopping, she would have to check the snares later – when a meaty hand landed on her shoulder, almost pushing her into the dirt. It was her oldest brother, Ron. He smirked at her and let her go, using his free hand to yank at the strap on his overalls.

"You don't want to go out in that, Mira," he said. "Little shrimp like you'll drown."

"I wasn't gonna," Mira said, her voice small. It often shrank in the presence of Ron, who seemed to take up all of the air in a room. From inside the house, she could hear the tinny whine of the radio, which meant Mama was probably feeding little Thomas, the baby. She liked to listen to tunes while she did it, but today the tunes sounded half-drowned themselves. "But I've gotta check the snares."

"Bring us back a nice fat rabbit," Ron said absently. "Do you got your knife? Sometimes they don't die clean."

"I've got it." Mira patted the pocket of her ratty dress. "I've done it before, you know. I'm not a baby."

Ron looked at her properly for the first time, narrowing his eyes.

"Don't much like that attitude off you, Mira. We all got our chores to do, even a little runt like you has to do somethin' around here. You got that? Or should I get Daddy's belt?"

"I got it." Mira took half a step away. She wouldn't put it past Ron to find a reason to beat her, and she thought she'd be willing to run into the rain to avoid it. Ron had thick red hair that fell in waves across his high forehead, and he was quite vain about it. He might not follow her into the downpour. "I don't mean nothing by it, Ron."

Ron opened his mouth to speak, but he was interrupted by a strange noise, a kind of shrieking howl that seemed to cut through the rain like a scythe. It grew louder for a second, becoming almost unbearable, and then it was gone. Just after that, there was a soft flash of yellow light, briefly turning everything beyond the lean-to an insipid, sour colour.

"What was that?"

Ron shrugged. "Just a flash of lightning." Mira noticed he did not meet her eye.

"What was the *noise*? It's not thunder, that comes after, and it didn't sound like thunder neither."

Her brother pushed out his lower lip, then shrugged. Talking about things he didn't understand was something Ron generally tried to avoid. Instead, he slapped her on the back, nearly pitching her into the dirt again.

"There you go, shrimp, the rain is stopping. No more shirking work for you."

Mira looked and saw that he was right. The rain was turning off like a faucet, abruptly reducing to a minor dribble then, as quick as it had arrived, it was gone. There was an expectant quality to the air which made Mira think of the hum of a tuning fork when it had been struck.

"I've got work in the lower field," Ron was saying, although Mira noticed he was digging around in his pockets for his rolling tobacco. Work in this case would mean smoking somewhere out of sight of Mama. "Go check the snares, Mira, and bring us back something juicy."

* * *

The cabbages were on the westernmost edge of the farm, the part that lay alongside the old wood. Mira and her older sister June had set up the snares along the dirt track that ran between, hidden in a handy strip of tall grass. They had figured that rabbits coming from the wood to eat their cabbages would have to pass through this strip of dirt, risking their rabbity necks for something crisp and green.

Mira walked along in the mud, noting the squelching sound as her boots stuck and unstuck, and the peaceful mounds of the cabbages, almost supernaturally green after their recent soaking. The first few snares she checked were empty, and that made her feel a little uneasy. She had no control over what the snares caught, but somehow it would be her fault when she went back to the house empty-handed. There had to be something.

Ahead of her she spotted a white shape lying across the dirt track, shockingly pale against the mud. Initially she took it to be a sheep – one of the Johnson's number, who lived on the other side of the wood. It was a fair trek for a sheep to make, but it wasn't impossible. *If it had gotten into the cabbages there would be hell to pay*, she thought. But then, as she drew closer, she revised her opinion. It couldn't be a sheep. Bones, perhaps? Had the rain uncovered some old cow bones? That would be impressive at least.

Around ten feet away, Mira stopped. The white shape on the ground was a child, although it was unlike any child she had ever seen. He was small and skinny-limbed, his feet and hands and head all appearing to be just slightly too big for his body; he was white like the moon is white, almost glowing with the power of it. The boy lay in the dirt curled up on himself, his big head pressed against his knees, his eyes tightly closed. He was completely nude as far as Mira could see, and one skinny ankle was caught tight in the rabbit snare. She had caught a boy.

"What are you doing there?" she asked indignantly. The boy did not respond. He looked so small and weak. She thought he must be no more than seven or eight years old, but there was something about the length of his limbs and his proportions that kept her from committing to that estimate. The hair on his head was downy and fine, not unlike that of Thomas. Like cornsilk, but white. Like a spider's web. "You can't just be wandering our farm nekkid, boy."

She looked again at the wire of the snare where it was biting into his skin. It had caught him and pulled tight, so tight it must be cutting the blood off to his foot, although she found it difficult to imagine he had any blood in him at all. Kneeling in the wet, she stuck her hand into the mud and yanked up the stake that kept the snare in place. A rabbit wasn't strong enough to move that stake, but a child could do it. *Although, not this child*, she reasoned. *He doesn't look like he's been raised on a farm.*

When it was free she set to dismantling the snare, untwisting the wire to loosen its grip on the boy's ankle. When that was done, she moved to slip the snare over his foot but the second her fingers brushed his ankle he was moving, slithering in the mud like an adder. He sat up, long fingers closing around her forearm like a vice.

"My darling, skin to skin contact with the likes of me is not advised."

His eyes were open, and they were a filmy pink from lid to lid. He was smiling too, revealing small, neat teeth like pieces of white corn.

"What?"

Mira shook his hand off and squirmed away from him. His voice was older than she was expecting. Much older.

"I take it the snare is yours?" The boy looked down at his ankle, where the wire was now hanging loose. His white skin was marked with flecks of black mud. "You've done me a kindness, I note. You could have left me to twist like one of your unfortunate rabbits."

"You can see? With those eyes?" Mira had assumed they were diseased somehow, but when he looked up at her it seemed very likely that he could see all things; that he could probably see right down to her marrow.

"Let's just get rid of this." The white boy slid his long fingers under the loosened wire and pushed it off the end of his foot. He grimaced while he did it, as though touching the metal itself was unpleasant. The snare had left a livid pink ring around his ankle. When that was done he got to his feet. One side of him was thickly covered in mud, and as he stood there he began to shiver violently. "This is a poor state of affairs, I must say."

Mira frowned, eyeing him warily. She didn't like to look but she could see no genitals on him at all, not even an angry little peanut like she had once seen gracing the hairy mound between Ron's legs. Instead the boy was entirely smooth in the space between his legs, and now that he was stood before her he seemed

61

even smaller and more fragile, somehow. She shucked off her denim jacket – made from Pop's old jeans – and pressed it quickly, awkwardly, around his shoulders. It dwarfed him.

"You'd best come back with me, I think."

* * *

When Mira returned to the farmhouse, the strange white boy cradled under one arm, it was to see Allen Mathis coming down their porch steps, his red leather hat folded between his hands. Mathis was a man from the town that everyone knew, because his businesses were, at best, dubious. Why he was at the house, or why Pop was standing at the door watching him leave, was a mystery. Despite herself Mira glanced up at the visitor, and as their eyes met he stopped, a slow grin inching up the side of his face like something spidery crawling out from a dark corner.

"There you are, Mirabelle. Me and your daddy were just talking about you. How are you?"

Mira swallowed hard. Allen Mathis did not even look at the boy by her side. His eyes seemed glued to her.

"I'm fine."

"Fine. Yes." Mathis gave her father – still standing on the porch – a look Mira didn't understand. "You're filling out well for a girl your age, Mira. Well, I'm sure I'll see you soon."

Allen Mathis wedged his hat back on his head and walked away, heading down their dirt track towards town.

"Who's that there?" asked Pop.

* * *

Mama quickly brought the boy in, washed the mud off him, dressed him in some of Mira's old overalls and a shirt that had been washed so often it had no colour left in it. Mama boiled a kettle and gave him hot tea to drink, and smoothed that white cornsilk back from his bony forehead.

Mira was perplexed. She had expected a hullabaloo, a to-do. Ron was out having a smoke still, or whatever it was he was up to, but Pop was there, in his customary seat by the stove, and June was sat at the table, a pile of darning in her lap. Neither of them had said much; they simply watched Mama fuss over the pale boy, their faces slack and their eyes watchful.

"I found him in the rabbit snare," she said again. "Just lying there naked."

"Poor little lamb," said Mama. "They're dangerous, those snares, I've always said so."

"You never did," Mira pointed out quietly. "What's his name even?" She shifted her eyes to the pale boy, who was sat on the good seat with his feet dangling. "What's your name?"

He regarded her with his milky pink eyes. "You can call me Rabbitheart, Mirabelle." Everything about him, she realised, was sly. "That's a special name for you only."

"He looks like a Tommy to me," said Mama, as though the boy hadn't spoken. "Like a Tom."

Mira frowned. She wanted to say *we already have a Thomas*, or *he just told us his name*, but she found she couldn't. Instead she said: "Where is the baby?"

"Sleepin'..." said Pop.

"Like a sweet little Tommy," said Mama. She reached over and brushed the boy's hair back from his forehead again. Rabbitheart didn't take his eyes off Mira. "Where did you come from, sweetie? Your parents must be worried sick. I'll have to send Ron into town to see if anyone's looking for you."

"There's no need," said Rabbitheart. "There will be no one looking for me, Mama, as I have no parents of my own. I'm all alone in this world."

"Oh my, surely not?" Mama leaned forward, and there was something in the movement Mira didn't like. It was hungry, somehow. "How can that be?"

"I'm an orphan," Rabbitheart said solemnly. "I've been wandering for a long, long time, looking for a family."

Mama shifted in her seat. The hungry look hadn't left her.

"Well, we'll just have to see what we can do about that."

* * *

That night Rabbitheart was put into Mira's tiny bed, and she slept on an old mattress on the floor next to it. She lay there for some time, looking up at the small, square window. Her room was the smallest, little more than a cupboard really, and it backed onto the main living area so when her parents stayed up late she would hear them walking about and talking. Through the window she could see the white pinpricks of stars; the storm had moved on and cleared off, as though it had never been there at all.

"Where did you come from?" she said into the dark.

"A distant land," Rabbitheart told her. Thanks to the confines of the room they were close enough that the boy would have to walk across her makeshift bed to get out, but even so she couldn't hear him breathing. Her brother Ron made a huge racket at night, sniffing and snorting and snoring. "It is always twilight there, and the bells are always ringing…" He trailed off.

"That sounds made up. There's no such place."

"Do you see how quickly they make you give up your bed? For a stranger? Not that big lump of a lad, who I strongly suspect could sleep standing up like a horse, but their smallest girl, still growing. And not growing enough, by the looks of you. Do they feed you properly, Mirabelle?"

"'Course they do." Mira frowned. It was true that she went to bed most nights hungry, but Ron and June did most of the work around the farm, so they needed the fuel – that was what Mama said. And little Thomas was growing so fast. Mira, they told her, had always been small and scrawny. She only needed enough to keep a bird alive; that was what Pop said.

"I'll make them pay for it," said Rabbitheart. "Because I have decided you are my particular friend, Mirabelle, and I look after my friends."

"What do you mean by that?" When he didn't answer, Mira sat up, leaning on her elbow. His face looked like a big full moon laying on her pillow, and his unsettling eyes were closed. "What are you going to do?"

But he still didn't reply. After a few moments Mira lay back down again and pulled the thin covers up to her nose.

* * *

The next morning Mama made pancakes for Rabbitheart, drowning them in the last of the maple syrup and cream. Mira watched the plate hungrily – she couldn't remember when she'd last had pancakes – and noticed that Ron too looked somewhat put out by this special treatment, but then it wasn't out of character for Mama to treat guests this way, on the rare occasions they had them. The boy held the knife and fork awkwardly, as though he'd never used cutlery before, and when he put the first chunk into his mouth he just sat with it, his cheeks bulging slightly. After a moment he began to chew laboriously, his pinkish eyes wet at the corners.

"There you go, Tommy." Mama beamed, and poured some black coffee into a tin cup for him. All the children drank coffee as soon as they could stomach it; they all needed to be up with the dawn. "We'll soon get some colour in those cheeks."

"I doubt that somehow," rumbled Ron. "You could leave that boy in the fields all summer and he wouldn't catch a tan. You can tell. He's one of them albinos, Mama. They're unlucky."

"Unlucky? Nonsense."

"What are you going to do with him?" asked June. She had Thomas, the baby, in her arms, jostling him slightly to keep him quiet. "We can't just keep any waifs and strays that get lost in our fields."

"He's got no one else." Mama moved so that she was standing behind the boy, her strong hands curled around the back of his chair. "We always need more bodies on the farm, don't we? We'll feed him up, get him good and strong, and then he can work with you and Ron and Mira."

Ron looked dubious. "Mama, I don't think a whole farm's worth of steaks could get that boy strong enough to lift an empty kettle. Look at him!"

Mira took a sip of her own coffee, dark and bitter on her tongue. There was never enough sugar for her.

"Don't talk such nonsense, he'll be fine," Mama said. "Tommy just needs to eat up what we give him and he'll soon be putting you to shame, Ron."

But Tommy, as Mama insisted on calling him, was bending his head back towards his plate, a strange expression on his white face. He jerked forward in one convulsive movement and vomited the half-digested pancakes over the table. Mama jumped back, alarmed, while June made a noise of revulsion. Mira looked at the ruined remains of the uneaten pancakes, now covered in sick; it seemed like a terrible waste.

"Oh goodness, Tommy, do you have a stomach bug or something?" Mama had knelt next to Rabbitheart and was wiping the corner of her apron across his mouth. The boy sat there and let himself be cleaned, a docile expression on his face. "This food is too rich for your blood. I should have known that. I'll have to find you something else, that's all."

* * *

When breakfast was done, the three children were hustled out the front door to their various tasks, while Rabbitheart hung back with Mama. Mira went to muck out the goats, a chore she found more attractive than many of the others around the farm; the goat mess wasn't pleasant, but she did like the goats, who were boisterous and curious, butting their bony heads into the flat of her hand. After that she went and found June at the back of the house; the girl was patching old sacks so that they could be reused. Her deft fingers moved ceaselessly over the fabric, not even pausing when she looked up at Mira's approach.

"What do you want, Mira-mouse?"

"Don't you think he's weird? That boy?"

June shrugged, turning back to her patching.

"You know what Mama's like. Got a weakness for little ones. Boys especially."

Mira knocked her boots against the back step, dislodging some pieces of mud and goat dung. It was a fine, warm day, likely to be uncomfortably hot by the middle of the afternoon.

"But he don't sound like a little boy. He doesn't speak like one."

"Foreign folk are strange," replied June. "Don't you have anything better to do than buzz around me? Go on now."

Leaving her sister to her work, Mira headed towards the front of the house again, intending to wash her hands a second time under the pump, and saw that Mama was sitting out on the porch with Rabbitheart in her lap. It was a curious sight. The boy was small, but he was still much too big to be cradled in a lap, his long, bony legs hanging down between Mama's, his slim white hands laying limp on top of his thighs. And then with a start Mira saw that Mama had her shirt pulled to one side, and Rabbitheart had his face pressed to her bosom. She was breastfeeding him.

"Mama!"

Her mother looked up sharply. "What do you want, girl? I don't want you disturbing Tommy."

"What are you *doing*, Mama?"

Abruptly Mira felt like crying. There was a soft, obscene sound as Rabbitheart let the nipple slip from his mouth. She couldn't read the expression on his face. Mama, however, looked exasperated.

"Oh come now, Mirabelle, you've seen me nursing your little brother for months." Mira noted that she didn't call Thomas by his name. "Are you suddenly squeamish? Don't be so ridiculous. I thought we had raised you to have more sense than that." Mama looked down at Rabbitheart, pushing her chin into her neck to do so. She smiled at him fondly, and in the shadows under the porch her skin had a greenish hue. "What could be better for a growing boy than mother's milk? If he can't stomach solid food right now, this will do nicely."

* * *

That night, Mirabelle woke in the early hours before dawn to find Rabbitheart missing from her room. Feeling stricken with fear for reasons she couldn't quite name, she slipped out from under her blanket and tip-toed through into the kitchen area. The old Crisco clock they'd saved up coupons for ticked away the seconds from its place on the wall, and the faucet dripped; otherwise nothing else was moving. Mira went up the stairs slowly, keeping to the boards she knew creaked the least, and peeked into each of the rooms. Ron was sleeping face-down on his narrow bed, his usual snoring a subdued rumble softened by the covers; Mama and Pop were indistinct shapes in the gloom, with Thomas' cot pushed into the far corner.

She found Rabbitheart in June's room. Mira's older sister was curled up on her side asleep, her usually stern face turned towards the wall and her long chestnut brown hair laid on the pillow behind her. The boy was kneeling by the bed, his head just behind June's, and he had a mouthful of her hair, which he appeared to be chewing slowly. When Mira stepped into the room, forgetting to be quiet in her surprise, he lifted his face towards her, his mouth filled with long dark strands – almost black in the dim light.

Mira felt a flutter of something frantic high up in her chest, like a trapped bird.

What is he? What does he want?

Rabbitheart smiled around the hair, his lips curling into a joyless crescent. Pieces of June's hair fell onto the pillow as though they had been cut with a knife.

They were wet.

* * *

The week crept by, and then two weeks. Mama continued to breastfeed Rabbitheart; Ron made a mild protest, complaining that the boy was much too old for such attention, and Pop gave some noises of agreement, but Mama was set on the path and would not be moved. Rabbitheart, for his part, said very little, at least in front of the rest of the family, and he did indeed seem to be filling out. His long stick limbs were growing thicker, and his large head started to look less incongruous above his bony shoulders. The white hair that so thinly covered his skull grew thicker, and with a tinge of colour that could have been blond; the fine, golden sheen of wheat, perhaps. His eyes were still pink and filmy, but they too seemed to be darkening in the centres, as though something else were coming through. Mama, meanwhile, seemed to be moving in some other, unknown direction. Her skin was greenish – it hadn't been a trick of the light after all – and she had become very quiet, saying very little and often staring off into space at odd moments. Sometimes she would go so still that Mira would be filled with panic. It was as though her mother had briefly become something inanimate, a woman shelling peas carved from green marble, left to lean carefully against the dining table. June did not talk about her hair, and got angry if Mirabelle brought it up; it was clear to Mira that there were patches missing, and her older sister also had a sallow complexion.

As Rabbitheart got stronger and put on weight, he spent more time outdoors with the men. Mira watched as Pop led him by the hand out into the fields, where no doubt he was lectured on the importance of soil and grains and the vagaries of the weather. When they returned from these excursions, Pop moved a little slower, taking slightly longer to climb the wooden steps to the porch, and at mealtimes he would often stare at his food for a while as though he'd forgotten what it was for. Rabbitheart continued to feed from Mama, even as he gained inches to his height, until when he sat in her lap his long feet could rest fully on the ground.

One day they had another rainstorm. Not as apocalyptic as the one that had announced the arrival of Rabbitheart, but a real belter all the same, churning up the dirt track into a long river of mud and thundering on the corrugated iron roof of the porch. When it was over, disintegrating into gusts of drizzle, Mira stepped down into a puddle, letting the water seep into her old boots. She felt electric, and on edge. Every day her life seemed to fall further off-kilter while every other member of her family kept on with their chores; tending the fields, feeding the goats, collecting the eggs. And all the while they grew quieter, stiller. Once, a few years ago, Mira's grand-aunt had taken her into town to see a museum, and she had wandered, rapt, around a huge room that contained glass cases filled with all manner of strange objects. Sometimes, after dinner, their living room reminded her of that museum – here there were things that had once contained life, perhaps, but were now unmoving.

She heard a soft tread on the boards behind her, and turned to find Rabbitheart standing there. Dressed in more of the family's old clothes, he could almost be mistaken for a real person. There was a faint pink blush across the tops of his cheeks.

"What are you doing to them?" she asked quietly.

Rabbitheart smiled. "Look at that, the sun is coming out. That's what I like to see in this world, the way the weather changes. We never get that back home, you see. It's all very dull." He took a long breath in through his nostrils, flaring them slightly. "Mirabelle, I am just doing what your mother wants. I am feeding. I am getting stronger."

"I don't... She doesn't mean like *that*."

"Doesn't she?" He shrugged. "She's very giving, your mother. Very generous."

"Why don't you just go away?" Mira lowered her voice to a hiss. "I don't want you here. No one does. Just leave us alone."

"Really, Mirabelle? You want to be left to your neglectful family, who barely notice you are here? I don't believe that's true."

At that moment, the door to the house opened and shut, and Ron came out to join them. Even he, normally so huge and solid and loud, seemed quieter; reduced somehow. Mira wondered what Rabbitheart was doing to him in the night, because surely he was doing something – but if he was eating her brother's hair, there was no sign of it.

"What are you doing in that mud?" Ron demanded, although without much fire. "Mama will be furious if you bring that muck back into the house on your boots, Mira."

Mira opened her mouth to reply, but Rabbitheart spoke smoothly over her. Much of the archness was missing from his voice when he spoke to the other members of the family.

"I don't want to get *my* shoes mucky, Ron. Will you carry me over to the back field?"

Ron considered a moment, and then crouched where he stood so that Rabbitheart could climb onto his back. To Mira it was like watching a pale spider scramble up her brother's tall frame, and she felt a shudder of revulsion pass through her as the boy wrapped his long arms around Ron's neck. He leaned forward to press his pale cheek to Ron's whiskered jaw, all the while keeping his eyes on Mira.

"Thank you, Ron." He nuzzled the larger man, like a cat, and Ron stumbled forward slightly, his eyes glazed.

"Let's get you out to that back field," he said, before trudging out into the mud.

* * *

Mira ran.

It was all she could think to do. It was a long way to the nearest town, but the town contained people like church men, police officers, doctors; folk who could perhaps help her family, or at least listen to her. She was sure that Pastor Blevins, for example, would hear her out even if her story sounded strange or unbelievable; it was Pastor Blevins who insisted that the Devil's agents were constantly at work in the world, and if Rabbitheart was anything, surely he was a devil? An unlikely demon come to eat her family up.

The mud on the dirt track was thick and treacherous, but she got down to the edge of the main road with only two slip-ups – each one plastering her dress in solid black muck – and arrived panting at their blue and yellow mailbox. She had time to note that it was stuffed with mail, that clearly no one had collected it in days, when the air began to ring with the sound of bells. Softly at first, a gentle jingle like the Santa Claus float at Christmas, and then louder, and louder. Mira cast around for the source, but the main road was empty, and she could see nothing that might be causing the noise. Instead, she noticed that the sky above her was turning the pearly lavender of twilight, even though it couldn't be more than midday at the latest. She looked up to check that yes, the sun was high in the centre of the sky where it was supposed to be, and the bells grew piercingly loud, as though to punish her for looking.

Mira fell to her knees, clutching her head. It was like being beaten, and when she pulled her hands away she expected to see blood on her fingers, surely leaking from her abused ears. Weakly, she shuffled back from the road, and the sound of bells lessened a tiny degree.

It was a warning. A barrier. A snare for unwary rabbits like her. There was no leaving. Not yet.

Covered nearly head to toe in mud, Mira made her way slowly back down the dirt track, the sound of bells gradually fading from her aching head.

* * *

When she arrived back at the farmhouse, Mira was not especially surprised to discover the bodies of her family, lying dead in the dirt.

They were green and quiet and still. When Mira bent down next to her mother and tapped her face, she found that the skin had hardened. It was like touching the shell of an egg, or a seed. Mira felt very still herself, as though everything inside her had stopped. The only one that was absent was the baby, Thomas, although she could hear him crying lustily from somewhere inside the house.

"They're nearly ready," said Rabbitheart from behind her. When she turned she found him standing on the edge of the wheat field, a shovel in hand. He had already dug four holes in amongst the crops; not wide, from what she could see. But they were deep. She was willing to bet that.

"Why?" The word dropped from her mouth like a stone. Her lips felt numb. "*Why?*"

"I'm growing you a new family," said Rabbitheart, easily enough. "A better one. Won't that be nice?"

Mira began to shake. Rabbitheart watched her for a moment, his strange eyes considering, and then he put down the shovel.

"Come with me, Mira. I want to show you something."

* * *

Inside the house it was quiet; Thomas had finally exhausted himself with crying and was making do with tired, snuffling noises. Mira followed Rabbitheart through the front room to the stairs, thinking that the place seemed like a museum again: people had lived here once perhaps, but not for a long time. On the first floor, he led her into Mama and Pop's room and, ignoring the whingeing baby, he went instead to the small, battered desk that her parents kept their papers in. There were still receipts scattered across it, and a tin cup half full of coffee sat on the edge.

"What is it?" Mira asked. She was wondering about the bells that had stopped her leaving the farm. If she put cotton wool in her ears, would she make it through? "What could you possibly have to show me?"

"I heard them talking to each other about it," said Rabbitheart. He reached into one of the drawers and pulled out Pop's business book, the one where he wrote up every penny the farm made or lost. It had a blue, ink-stained cover. "They thought nothing at all of speaking in front of me, your father and your brother. I think they thought me a halfwit." He opened the business book to a certain page and handed it to her. "The third row down, my darling Mirabelle."

She recognised her father's handwriting easily enough. In the row where he normally listed the things the farm sold – wheat, eggs, cabbages, goats – he had listed her name. In the row where he listed who had purchased their products – whether it was old Missus Duckett from up the road or the general goods store in town – he had written 'Mr. Allen Mathis'. The selling price was three hundred dollars.

"I... what does that mean?"

"Do you know the business Mister Mathis conducts, Mirabelle?" Rabbitheart frowned. "Being a good girl, a sweet girl – the sort of girl that would free a strange boy from a rabbit snare – I doubt that you do. And believe me when I tell you that you would not have enjoyed the life your dear parents were attempting to sell you into."

Mirabelle looked at her father's writing again. At the end of the row, he had written a date some ten months in the future. Her fifteenth birthday.

She closed the book.

In the end, she helped him. Together they dragged Ron's stiff, greenish body to the hole and then upended him, sending him feet first into the ground. He slid in and fit snugly, like a round peg in a round hole, and Mira was reminded of sowing cabbage seeds, or pushing wooden poles into the dirt to grow sweet peas. Together they fitted him with a flat cap of earth, and moved on to Mama, and June, and Pop. When they were all safely planted away, Mira fetched the watering can and added a sprinkle of water to the already damp earth. It seemed like the right thing to do.

"Now is the growing season," said Rabbitheart when they were done. "But in my land, the seasons are all much of a muchness. This shouldn't take long at all."

* * *

Over the next few days, Mira watched, fascinated, as four thick green shoots sprouted from the burial mounds. They were the greenest things she had ever seen, making everything around them seem dowdy by comparison, and they shot up, reaching for the sky like thirsty rockets. Huge fleshy green leaves unfurled by the third day, and the stems thickened up to support them until the plants were enormous. On the fourth day, buds were apparent, and on the sixth the strange plants flowered; long, spindly lavender petals, almost like a thistle, burst from tight green pockets. Mira leaned in to smell them, and then took a hurried step backwards. They smelled like rotten flesh, sweet and sickly.

On the eighth day, there were seed pods. They hung beneath the exhausted flowers like engorged green beans, each as long as Mira herself. Sometimes, when she watched them – which was quite often – she saw them twitch, like a dog in the midst of a dream.

And then on the tenth morning, Rabbitheart woke her up at sunrise, a broad smile on his face. In the early morning light she had a moment to note how much he had changed since she had found him in the rabbit snare – his head was no longer bulbous or strange, and his blond hair curled around his ears like any farmer's son. Together they went out to the wheatfield – the wheat itself had withered away and died, all of it, around the second day – and stood before the plants. The third seed pod was moving, convulsing almost.

"It's time, Mira," Rabbitheart said softly. "Are you ready? These will be the first of your new family."

The pod split along its bottom-most edge, and a slippery white shape slid out onto the dirt below in one sudden movement. It was a child, or a child-shaped thing at least. It had skin the colour of snow, and its eyes, when it opened them, were pink.

"How many will there be?" Mira asked. The thing in the dirt mewled and wriggled. "In the end, I mean?"

"Oh Mirabelle," said Rabbitheart. "Now that we've found the way through, our numbers will be unending."

The Original Occupant

Adam L.G. Nevill

REASONS for the male midlife crisis are well documented, so I need not trouble the reader with too detailed an interpretation of the affliction. But the consequences arising from the death throes of youth, and an individual's grapple with a more precise awareness of its own mortality, were extraordinary in the case of William Atterton. Word of his dilemma came to me through Henry Berringer.

William Atterton, Henry Berringer and I were all fellows of St. Leonard's College and shared the same alumni affiliations, including a club in St. James where Henry and I enjoyed a regular dinner on the first Friday of each month, complemented by a stroll along the Mall with cigars to close. There were many predictable aspects to our dining ritual, chief among them a discussion of Atterton and the precarious life he led.

It was towards the end of June that Henry updated me on the latest 'Atterton news'. Only a few weeks earlier Henry had bumped into our mutual acquaintance in Covent Garden carrying 'a hundredweight' of travel books and self-sufficiency manuals. Over an impromptu luncheon, Atterton told Henry of his intention to resign from his position in the City in order to pursue a "far simpler existence in the sub-arctic forests of Northern Sweden. Four seasons, if nothing else. I'll see it through for one entire year. And for the first time in ages I'm going to be aware of my surroundings, Henry. The changes in nature, the sky, the birdsong, the very air—"

"The ice and snow," Henry was compelled to interject.

"Yes, damn it! The ice and snow. And I shall lovingly observe every crystal and flake at my leisure."

"Which will be considerable," said Henry. "Would not a couple of weeks or even a month out there be more prudent?"

"No! I'll not be one of those look-at-little-me chaps, alone in a cabin for a fortnight. You won't understand,

Henry, but I'm realising more and more that my whole life has been a matter of compromise and half-measures. To tell you the truth, I'm not sure I ever pursued a real dream of my own. I can't even recall how I came to be this person, or what I ever wanted to do in life. But I do know one thing: that after thirty years in the City I've not done it."

On hearing this news, I immediately drew the same conclusions as Henry. We were both unsure precisely what Atterton was escaping from this time, because this plan certainly had the makings of an escape and there were plenty of reasons for one. Though I risk sounding like a gossip, Atterton had always been something of a meddler. Particularly in the pockets of others. Some years ago, he made property speculations in which several dear friends lost considerable sums of money. His involvement in a restaurant is alleged to have caused its swift closure, and his mismanagement of several accounts led to the impoverishment of at least one pension fund. To exacerbate his fiscal troubles, at the start of what we shall call his *crisis*, there was evidence of meddling both in a friend's marriage and then with a colleague's daughter, working as an intern at his firm, with barely a weekend to spare between the two affairs. As to his resignation from the company, there has been some talk in the City that it was not entirely a matter of choice.

But during discussion of this Scandinavian venture, Henry had never seen the man's face so animated. He described Atterton's eyes as being fixed with a peculiar quality akin to euphoria. Atterton was a committed man.

"And what, dare I say, will you do for one entire year in the woods?" Henry had asked him, shortly before paying the bill for their lunch. This was the only question that Atterton wished to be asked on the matter. Beside his fondness for Thoreau's *Walden*, and his long-eulogised backpacking holiday in Scandinavia as a student, Atterton had this to say: "Walk. Swim in the Alvar. Sleep outdoors. Explore. Get back to my sketching. I haven't touched a pencil in twenty years. There won't be enough hours in the day. And you should see the place I have purchased for my exile, Henry. What they call a *Fritidshus*, or *Stuga*, meaning summer house. It's thirty kilometres from the nearest town, and situated in a prehistoric forest festooned with runestones. There's even a wooden church that has been around since the fourteenth century. I shall be suffering from brass rubber's elbow by the end of summer."

Henry was beginning to share Atterton's excitement and feel the first twitches of envy, until he inquired how they might stay in touch.

"Now there's the rub, Henry. No phone masts where I'm going. And I'm not even connected to the mains. I shall be drawing my bath from a well, running a generator on oil and cooking my freshly caught fish on a wood-fired stove. It's all very basic. I plan to spend my evenings by the fire, Henry, reading. I'm taking the complete works of Dickens and Tolstoy for starters. So I anticipate we will be corresponding by letter."

Henry was not the sort of man to dampen a friend's spirits, but as Atterton held forth about his plans for isolating himself in the backwoods of another country, he was filled with a schoolmarmish suspicion that things had not been properly thought through.

"I want to be tested again, Henry. Really tested." As indeed he was, but not in the manner that he anticipated.

* * *

So, in early August, into the wild ventured Atterton, accompanied by a large collection of books and several cases of warm clothing, leaving Henry with the sole task of checking on his flat in Chelsea to flush the toilet from time to time, and attend to other matters in a bachelor's absence. And so too, towards the end of August, began their correspondence. Which swiftly failed to take the course that either man envisaged.

I spent the remainder of the summer and most of autumn abroad, but on my return Henry and I fell into our first Friday of the month routine. But my dear friend was much changed. At his request, we took possession of a table close to the kitchens of the club's dining room, rather than our usual seats overlooking Green Park. During dinner Henry also displayed all the signs of high agitation, which were only partially relieved when the staff closed the curtains. "I tell you, I've had enough of damn trees in a high wind," he said, and waved away my invitation to take our stroll along the Mall. Instead, we retired to the library with a decanter of brandy, where he promised to explain his mood and the events of the summer, which served as the cause of his discomfort. It became immediately apparent that Atterton, or 'poor Atterton' as Henry now referred to him, was to be the sole topic of conversation as tradition dictated. Only this time the tale Henry told was different from any other that I had ever heard, and must have influenced my decision to take a cab home to Knightsbridge, forgoing my usual walk home around the leafy perimeter of Hyde Park.

"I can well understand a sophisticated man's desire for solitude in a more natural environment, and even his yearning for a more historical way of life, but I did fear that a lack, or, in Atterton's case, a total absence of society could lead to an excess of inner dialogue, which can only result in one's consciousness turning upon itself. And during our brief correspondence, it appeared that just such a thing had befallen the poor fellow.

"There were three letters, and only the first one contained any trace of his initial enthusiasm for this Swedish venture. I can be prone to an underestimation of my fellow man, but it was never the selection of supplies, gathering of fuel, the workings of the generator or the outdoor orientating skills that gave him trouble. On the contrary, during his second week out there, he'd removed a ghastly decoration of horseshoes from the property, was repainting the house in the traditional deep red of the area and replacing roof slates with an enthusiasm befitting a scout on a camping trip. He was hiking well into the bright nights, had begun fishing in local waters and had completed the Everyman editions of both *Bleak House* and *Little Dorrit*.

"But after reading the second letter, I couldn't help but suspect that Atterton had become uneasy in his surroundings. The valley – no more than twenty kilometres across, in northeastern Jämtland – was entirely cut off. I mean, that was the whole point, to get away. But the area's sparse, and mostly elderly, population seemed to have exercised a wilful obstinacy in remaining divorced from modern Sweden.

"Despite the incredible beauty of the land, and its abundance of wildlife, Atterton believed that the local population were committed to turning tourism away at the door. Atterton's Swedish was almost non-existent, and their English was uncharacteristically poor for Scandinavia, so what little contact he had with his nearest neighbours, during his walks, was only ever conducted at the border of the valley, and he found it to be entirely unsatisfactory in nature. The people there had either taken to some sect of Protestantism with a fanatical bent, or were observing the dictates of some kind of folklore to an irrational degree. They spent far too much time in church, and any building or fence or gate he came across on his wanderings was festooned with iron horseshoes.

"And what's more, they seemed wary of him. Not afraid of him, but *for him*, he felt. Once or twice, at the general store and post office, that he cycled ten kilometres to reach, he'd been told about 'bad land', or some kind of 'bad luck' in the area. An elderly man who had learned some English in the merchant navy advised him to leave well before the end of September, when what little summer congress that frequented those parts would migrate to other places before the long night fell. What was equally alarming was the manner in which other Swedes appeared only too happy to avoid the place. Odd, considering the plethora of standing runestones and several wooden churches of immense antiquity dotted about the woods. Even trails for hikers seemed to circumnavigate the region on every map.

"Atterton did admit, however, that his curiosity about the region far outweighed his reservations; a remark which sounded a chime of alarm inside me, knowing how our mutual friend could be impervious to reason and logic in his passing enthusiasms.

"Anyway, another four weeks passed before I received the next letter. And moments after reading his hastily scribbled handwriting, I made a cursory inspection of airline timetables and looked into car hire in Northern Sweden.

"Here, see for yourself." Henry handed me the third letter from Atterton.

Dear Henry

I plan to be gone from here by the week's end. I anticipate arriving in London a few days after you receive this letter. I cannot alarm you any more than I have alarmed myself, Henry, but there is something not right about this place. With the late sun gone, the valley has begun to show me a different face. I no longer spend much time outdoors if I can help it.

Do not think me foolish, but I am not at all comfortable with the trees after midday. As for this wind, I had no idea that gusts of cold air could create such a sound of violence amongst deciduous woodland; it's unseasonably strong and cold too for autumn, and savage. The forest is restless, but not quite in the same way that a wood is animated by air currents alone; I believe the core disturbance comes from the standing stones.

They were benign in midsummer; though even then I was not particularly fond of that hill on which the circle stands. But I have made the very grave error of visiting that place when the sun is behind the clouds or going down. And I believe I may have interfered with some kind of indigenous custom.

I can only imagine that it was some of the locals who had tethered the pig inside the stones. You see, while I was out walking yesterday evening, I heard the most desperate and baleful cries, carried on the north wind from the direction of the circle. I went up and found a wretched boar tied to the central plinth. Surrounded by enough dead fowl, strung up between the circle of dolmens, to satisfy a large appetite. Some kind of barbaric ritual in progress. The plinth had been literally bathed in the blood of the birds. I found it appalling. So, I cut the boar free, and wished him well as he made haste into the forest. But, in hindsight, I believe he had been installed there for my protection. As some kind of trade.

You see, the entire time I was among the stones, I felt that I was being watched. You get an extra sense out here in the wild, Henry. You come to trust it. And I believe the scent of blood, and the shrieking of a pig, had attracted something else to that place. I felt a presence in the wind that seemed to come at me from all points of the compass. Air that cut to the bone and left me damp inside my clothes and hair and the very marrow of my bones.

I didn't hang around. I set off for home feeling more peculiar than I can adequately describe. To be honest, I became more frightened than I had ever been as a child at night. But my fear was combined with a sort of disorientation, and a conviction of my utter insignificance out here amongst these black trees. The noise of them, Henry. It felt like I was being shipwrecked by an angry sea.

I'd not gone far before I heard a dreadful commotion from the direction in which I had just come: the freed boar in some considerable distress. Though it sounded frightfully like a child at the time. Then its cries ceased with an abruptness worse than the preceding shrieks.

I fled. Fast as I could. Ran till I thought my heart would give out. Cut my head badly on a tree branch and smashed up a knee on a tree root when I fell. And through the trees the cold air chased after me. Along its whining gusts came a howl of a nature that I am convinced will echo within me for some, if not all, time. There are wolves and bears and arctic foxes this far north. Perhaps I had even heard a wolverine, or so I told myself. I've heard the baying of jackals and the roar of great baboons on safari too, but yesterday I was ready to wager that nothing in the animal kingdom could utter such a cry in the mêlée of the hunt. There was an awful note of triumph in it. And I'm convinced that whatever issued the howl followed me back here, Henry. Last night I heard something outside, in the paddock at the rear of the house. And this morning, I found prints. Not even bears make such tracks.

Suffice to say I have seen and heard enough. This Friday I shall make my way to the airport in Östersund. By then, the rest of my things will be packed and the house shuttered for the winter. The sun is still bright and strong in the morning and I can sense things are more reasonable here at that time of day. I shall wobble and wince up to the post box this morning on my bike to post this letter. And while I am there, I shall arrange from the callbox for the transport company to come for me and my gear in two days' time.

Your fond friend
William Atterton

In silence I passed the letter back to Henry, and he continued with his story.

"I waited anxiously for the week to end and even made a hasty call to the Swedish consulate, only to discover the nearest local authority to Rådalen was some eighty kilometres away from Atterton's *Fritidshus*. As I had no crime or accident to report, and was frankly too embarrassed to paraphrase the content of his third letter over the phone, I decided it best I set off for Sweden myself the following Monday. Even if we passed each other in transit, so be it; I'd like to think that one of my own friends would act as I did, should they ever receive a letter of a similar nature from me, while I'm abroad. The least I could do was accompany poor Atterton home and assist him in procuring professional treatment for his nerves.

"On the first plane to Stockholm early on Monday morning, an elderly Swedish gentleman sitting beside me asked if I required any assistance with the map that I'd spread across my lap. He had seen me struggling with four reputable travel guides too, in which I sought some information about Rådalen. There was mention of the counties inside Norrland, but little on Jämtland, and nothing at all on Rådalen. So I took advantage of the passenger's kind offer and made some inquiries about getting to Rådalen. To which the gentleman immediately asked me a question as direct as his gaze. 'And why would you wish to see Rådalen?' Just like most of his fellow countrymen, the man spoke excellent, direct and concise English.

"I was temporarily at a loss for an explanation, but the gentleman informed me that he was originally from the south of Jämtland, though hadn't lived there since his teens and rarely visited any more. But though most of Sweden was ignorant of the reputation of Rådalen, those of his generation who originated from the area were unlikely to forget the stories that they were told as children. Many other parts of Sweden were more *amenable* to visitors, he said, than Rådalen. As a youth, he was forbidden to ever roam that far north.

"Of course, I humoured the man, and tried my best to keep an expression of scepticism at bay. I asked him for more detail about this *reputation* and mentioned my friend's recent residence there.

"He proceeded to tell me of things that had survived in the oral tradition, as opposed to those recorded by historians, which detailed the survival of... I guess you would call it folklore, or a belief system that had been observed long before the aggressive colonisation of Sweden by the Christian Church. Apparently, even during the early twentieth century, animal sacrifice was still common at the end of each summer to placate the original occupants of the forests, prior to the privations of winter.

"It was claimed that these original occupants of the woods – or *Rår* – were ghastly things, and the basis for monsters in local legends and so forth. And it had always been believed that the forests were unsafe if certain precautionary measures were not taken. Foresters and huntsmen could no longer roam, women could no longer collect firewood, and children would be unable to play freely. Then, in the seventeenth century, the custom of offering gifts was violently suppressed during a period of puritanical fervour, intended to sweep away the last vestiges of pantheism in Northern Sweden. But immediately after the censorship, this fellow claimed, a spate of disappearances ensued in northern Jämtland. First livestock, then the more vulnerable human elements of the local communities went missing. And it was from this period that a particular warning originated – *Det som en gång givits har försvunnet, det kommer att återtas* – which the gentleman translated into English for me: *What was once given, is missing. One will come to fetch it back.*

"This script was erected on gateposts and signs as a warning to visitors, and was usually accompanied by the horseshoe, a symbol that made the *Rår* particularly uncomfortable due to its aversion to men on horseback.

"Though temporarily suppressed, the late-summer gifts were soon offered again from the places designated for such transactions. And this originally began in an age when colonising Norsemen, and the original occupants, had made these uneasy treaties. This time, the Church turned a blind eye, silently acknowledging a local problem beyond its brief and power to correct.

"But things were different. The tastes of the original occupants were said to have changed. Changed back to an older *baseness*. During the interference of the Church, the *Rår* had rediscovered a taste for a different kind of flesh. And unscrupulous members of the local populace were soon said to be giving succour to the revival of such an enthusiastic appetite. Hence the long-standing tradition of missing travellers in Rådalen.

"Gradually, the local communities withdrew from the affected area to put themselves beyond reach of the very territorial *Rår*, abandoning homes and churches as they migrated south and east. And in time, such observances of old lore struggled to survive in the age of reason and science. The local lore was seen as folly by all but a few who lived closest to the valley. This area is now a long-neglected portion of the national park, though the gentleman did hear something about a property developer rebuilding or renovating old villas to sell off as summer houses. But the idea had never taken off. With such a slender population, there is little infrastructure and almost no local services in the area. 'It must be one of these your friend has purchased,' he said in closing, just as the smoked salmon and caviar were served to us by a stewardess.

"I had listened with interest and some disquiet, but my unease soon turned to irritation. I was willing to venture that such talk and spurious conjecture amounted to nothing more than the fairy tales composed to prevent children from getting lost in the forest. Somehow, it must have all taken root in Atterton's isolated imagination, and then the foolishness must have flourished; no doubt cultivated by the dying of the light as winter approached. So, the sooner I reached him and returned him to the observable world, the better.

I say 'observable' because I've always championed a motto among those with a bent for psychics, ghosts and visitors from other galaxies, and that is that *I trust my own eyes. If it exists, then let it show itself.*"

At this point in his narration, I was surprised at the manner in which Henry gulped at his brandy.

Descriptions of travel by untutored pens can be as dull as slide-shows of holiday photographs, so I will not blunt the reader's concentration with details of Henry's journey through Sweden to the Jämtland region, and then on to the periphery of Rådalen. Suffice to say, he acquired his rental vehicle and a better map. But the closer he drew to Atterton's location, the more difficult the journey became.

"The moment I left the main arteries to move inland on secondary roads, I found myself overwhelmed by the impenetrable nature of the forest. I'd never seen such a place in Europe before. A true, virgin wilderness, as much of northern Scandinavia still remains; boreal forest surviving from prehistory, unmanaged, and probably still boasting miles of woodland where no human has ever set foot.

"About sixty kilometres from Rådalen, there was some evidence of summer housing scattered about through the trees; small wooden houses built in the vintage rural style and painted a dark red. These must have been the remnants of the settlements that drew away from Rådalen in the eighteenth century, and the buildings were now used for summer holidays, but were empty that late in the season.

"The buildings thinned and then practically disappeared when I couldn't have been more than twenty kilometres from the valley. The road surface turned from tarmac to gravel and, in places, was barely wide enough for a single vehicle. And even in the late sun of the afternoon, I couldn't prevent myself thinking that the last of the buildings that I spied through the trees, on higher ground, suggested a greater air of abandonment than the others. The very structures seemed to suggest that they had not drawn back far enough from the darkest, ageless fathoms of the valley. I even fancied that some of the little *Stugas* were in the process of peering over their gabled shoulders in fearful anticipation of what might be approaching through the trees.

"Chiding myself for a betrayal of reason, I shut down that train of thought. But even the unimaginative, in whose number I would include myself, retain enough of their primal instinct to fear the shadowy expanses of uncultivated forests. Particularly as dusk settles through the clouds to tint the very air before your eyes, promising a nightfall so dense as to cancel visibility in every direction. It was no longer any surprise to me that legends of the *Rår* and human sacrifice lingered in these valleys. It was the perfect setting for such fables. But stories they were, and I had a troubled friend to find.

"When I could not have been more than ten kilometres from Atterton's *Fritidshus*, I found myself making repeated stops to study the map. The light was fading and the road curved about to such an extent that I no longer knew which direction was north and which was south. I'd become lost. I was tired and hungry by this time too, the best of my concentration was long gone, my temper was beginning to spark, and my sense of awe at the forest was fast turning to dread. I wondered if I'd have to spend the night on the backseat of the car.

"But, to my relief, after another five minutes behind the wheel, I spied a church steeple through the passenger window, during a brief break in the woodland bordering the road. Hoping to find someone who could direct me to Atterton's house, I drove toward the steeple on what amounted to no more than a track.

"The church was a long, single-storey, timber affair, with a steeple that also served as a bell tower, surrounded by a well-tended meadow cemetery. But my brief optimism began to drain when I noticed that all of the windows were shuttered. And around the arch that topped the little gatehouse, providing access to the grounds through the dry-stone wall, an inscription had been carved into the wood between two black horseshoes: *Det som en gång givits har försvunnet, det kommer att återtas – What was once given is missing. One will come to fetch it back*.

"Alone, lost in a national park, hours' drive from the nearest town, and before a churchyard with a chilly dusk assembling about me, this warning was just about the last thing that I wanted to come across. And no sooner had I advanced through the gate and approached the church doors than I noticed another configuration of horseshoes nailed about the porch canopy, to protect the entrance of God's house. If indeed these primitive iron symbols were used to ward off evil spirits, then why would a crucifix not suffice?

Perhaps, an irritating voice cried out inside me, *because a cross is not recognised by eyes older than the origin of that symbol*. I turned an involuntary shudder into a vigorous shake of my cramped limbs, my tired muscles and frazzled senses, and I investigated the building.

"My knocks went unanswered, as did my calls, and there was not so much as a single notice in the glass-fronted display case beside the door.

"At the rear of the property I discovered a collection of large granite runestones, suggesting to me this was the site of a far older cemetery. And while I looked at them, all about me the shadows thickened between the boughs and trunks of the trees, the leaves darkened as the light thinned, and I pulled up my collars against the buffets of a cold wind. I was forced to remember Atterton's last letter. I didn't linger long and made my way back to the car.

"Eyes burning and head thumping, I made another frustrating scrutiny of the map under the overhead light. Pretty soon the headlights would have to go on as well. I was just about to utter another string of curses when I noticed the tiny symbol of a cross on the map, which seemed to be an indication of the church that I was currently parked beside. If this was the case, then all I needed to do was turnabout, drive to the crossroads that I had passed no more than two kilometres back, and take a left. A road or single track would then take me to Atterton's *Stuga*.

"With my sense of direction recovered, I managed to find the house without further mishap, at 6:45 p.m. A small, pretty, red building with white awnings and porch, set in a grass paddock about which the white picket fence was not so much surrounded as engulfed by the encroaching forest. I could see no more than a few feet along the leafy tracks that ran between the great trees and then vanished into a darker immensity.

"There was no answer to my rapping on the door, or to my calls as I circled the house with a growing sense of alarm. I recalled Atterton mentioning his removal of a plethora of horseshoes from the walls of the house, but it now appeared that they had been nailed back, and with haste and little regard for symmetry. The windows had also been boarded over with any material at hand: bits of broken furniture, firewood, planks torn from the outhouse. Surely this was not what he referred to as shutting up for the winter? So, had he come to believe himself besieged by a creature from a fairy tale?

"Upon a closer inspection of the windows, even in the failing light, I happened to notice a disturbance in the flower beds beneath the windows at the rear of the property. The soil had been thoroughly trampled and the plants had been raked out. So had some inquisitive moose come nosing up to the windows to eat flowers or peer in through the glass? Or perhaps a bear had been enticed out of the woods by the scent of Atterton's fish supper? And had the noises from such a commotion transformed themselves, inside Atterton's unstable thoughts, into what he perceived to be a threat from some monstrous intruder?

"Running my fingers along the woodwork of the sills, I discovered a series of deep scratches in the timber, which may have resulted from his hasty and inept attempts to seal the windows. And yet, despite my stubborn recourse to reason, I was struck by a notion that these marks suggested the attempt of a powerful animal to gain access to the interior.

"But one thing did seem irrefutable: isolated and over-stimulated by the oppressive forest once that summer had gone, Atterton must have succumbed to panic and fled. For I was sure that he was no longer a resident of Rådalen.

"By this time, night was falling fast and an icy wind was causing a noisy commotion in the treeline. After over fourteen hours of continuous travel – including two plane journeys and a long drive – I needed shelter, food and rest. Going back the way I had come in the darkness would have been idiotic, so I made a quick decision: I would break in and get a fire going, first forcing the door with a tyre iron or a tool from the shed.

"But I'll admit, by that hour, it was not only exhaustion that spurred me on: I found the heavy, tense valley air peculiarly unpleasant. From out of the gloom came the odours of leaf rot and wet soil, and, if I'm not mistaken, the night air was also tainted by the smell of animal spoor. Not as searing as the pig, but less earthy than the cow. Something sharp and doglike. Perhaps Atterton had been using a local manure to cultivate the gardens? At any rate, I wanted to be spared the stench.

"Using a spade from the shed, I levered the lock out of the door-frame, and into the dark house I made my way. Guided by the twilight, I found an oil lamp in the kitchen and got it lit before checking the rest of the ground floor. The ceilings were much lower than I expected and the whole place reeked of timber, wood smoke and paraffin. Wherever I found them, I lit the lamps.

"As Atterton had promised, it was basic. Plainly and simply furnished and painted white throughout. The interior of the place reminded me of both a skiing chalet and a child's playhouse; everything seemed small, and cramped, especially the beds in the two upstairs bedrooms: little wooden boxes built beneath the slope of the roof.

"And while I searched about, I realised that Atterton had never finished packing. It appeared to me that he had started stuffing his clothes into cases, in the master bedroom, and to box his books in the parlour, only to have stopped, or been interrupted.

"In the kitchen, the surfaces were also littered with the rubbish produced by the last few days of his occupancy, and the metal bin beside the back door was full. That door was now sealed by uprooted floorboards. He'd been eating out of tins and rationing water out of a collection of enamel jugs. There was a pile of firewood beside the range, brought up from the dry-goods cellar, in which I found the remainder of his supplies.

"So, I reasoned, Atterton had nailed himself inside the house, remained there for a few days and then fled. What else could I make of the evidence?

"I helped myself to some crackerbreads, pickled herring and some interesting local beer, while pondering his disaster. I decided that I would wait until dawn and then make a cursory inspection of the surrounding terrain, in case he had injured himself, or completely lost his wits and was out there now like King Lear, raving on the blasted heath. I'd then drive to the nearest settlement to notify the authorities of the condition of the house, and Atterton's mind, in case a more thorough search of the locale needed to be arranged, or his whereabouts traced through airline records and so forth. Until then, I'd make camp in the parlour where I would get a fire going. I'd sleep in the chair, wrapped up in blankets.

"With the majority of the oil lamps arranged about the room, and a fire roaring in the grate, I tried my best to relieve the oppressive gloom of the place. I'll admit it, the place and its atmosphere unsettled me greatly; every window nailed shut and reinforced with oddments of wood, horseshoes hammered on the outside of every interior door, the wind crashing about in the trees outside, or buffeting the walls and whining under the room beams. And as night fell, the entire structure of the house was beset with all manner of groans, creaks, bangs and sly draughts. How Atterton could have even contemplated a year alone, out here, was beyond me. In itself, such a decision suggested the onset of mental illness, and it seemed his sanctuary had quickly become a prison – a theory confirmed by what I found amongst his papers.

"Besides his jottings detailing his chores and repairs and intentions to begin a vegetable patch, I discovered some heavily scored maps; they indicated the paths he'd trekked, waters he'd fished, the circle of stones on the high ground to the east of the property, and a loose folio of charcoal sketches. Amongst his drawings, there were depictions of the house from various angles, trout he'd caught and the church I had seen; all of which I took to be his earlier work, before his obsession with the stones took precedence. You see, there were scores of rubbings from the runestones on the hill, and dozens of sketches of the circle from within and without its rough boundary. And as I flicked through the papers, I noticed how he'd begun to incorporate text with the pictures. One page in particular caught my eye. It was titled 'From The Long Stone' and featured a rubbing from a weathered granite dolmen. Below, he'd added definition and detail to the etching's crude suggestiveness with a set of cutaways and expansion sketches. It was these convincing embellishments to which I took an instant aversion. *So what am I to make of this?* he'd written at the foot of the page.

"What indeed? If Atterton's sketch was to be believed, upon the stone was carved a silhouette of something both too tall and too thin to have been a man. A creature with long, simian arms and clawed feet and hands, that appeared to stride across the face of the stone, while pulling behind itself a smaller figure, by the hair. The second character in the piece must have been a child, and it was being taken to what seemed to be a depository of bones chiselled on the far side of the stone; that is, if the pile of sticks were skulls, ribs and femurs and so forth.

"My eyes didn't dally upon the sketch, I can assure you, and I began to take a keener interest in the violence of the wind about the little house. The timbers were being harangued by these swooping blasts, from every direction, and I was at once reminded of how the noise of a strong wind in old timbers can produce the sounds of occupancy in empty rooms, particularly those above one's head. I had another suspicion that the elements were building to something, or heralding an arrival. I could have sworn there was some kind of anticipation in that wind.

"After perusing Atterton's final sketch, I confess to getting out of my chair in order to move it away from the window behind my head.

"You see, the last picture contained a rough impression, made by an unsteady hand, of the tracks Atterton claimed to have discovered *outside the gate, at the rear of the garden* and *under the parlour windows*. They were certainly the prints of a biped, not dissimilar to the human foot in shape, apart from the size and length of the clawed toes, including a sixth on the heel; this was akin to that of the cat, used for disembowelling its prey. As a footnote, Atterton had added the date of composition too: four days prior to my arrival. He'd embellished that drawing with a comment: *No longer deterred by horseshoes or fire, it meant to get in.*

"I tried to persuade myself that this was more concocted evidence produced by a deeply disturbed mind; one driven to extremes of fancy and conjecture, delusion and suspicion, by the windy rigours of this climate and the haunting aspects of the landscape.

"I put down the sketches and took a firmer grip of the fire poker, longing for a more fitting distraction from the dark and the relentless wind than Atterton's illustrations. I had a go at *Great Expectations*, but my concentration was repeatedly fractured by sudden squalls against the walls of the parlour that made the foundations shudder and the lamps flicker. But some time after midnight, I mercifully succumbed to a fatigue peculiar to travel, fresh air and new surroundings, and I nodded off in my chair. Neither the angry roar of the gale nor the thumpings about the roof could stay my eyelids any longer.

"But a heavy crash, filled with the splintering of wood, brought me around soon enough and straight to my feet.

"About me in the parlour, the fire was no more than red embers and two of the lamps had gone out.

"The terrific noise had originated from the front of the house, and the most vulnerable spot, or so my senses cried out. Even with two metal latches in place, I had broken the main lock earlier, and it was the only access point not secured by six-inch nails and timber. I surmised that Atterton must have left that exit clear to make his final escape. Unable to spend another night trapped like a rabbit in a burrow, he must have made a dash for it, during his last morning.

"With the lamp and the small axe, used for breaking up the kindling, I stumbled through the parlour, into the dark kitchen and towards the little reception room that housed the front door. And the thought came to me then: *it could be Atterton trying to get inside*. Who knows what hours he kept out there? He could have been half-lunatic by then. But when I saw the state of the door, I soon shook off the last swaddling of sleep. At once, I abandoned my theory about Atterton breaking in. And besides that, I never had the breath to call out his name.

"Both hinges and latches had been ripped from the wall and now hung from a flattened door. It had been smashed inwards from the outside by considerable force. Did a man have such strength? Even a madman?

"The freezing night air hit me with a *whump* that failed to dispel what I would call an intensification of the stench that I had smelled seeping from the trees around the garden earlier: the damp of an unlit forest floor tinged with a bestial pungency; the raw miasma that strikes one near the stained concrete of the zoo cage. And it filled the house.

"I found it impossible to even step onto the porch and investigate. I dithered in the hall and suddenly comprehended Atterton's belief in the necessity of barricades: someone, or *something*, was terrorising the property under the cover of moonless nights. An assailant of significant size and power.

"I held the lamp up and tried to shed some light on the doorway and whatever lay beyond. Screwing up my eyes, all I could make out was the end of the porch and a murky impression of the grass below the steps.

"The lamp flickered and was nearly doused by another gust of wind that whipped across the paddock from the treeline. 'Who's there?' I called out, and in a voice that broke like an adolescent's.

"I put the lamp on the floor beside my feet and went to raise the door when I heard the sound of a footfall. Behind me. In the kitchen. The dark kitchen that I had just come through, wide-eyed but drowsy.

"Then another floorboard creaked. Followed by the sound of a snort; the kind a bullock might make.

"Whatever had smashed down the door was inside the house with me. I stopped breathing and felt disoriented by an acute terror that I cannot begin to articulate. I whimpered like a child and I cringed as if anticipating a blow from behind. One more sound from the darkness and I was sure that my heart would stop beating. I could not bear to turn my head and see what now stood behind me.

"Then I heard it again. The squeak of a floorboard beneath another step taken, closer. And there was something at the end of the sound, a scratching, that inserted the picture from Atterton's sketches into my mind: a long foot, tipped with claws, but now moving across a wooden floor toward me.

"I sprang about-face and knocked the lamp on to its side with a clatter that made me suck in my breath, and cry out, 'Oh, God!' At that moment, I saw the intruder, bent over and tensing long limbs inside the kitchen.

"I say I saw *something*. I only saw a silhouette for a moment before the lamp spluttered out. But in that crouching figure I am sure I detected a wet snout, yellow canines and blood-spoiled eyes in a black face. The head was close to the ceiling, against which it was stooped over, unable to stand upright, even with its spindly legs bent at the knee.

"I ran out of the building and into the darkness, and in the direction of the car. Which I hit with my knees at the very same moment as the door to Atterton's house was slammed hard against the floorboards by a heavy weight landing upon it. That noise, I assumed, was of the door being trampled, or run over, and it signalled that the trespasser was now outside *with me*.

"From force of habit I'd locked the car and activated the alarm, which I set off after striking the vehicle at full pelt. It was the shrieking of the alarm, I believe in hindsight, that saved my life. It must have momentarily stunned my pursuer, and given me enough time to grab the keys from my jacket pocket and get the car unlocked and my body eventually into the driver's seat. Had those valuable few seconds not been purchased, I am sure that I would never have left Rådalen. And leaving the place, I am convinced, is something that Atterton never managed to achieve.

"I stalled the car three times. Once because I had left it in gear. The second time because the engine was cold. And the third time because, when I turned the lights on, I caught sight of something in the rear-view mirror, all lit up in red, that made me take both feet off the pedals in shock.

"When I managed to get the car moving, across the paddock and onto the narrow entry road, driving faster than caution advised, *it* kept pace with me. Sometimes behind, loping along the track, a few feet back from the bumper, and sometimes alongside me in the trees at the side of the road. At least I think it was my pursuer that rubbed and scratched up against the car like that. And as I slowed down to take the bends in the road, something outside the vehicle tried to hold the car still. It meant to have me that night, and I believe it tracked me for over ten kilometres.

"I drove through the night and into the welcome dawn, straight on to Kiruna, where I raised the alarm about Atterton. That was before paying over two thousand pounds for the damage sustained to the car's paintwork and, in some places, to the actual steel of the door panels."

* * *

It was a much paler and strained figure who finished the story for me in the library of our club. The epilogue

Henry only managed to deliver after another glass of brandy:

"They never found him. A removal company sent a van the Friday before my arrival, but found the property much the same as I found it: deserted and crudely boarded up. Atterton never set foot on the plane. He never left the valley.

"Just as the first snow began to fall, the forestry commission and army searched the area and found no trace of him either, and could shed no light on his disappearance. They even used a helicopter to search the valley, but found nothing unusual except an abandoned bicycle, about ten kilometres from the *Fritidshus*. Though the ownership of the bike was never established, I think it must have been his.

"In Sweden, poor Atterton is still listed as a missing person."

Summer Bonus

Lee Murray

THE TWIN-CAB truck rattled down the gravel drive towards a tired weatherboard farmhouse flanked by a flotsam of equally tired but serviceable outbuildings. There was a large vehicle shed, a rickety wooden barn, and several assorted trailers and caravans, including, no doubt, the one Kate would share with Laurel for the next three months. Kate hoped the girl didn't snore.

Though they'd both come from the UK on the same flight, she'd only met Laurel this morning at Auckland airport, both of them boarding the bus to Northland to a one-street wonder of a town with an unpronounceable Māori name, and then getting off and wilting in the heat at the bus stop – Fiona, a friend who'd tended bar with Kate a few years back, the one who'd set up this gig, had given them instructions to wait until someone came to pick them up – and in all that time Laurel had barely let up the chatter. For nearly seven hours now, Kate had nodded and clucked through Laurel's extensive travel stuff-ups, how she knew Fiona – childhood friend; they went to preschool together – a blow-by-blow account of her recent break-up with an unrelenting capitalist named Simon, and the subsequent personal epiphany that led her to throw in her studies for a summer with the Farm Volunteer Scheme in beautiful Ow-tia-rower – her first time in this amazing country – until she could work out her next move. Something in conservation, she'd speculated, or the environment. Maybe with Greenpeace. In any case, she wanted to do something relevant with her life, you know?

Kate did know. For years now, she'd been flitting from job to job, looking for meaning, or at least something that raised her pulse from barely dead. Then Fiona had called asking if Kate was interested in taking over her spot on this farm in New Zealand. "Free food and board in return for a few hours' work a day. No drunks for miles, and no going to bed with stunk-up hair. Job starts in a week."

"A week? Won't I need a work visa?"

Fiona giggled. "Nah. Just say you're on holiday. It's what I did."

Kate was totally over the job at the rental car company, and it wasn't like she had anything better to do, so she hit up her parents for the plane ticket money – spun them the usual blah-blah – told her boss to shove it and cleared out her desk the same day.

"So I bought two bottles," Laurel was saying. "And believe me it was hard to get in the middle of a UK winter. The woman at Boots looked at me like I was some kind of idiot. But I wasn't going to take no for an answer. English petals burn quickly, right Kate?"

Nodding yet again, Kate squeezed out a small smile. It wasn't that Laurel was unlikeable, or even unbearable, just a tad exhausting. Or maybe that was the effect of a god-awful thirty-hour flight talking. Either way, the graunch of the brake was a relief.

"Right then," said the driver, putting an end to Laurel's commentary on the merits of Factor 50 sunscreen. "You'll want Sarah," he said through thin lips. A rough voice from a face like chipped stone. "She'll be inside." He tilted his chin towards the house, then hauled open the door and stalked off towards a flaking black trailer, leaving them there.

"Okay then," Laurel said brightly. "I guess it's just us."

She clambered out of the truck, shouldered her backpack and, clutching her winter jacket, trudged across the gravel to the front door. Kate snatched up her backpack from the flatbed and followed her.

"Hello, the house," Laurel said.

Hello, the house? Kate resisted the urge to roll her eyes.

"Hello?" No answer. Laurel shrugged and pushed open the door.

They stepped inside, blinking in the sudden gloom.

A black and white sheepdog surged around Kate's knees, its nails clicking on the linoleum floor.

"Oi! Shoes off in here," snapped a woman in her mid-forties, with old eyes and slumped shoulders. Sarah, presumably. Her yell startled the dog and sent it scuttling under a fraying armchair.

"Oh! I'm so sorry," Laurel blurted. "Of course. I should have realised. That'll be the jet lag, making my brain fuggy. We'll just put our shoes over here..."

Letting Laurel do the talking, Kate shucked off her backpack and set it down beside her shoes on the rubber mat near the door. Waited in her socks on linoleum that had to be forty years old.

They weren't alone in the kitchen. At the table, in a thin t-shirt, an influencer-hot twenty-something was hunched over a newspaper, his fingers hooked around an enamel cup. He was wearing earbuds, but their movement must have alerted him because he lifted his head. He considered them a moment, slow and casual, then turned his attention back to his newspaper.

"All right then. No harm done," Sarah said, softer now. "Sit yourselves down, girls…" A question.

"I'm Laurel and this is Kate."

"Hmm." Sarah lifted a massive teapot, sploshed tea into a couple of pottery mugs, and pushed them across the table, followed up with a jug of milk and a basket of still steaming cheese scones. That done, she said, "Welcome to Pine Farm. I'm Sarah and this is my nephew, Jayden." Jayden didn't hear. He was in his own little world, plugged into an unknown soundtrack. "We hope you'll have a memorable stay. I'm assuming Fiona told you our rules?"

Laurel's mug chinked against her teeth. "Rules?"

"Yes. We don't have a lot. Shoes off in the house. Set mealtimes. Farm vehicles have to stay on the property. Those sorts of things."

"Oh, we don't have a problem with those," Laurel gushed. "Right, Kate?"

Behind her second mouthful of cheesy scone, Kate gave a quick nod.

"We ask you to put in a half-day's work every day. You can choose morning or afternoon. Most of our Farm Volunteers prefer to work mornings when it's cooler and spend their afternoons on the beach."

Jayden folded the newspaper and took out his earbuds. There was a sharp scrape of wood on lino as he got to his feet and carried his mug to the bench.

"Fiona didn't mention a beach," Laurel said while Jayden emptied the dregs of his tea into the sink. "That's a nice surprise."

"The beach borders the farm to the east," Sarah went on. "There are tracks through the bush to the bottom of the cliff. Jayden can take you tomorrow."

"Sure." His voice was like melted chocolate. "I'd be happy to."

"So if you girls would just give me your cell phones now, Jayden can show you to your accommodation—"

"Our cell phones?" Laurel squeaked. "Why?"

Jayden sucked air over his teeth. Shook his head. "Sounds like Fiona didn't tell them."

Sarah sighed heavily. "You can send a quick text to your families now to let them know you've arrived, but after that we'll need to hold on to your phones until the end of your stay."

Kate swallowed her mouthful. "The *whole* three months. That's a bit harsh, isn't it?"

"I'm sorry. It's not just a lifestyle choice. We don't want hordes of people turning up here. There's a conservation site on the beach – a protected species."

"Wow, that's so amazing. What sort of species?" Laurel asked.

She was missing the point. They would have *no phones*.

"Dead girls' eyelashes," Jayden said in a spooky voice. He lifted his hands and wiggled his fingers in a parody of a ghost. Laurel tittered like a schoolgirl.

Sarah flicked her nephew an odd stare. "It's a colony of filamentous red algae" – she raised an eyebrow at Jayden – "*commonly known as eyelash seaweed.* It lives on a rocky outcrop jutting into the sea. There are only three populations left, maybe only two since the Kaikōura earthquake. Ours is the only North Island site, so the government gives us an annual grant to ensure it's left alone. We're the guardians."

Her hand in her pocket, Kate fingered her phone. "It's okay. I won't say anything." Meanwhile, bloody Laurel had opened hers and was dutifully firing off her final text.

Sarah folded her arms across her chest. "Sorry, Kate, but those are our rules. We can't afford any photos getting out. I get that it can be hard – we've all become so addicted to social media – but honestly after a few days, most people don't even miss it."

"Come on, Kate. It's only three months." Laurel pushed her phone across the table.

"Trust me," Sarah said, her mouth stretched too wide, like a smiling skeleton. "You won't even notice. It's so beautiful here."

"What if I don't want to?" Kate said. What was the big deal, anyway? She'd already said she wouldn't tell.

Sarah's expression hardened. "Then I'll have to ask you to leave."

"Kate. We just got here," Laurel whined.

Jayden strode across the room and picked up the backpacks. "Good point, Laurel. You've both been travelling for days. Give Sarah your phones for now, and if you still want to leave tomorrow, I'll get Sean to drive you back to town in the morning."

Scone weighed in Kate's stomach. This wasn't right, blindsiding them like this. She felt like a rabbit with her foot in a trap. "You know, I'll just call an Uber now."

Jayden laughed. "Yeah, they don't come out here."

Something crept across her nape. She wanted to say she'd walk, but the trip in the truck had taken forty minutes. She'd be stumbling along that rocky back-road with her pack in the dark. It would probably take her until morning to get there.

"Just give her your phone," Jayden said softly.

"Kate," Laurel said again.

One night. Kate thumbed off the device and handed it over.

Minutes later they were following Jayden across the driveway towards the trailers, getting their first proper look across the farm, at the rows upon rows of vegetables, the stand of dark pine trees to their left, and the gently sloping paddocks to the east, where, a half mile away across a patch of bush, the ocean glistened like new-car paint in the afternoon sun. It was idyllic. Just as Fiona had promised.

"Weird that Fiona didn't tell us about the draconian phone rules," Kate whispered to Laurel.

"Maybe she just didn't miss it, like Sarah said."

"I don't know. Does this place seem off to you?"

"It seems amazing to me."

Laurel wasn't talking about the ocean. Opening the door to a dented white caravan, Jayden was heaving their backpacks inside, the muscles of his back rippling under the thin t-shirt. He straightened up and ran a hand through his hair. "There you go, ladies," he said, pointing to the adjacent trailer. "If you need anything, that's me there. And Sean's is the black one."

He gestured for Laurel to enter. "Dinner's at six," he said, taking her hand as he helped her up the step. "I'll see you both then."

When her turn came, their fingers touching, Kate considered his chiselled cheekbones and smouldering black eyes. It was only three months. Might not be so bad, after all.

* * *

A month went by. Two. Sarah had been right. The first few days without social media had been excruciating – Kate's hand automatically going to her pocket, searching for her device – but once she'd survived the withdrawal, it was as if Kate had never been on it.

This place was worth a million likes. On the edge of nowhere, it had wormed its way under her skin with its hot days, clean air, and endless skies. The gig was hard, but it was satisfying, too. Mostly, Kate and Laurel worked in the farm's vast organic garden: sowing new crops, digging in compost, spraying the plants with soapy tomato-leaf spray, and dealing with the slugs. Occasionally, Kate would help Sean fix a chicken coop, re-wire a fence, or repair the rusting tractor. Each day she discovered muscles she didn't know she had, but in a good way. The kind that made you eat well and sleep better.

Only the 'home kill day' had been nasty. Kate and Laurel had tossed a coin, and Kate had lost.

"Oh thank God," Laurel said when it came up heads. "I couldn't bear to watch. I hate blood."

"You people," Sean scoffed as he manhandled the first squirming sheep from the pen. "Where do you think your fucking meat comes from?" He slit the animal's throat with a knife as long as his forearm, quick and matter of fact, like an assassin. The sheep's bleating ceased in an instant, the sudden quiet chilling. Its blood glutted from the wound; some of it spilled over the sides of the bucket, spattering Kate's hands.

"Hold that still!"

"Sorry," Kate mumbled. She'd been distracted by the frothing bubbles.

"Supermarket meat looks like it's made in a lab. Grey slabs under plastic wrap. Tastes like bloody cardboard, too." Sean twisted, giving the dog a vicious kick to the flank. "Get the fuck out, Tip!" The dog skulked away.

Sean set about skinning the sheep while the dead animal was still quivering. Kate trembled too. When he'd cut out the liver and heart, she loaded the stinking stomach contents into a wheelbarrow and heaved them into the offal pit up near the pines, sending a cloud of black flies into the air. Then Sean was yelling at her to fucking hurry up and hold the bucket while he killed the next one. She didn't mind Sean. Sure, he was ornery, all sharp edges and grunts, but Kate had worked a bar for a year and saw it for the armour it was. Everyone was running from something.

If 'home kill day' was the worst, afternoons were the best. Kate, Laurel and Jayden would grab their towels and trek the half-mile across the paddocks and through the bush to the sandy beach at the base of the cliffs, where they would swim and sunbathe and swim some more. Kate even read a book. First time in years. It was wonderful.

They stayed at the south end of the beach, away from the protected outcropping, although Jayden had taken them to see it that first full day. They had clambered up and over the outcrop, Jayden helping Kate and Laurel navigate the length of the rocky ridge until they had ventured well past the line of white breakers. It was slow going. The rocks were treacherous, with their dark shadows like spilled coffee, and the sharp edges which bit into Kate's instep through the soles of her trainers.

"Are you sure we should be doing this?" Laurel called from the rear. "Sarah said the seaweed was protected."

"It's fine," Jayden reassured her. "I'll just call this visit my regular surveillance."

Suddenly, there came a low moan, like a woman in pain.

"Someone's already here," Laurel said.

They stilled as the moan came again.

"It's the ghost of my grandmother," Jayden said gravely, then he chuckled. "Nah. Just kidding. It's the blowhole. It makes that noise sometimes. It's just up ahead." He pointed out the hole.

"Oh my God," Kate gasped. "I didn't see it. I nearly stepped right there." Nearly stepped inside that dark maw, where the ocean growled and ground its teeth, and its foul spittle foamed over the rocky lip.

"Careful." Jayden caught her hand and drew Kate away from the edge. She hadn't realised she'd been creeping towards it, mesmerised by the surge. "Fall in there and you'll be feeding the fishes," he said, "your bones pulverised to sand."

"Don't stand so close, you two," Laurel said. "You're freaking me out."

Jayden took a step back. "I know, right? That moaning makes your skin crawl. I felt the same, the first time I came up here. Before our family took over the farm, back in the Seventies, a Māori family lived here. They called this blowhole a tipua."

"What does that mean?" Laurel asked.

"An uncanny thing. The seaweed's over here." He led them carefully around the blowhole's edge, and a few yards further on to where the seaweed glistened in a rocky depression. After the adrenaline-rush of the blowhole, it was mildly disappointing, although Jayden had been right: the silky black tendrils really did resemble a woman's eyelashes. Talk about creepy.

Tinged red, they undulated gently in the swell, millions of tiny fingers reaching out for some unknown goal. And all the while the blowhole continued its pitiful moaning.

Kate shivered.

"Let's go back," Laurel said.

"Seems like a lot of fuss over a tiny bit of algae," Kate said, when they were safely on the beach and heading back to their towels.

Jayden shrugged. "It's pretty special. Apparently, that eyelash seaweed, or a relative of it, has been around for over a billion years."

"So back when recordings first started, then," Kate said.

Jayden grinned, the corners of his eyes crinkling. "Something like that."

Kate's pulse had flickered for the first time in ages.

Shagging Jayden was an unexpected summer bonus. Late nights rocking his trailer. Once in the bracken deep in the pines. In the sea out past the breakers. They didn't talk much. It was all about the sex. Except that one time when the blowhole had been especially mournful, she'd asked him what his plans were.

"I plan to live here forever, seducing beautiful English farm workers, sowing crops, and getting a tan."

She laid her cheek on his chest, curled her finger in his hair. "But don't you have dreams? Don't you want to get a degree, or travel, or something?"

"Nah. I can't leave. I mean, things are better now since we got the government grant for the seaweed, and the Farm Volunteer Scheme helps, but Sarah needs me. Way back we had family around to work the land, but these days no one wants to live so far from town. I'm all she has left."

"There's Sean."

"Sure. Sean keeps an eye on the place, but it takes more than two people to nurture the land. I don't mind. I like it here. Plus, the sexy English farm girls are a nice bonus." He'd turned her over then. They had just enough time for another round.

Naturally, he was sleeping with Laurel, too. Kate wasn't stupid. What else would they be doing all those hours she'd been reading the battered Stephen King paperback? Exploring, they said. *Right.* She shared a caravan with Laurel and had seen her pink English-petal bottom. Let's just say Laurel wasn't always *that* conscientious with the Factor 50. Kate didn't care. She didn't own Jayden and if he had enough energy for the both of them, why shouldn't Laurel have her fun?

And then the first summer thunderstorm had come, and Sarah told her about the real summer bonus.

* * *

They were in the barn, the pair of them loading potatoes into 4kg sacks. Even inside, the air zinged with ozone and dirt and the promise of autumn.

"At the end of every season, we give out a bonus to our Farm Volunteers," Sarah announced.

"That's brilliant," Kate said. Food and board and sex were all very well, but the real world used actual money.

"Only for one of you, though."

A shadow flickered: Sean passing in front of the barn in a crinkled oilskin, his whistle carrying over the thwack of rain on the roof.

"Okay," Kate said slowly, her mind racing.

"You've worked really hard, and shown respect for our life here, so we think you should be the one to receive it."

"Wow, that's—"

"But you'll need to kill Laurel first. Offer her body up to the blowhole."

Dropping a potato, Kate laughed out loud. "That's funny. Kill Laurel. You had me going there for a moment." She bent to pick up the spud. Except when Kate straightened, Sarah wasn't smiling.

"I understand if you need some time to think about it. I can give you a couple of weeks. After that, I'll have no choice but to offer the bonus to Laurel."

No. She was joking. She had to be, right?

"This is ridiculous. I don't want to kill anyone."

Sarah jerked her head, eyeing Kate like a chicken might consider a worm. "So, you're okay with the bonus going to Laurel. Jayden says you're both eligible."

Did she just say eligible? Her skin tightened, her breath catching.

"Do you want the bonus or not?"

Kate lifted her chin. "I won't do it, and Laurel won't either. She can't even bear the sight of blood."

"Hmm," Sarah said, and that single syllable made Kate's marrow go to jelly.

"Look, I don't need any bonus. I don't want anything from you. I'll pack up my stuff and go right now. If Sean won't drive me, I'll walk to town." Kate shoved aside the bag of potatoes and strode towards the caravan, but now Sean hovered at the entrance of the barn, blocking her way. His expression chipped stone.

She whirled to look at Sarah.

"That's not how this works," the woman said quietly. "The land demands a sacrifice. If we want it to support us, we need to feed it."

* * *

Kate went back to work, carrying out tasks like an automaton, and always with Laurel's cheery chatter in her ear. Kate needed to tune her out. She needed to *think*. Process. She had two weeks to make up her mind. Except making up her mind meant killing Laurel.

She'd run, of course. Take one of the farm vehicles. Only Sarah and Sean were too canny to leave the keys lying around. No matter. She'd leave her gear, her phone, everything, and sneak away through the woods. Her flights were prepaid, so all she needed was her passport.

Precious days passed while she waited for her chance. The problem was, whenever she filled her lungs to run, Sean was there. Even at night when she slipped out of the caravan, he would be waiting and watching just outside his trailer, the glow of his cigarette a tiny beacon in the darkness, and Kate would be forced to go back inside.

She was running out of time and close to panic. The days were too hot. Sarah was always watching at the windows. Sean was always carrying that knife. Even the dog was different, snuffling at her legs and whining as if it knew what was coming.

Thankfully, Jayden could read the room and left her alone, electing to spend more and more time with Laurel. Kate would catch them emerging from another one of their afternoon explorations, their heads pressed together, talking quietly. Fingers touching. Exchanging sly looks.

When the two weeks were almost up, they were at the dinner table when Kate noticed that Laurel had filled out. Her skin was glowing. The result of all the healthy food Sarah was feeding them, or something more? Kate's pulse skipped a beat. Could Laurel be pregnant with Jayden's baby? And if she were, what would that mean for Kate? Would Sarah renege on her offer? Was Laurel already plotting to kill Kate? Laurel couldn't abide blood, but then again, mothers have been known to kill for their children. Fathers, too.

Kate lay awake in the caravan that night, listening to the whistle-sigh of Laurel's breathing.

* * *

The deadline came, and Kate was still wracked with indecision. Did she actually have it in her to kill another human being? Did Laurel?

Then, out of the blue, the opportunity presented itself. Sean stepped away to help Jayden wrestle with a stubborn tree stump, leaving his knife unattended against the side of the house. She picked it up. She would use it to defend herself. To get away from here. Only there were three of them and they were waiting, expecting her to flee. Meanwhile, bent over the capsicums, Laurel was culling the unripened green orbs to make room for the red ones, and in the middle of a diatribe about the impact of microplastics on the world's oceans. It was either Laurel or Kate. There was only one decision. Kate stepped up behind her and made a clean slice across her throat. One fluid movement. Laurel sputtered once, her bleating replaced by the silent rush of blood. She crumpled, and Kate went with her, holding her there among the rows while she bled out.

Although the body was warm and malleable enough to be loaded into the wheelbarrow, the half-mile trip across the paddocks took a while. Laurel was a dead weight, and more than once the grassy ruts and hollows caused the barrow to topple, forcing Kate to load up her stiffening body again. Tip didn't help; the dog kept sniffing around, darting in occasionally for a slurp at Laurel's bloody fingers. Kate chased him off.

There was no getting the wheelbarrow through the bush track. Kate dumped Laurel out for the last time and dragged her through the trees by her arms. It took over an hour, tugging and pulling and yanking her down the track while Laurel stared up at the sky. Kate was nearly dead herself by the time they emerged from the trees. Her lungs were burning, and her arms and legs were covered in cuts and scratches. Sweat trickled down her forehead. She took a moment, looking across the sand to the ocean, while she heaved in great gulps of air.

Then she hauled Laurel across the sand and waded into the water. Walking parallel to the shore, she floated the body the length of the beach, savouring the cool of the water against her legs. It was almost peaceful.

The final climb took the longest. Kate had no choice but to roll, drag, cajole the body up and over the rocky outcrop. Laurel's limbs snagged and her head bumped. Chunks of her flesh tore away, smearing the rocks. More than once the body tumbled into a crevice. Relentless, Kate hauled it back up.

She made it to the top. To the blowhole. The rocky lip glistened. Spray leapt from the hole, as if some ancient creature was salivating below.

Bracing herself against the rocks, Kate heaved the body in. It flopped and jerked over the edge, then disappeared into the black chasm. Spray misted and the sea surged up, then dropped away. *Bones pulverised to sand.*

Beneath the rocks, a woman moaned.

Kate stared at the hole. The afternoon burned on.

When at last Kate turned away, three sentinels were watching her from the far end of the beach. *The Guardians.* Well, let them look. She'd only done what they wanted. Hadn't they been grooming her for this the entire season? Why else would Sean suddenly leave his knife leaning against the house?

She stalked past them, back to the farmhouse.

* * *

Kate sluiced out the barrow. She took the shovel and dug in the blood around the capsicums. She packed Laurel's gear, including the sheets, and burned them with her own bloody clothes in a forty-gallon drum out behind the barn. Then she showered, taped up her cuts and scrapes as best she could, and packed up her own gear. Finally, she slipped her passport into the pocket of her jeans.

She crossed the gravel driveway and entered the farmhouse, shucked off her shoes.

The guardians were at the table, drinking tea and eating scones.

"It's done," Kate said. "I want the bonus and a ride into town. Now." She'd meant to sound gritty, like the killer she was; still her voice wobbled.

Sean grimaced. "Sorry, Kate. Not today." He lifted the knife from under the table and laid it alongside the massive teapot.

The air went stale. Kate backed away. *Idiot!* How could she have forgotten the knife? "No!" she wailed. "I did what you asked. You promised me the bonus."

Sarah clucked her tongue. "I said you were *eligible*, but you had to kill Laurel first."

"I did kill her!" Kate's blood ran cold. *Oh God, oh God, oh God.* She glanced for the door. Why had she taken her shoes off? "You're going to kill me, aren't you?"

"No, babe, you're wrong," Jayden said. "We're going to let you go. That's the bonus. You're the one who gets away."

"If you're thinking of running to the police, remember you're the one who killed her," Sean said.

"So, you're free to go, Kate," Jayden said. "You just have to do something for us first."

Kate trembled. *What something?*

Getting to her feet, Sarah opened a drawer in the sideboard and pulled out Kate's cell phone. Handed it to her. "We need you to call two friends."

* * *

Years later, Kate was working the emergency room when she spied a woman waiting outside one of the consult rooms. Her heart thundered beneath her ribs. She knew that woman.

It's her. Fiona.

A scream bubbling in her throat, Kate pushed it down with a breath, taking a moment to observe Fiona from the nurses' station, feigning interest in something else just as she had the day she'd pointed out Cady and Jen to Sean while they waited at the bus stop.

While they waited for their turn to spend a season at Pine Farm.

Not knowing what was coming.

Fiona must have felt the intensity of Kate's stare, because she glanced back.

Old eyes. Slumped shoulders. A universe of pain stretched between them. All the should-haves and would-haves, all the whys and why-nots. The late-night internet searches for news of their friends. The times they wanted to pick up the phone, call the police, and admit everything. The never-ending nightmares. The crushing guilt. The horror.

Kate exhaled slowly.

Fiona gave her the smallest nod, then she parted the curtains and ducked inside the consult room. Somewhere along the corridor, a woman moaned softly.

The Druid Stone

Katie Young

WHEN YOU grow up near the moor, the myths that have sprung forth from this gloomy, wind-blasted landscape over the centuries are rooted in you. They find their way into your bones before you're even born. The scrub and stone here is steeped in tales of pixies that conjure mist to confuse hapless wanderers, phantom hands that materialise in front of unfortunate drivers to force them from the road, and even the Devil himself, enticing mourners from the Lych Way and into the treacherous bogs of the wastelands.

Clinging to the south-west slope of the West Dart Valley is the gnarled and ancient oakwood, its twisted trees anchored in between granite boulders, long since tumbled smooth by the river that runs through it.

As a pragmatic child, I was sceptical about the stories of human sacrifices, ghosts, and hellhounds, but the very corporeal threat of venomous snakes was more than enough to keep me out of that forbidding tangle of trees and moss. As teenagers though, the enveloping, verdant stillness of the wood became a haven for me and my friends when we wanted somewhere quiet and secluded to share bottles of pilfered cider and smoke weed. The temptation of an illicit buzz overrode any vestigial fear of druids and adders, the latter seemingly more afraid of us than we were of them. And if Old Scratch really was lurking in the shadows, we figured he'd give his profane blessings and leave us to our small sins.

It's been almost twenty years since I last set foot in the wood. You know how it is when you leave home. At first you just want to get away from the same mundane haunts inhabited by stifling neighbours who know your entire history. You crave the different and unfamiliar. A clean page for a new chapter. You meet people who ask you questions about your hopes and dreams instead of making assumptions based on the kid you were. You can reinvent yourself.

Visits home become fleeting, dutiful, and less frequent with the passage of time. Christmas, Easter, birthdays. Obligatory weekends snatched between long stretches of work and endless, more pressing, commitments. The friends you whiled long summers away with are no longer around, and you realise that home isn't actually a place at all. It's a specific configuration of love and time. A constellation of stars that will never align again in your life. A collection of memories to be treated as something fragile and precious, like pieces of amber. Coming back to where they were formed feels more like a small desecration each time. You've become a ghost in the old places.

I leave the comfort of my hotel on a grim afternoon in early September. The sky is dappled silver and white like the belly of a great fish, and the drizzle is the kind that soaks you through rapidly. I can barely see the edge of the wood from the path along the ridge. It's just a dark smudge in the distance until I'm almost upon the boundary, when gnarled shapes begin to emerge from the fog. It's not hard to see why this place has instilled fear in locals for hundreds of years. Some areas just give off a vibe. *You're not welcome here.*

At least the good weather held for Dad's funeral last weekend. Not so long ago, I'd have spent the August Bank Holiday at a music festival, celebrating summer's last gasp with friends. But most of them have small children now, and they're not up for all-night partying anymore. They're all exhausted husks of themselves. When we see each other these days, they smile and nod and try to engage, but their gaze is always fixed on a point somewhere over my shoulder, ever vigilant in case little fingers are getting into things they shouldn't be, listening for bumps and scrapes and spats. They're all so different, and I'm in stasis – the same person I always was – except now my younger colleagues don't get my pop culture references and I have a dead dad.

I take a gulp of water from my flask. In hindsight, I probably shouldn't have had that fourth glass of wine in the hotel bar last night. Despite the damp and the first hint of autumn chill on the wind, I feel sweaty under my arms and my mouth is dry. Still, a brisk walk should blow the cobwebs away. I can feel the start of that jaded, bleak mood starting to encroach on my thoughts, and exercise will help stave it off. At least until the sun sets and it's time to open another bottle.

I'm at the edge of the wood now. The terrain always looks hostile at first, and it's even quieter than I remember. Maybe it's something to do with the way the trees are blanketed in thick lichen, deadening the sound. Slipping in between the trunks is like entering a cathedral. The cool shade, the hush, the inexplicable feeling that you're exposed to some sentient presence beyond the scope of your human understanding. They say animals have a sixth sense. Maybe that's why they lie low in the oakwood. All but the snakes. I pick my way carefully over roots and scree made slippery by the rain on moss.

My mother has always been the outdoorsy one in the family. She used to rally Dad for daily constitutionals, her enthusiasm eventually rubbing off on him though he was loath to admit it. She didn't make it back from Spain for the service. Apparently, she couldn't find someone to look after the dogs at short notice, and she doesn't like flying alone. She and my stepfather sent flowers. It's such a shame seeing all those bouquets and arrangements, knowing they will wilt and die in a matter of days. Death begetting more death.

In the days when I'd come here to get wasted, I didn't understand my mum's fondness for gardening and long hikes. I couldn't have thought of anything duller back then. But now I get it. It's important to mark the seasons. Everything seems to be speeding up, and if we don't take time to just be still and to let ourselves feel the natural rhythms and courses of things – well, then we're lost. In the end that is all there is. Endless cycles of death and rebirth. The only constant.

I watch my feet. It's so easy to turn an ankle in here and no one knows where I am to come looking for me. I stumble across the fly-blown carcass of a magpie at the bottom of a rowan tree. Its eyes are missing but its feathers glint in the low light, jewel tones like an oil slick on water. Tears prick my eyes suddenly, and I blink them away. I know it's not really the bird I'm crying for. "Rest in peace, little one," I whisper as I make my way further into the copse.

The rain gets heavier as I scramble over the rocks, water collecting on lichen-festooned branches that look like the giant, hairy arms of prehistoric creatures reaching for me. Every now and then a big splotch drips from a bough and trickles down the back of my neck. In ancient times, the entire moor would have been forest, before Mesolithic hunters cleared the land. This wood is a relic; a tiny, incorruptible piece of something far bigger and long gone. I try to imagine how vast and impenetrable it must have been. Wild animals hiding in the darkness. Snakes coiled under the mulch. Humans back then must have felt more prey than predator, until they found a way to flip the odds in their favour with cleansing fire. Even then, we were trying to bend the world to our will, burning Mother Nature for a witch.

The first time I hear voices nearby, I think it must be birds. I stop and listen. No – definitely people. I take a deep breath and try to quash the irrational anger I feel at having company. This place is on every rambler's bucket list now, there are pictures of its arthritic trees all over the internet, but although I haven't lived here for two decades, I still feel that the wood is mine somehow, and other walkers seem like trespassers.

"Just calm down! We're in Devon, not Death Valley!"

I watch as a middle-aged couple in shorts, windcheaters and bobble hats come into view. They're arguing. The woman is tucked into the man's side, supporting his weight on her shoulder. He is limping and wincing.

"Everything okay?" I call, alerting them to my presence. They look at me and stop in their tracks.

"No!" says the man, irritably. His skin is pallid, even in the drab, green-grey light of the wood.

"Sorry," says the woman, sheepishly. "We've had a bit of an accident. I think he trod on an adder. He's been bitten."

"Oh," I say. Despite the constant warnings from my childhood, it occurs to me I've never actually seen a snake here, much less heard of anyone being bitten. "Well, they're venomous but not deadly. You should get it checked out, though. The nearest hospital is about ten miles west of here. It's only fifteen minutes by car."

"It's all puffed up! Look!" the man complains through gritted teeth.

I repress the urge to roll my eyes. I bet if his companion had been struck, she wouldn't be making nearly as much fuss.

Still, the guy's calf does look red and inflamed. Maybe he's one of those super allergic people.

"Do you have a phone we can borrow?" the woman asks. "Neither of us can get a signal."

I pull out my phone and check the display. No bars.

"Shit!" I say. "Sorry. It's usually fine up here. Maybe there's a mast down or something."

"Do you think you can make it back to the car park?" the woman asks the man.

"You must be fucking joking!" he snaps. "It's a half-hour walk. This is agony. I feel dizzy. I need to sit down."

The woman looks at me apologetically, embarrassed by her partner's outburst. They're both wearing wedding bands. Married couple, then. She helps her husband over to a boulder and he lowers himself down, grunting. I stand and watch, feeling simultaneously useless and annoyed that my peace has been shattered.

"Right, well we can't sit here all day," the woman says. "You stay put and I'll run back to the hotel for help." She looks at me expectantly.

"I can stay with him until you get back," I offer, hoping I don't sound as reluctant as I am.

The woman smiles her gratitude, but her husband just scowls and resumes prodding at his swollen leg.

"I'll be as quick as I can," she promises, picking her way over the slick rocks.

"Careful," I warn. "Don't want you breaking an ankle!" I regret the words as soon as they're out of my mouth. I watch her leave and then turn my attention to the guy. He's sat there picking green fuzz off the rock he's sitting on with his thumbnail. Anger wells hot in me.

"Hey! That probably took hundreds of years to form. You're destroying a living organism."

The guy glowers up at me.

"It's just moss," he says, like a sulky kid.

"You have no idea what it is," I reply. "It could be lichen. A rare one."

"So? Same difference."

"Well, actually a lichen is a composite organism." I don't know why I feel compelled to educate this asshole and make myself sound like a total nerd in the process, but I can't stop talking. "Lichens are made up of an algae and a fungus in a symbiotic relationship. Two separate things that can't exist without one another. And, like I say, it's probably a lot older than you are." The guy stares blankly at me. "And more intelligent," I add under my breath.

"I hate the bloody countryside," he states finally. "I'll stick to Ibiza in future."

"Fucking tourists," I mutter.

"What did you say?"

"Nothing!"

I smile in a way that doesn't remotely reach my eyes and silently curse the polite social conventions that dictate I have to babysit this man-child.

The last time I spoke to Dad, he told me he'd been spending more and more time up here on the ridge. Since the divorce, I suppose his retirement wasn't all it had been cracked up to be. He was furious about the litter he saw strewn about at the height of summer. Apparently, some days there were literally hundreds of visitors. Energy drink cans, fag butts, and fast-food wrappers left by *disrespectful townies*, as he called them. People carving patterns into the velvety organisms covering the boulders, obliterating in the blink of an eye life that would take generations to reform. He seemed anxious and distracted. Looking back, I should have noticed he was acting out of character. I assumed it was an age thing; that without Mum to bolster his moods, he'd just get increasingly bitter and befuddled and short-tempered.

He mentioned there'd been a few incidents recently. Some lads came here one night to sniff glue or something and got into a fight. One ended up stabbing another and leaving him to bleed out. Then Dad said something weird. Something I wish I'd pressed him on in hindsight. He said the woods were waking up. He said the trees were putting thoughts in people's heads. Dark thoughts.

I finish my last dregs of water.

"Give us a swig," says the rude man with the snake-bite.

"That was the last of it. Sorry."

He huffs out through his nose and a fleck of snot lands precariously close to my boot. I suppress a knee-jerk urge to punch him in his stupid red face.

"I wasn't planning on having to share my supplies or my time with an ill-prepared ingrate who doesn't look where he's treading."

"Yeah, well, don't do me any favours, you stuck-up bitch," he hisses.

"Fine. I'm out of here. Good luck, dickhead! I hope you don't die before you can get the antidote!"

I turn and head off, a flurry of insults following in my wake. I feel kind of bad for the guy's wife, but I don't owe these strangers anything. Fuck them. Something about the man gives me the creeps anyway and I just want to be alone with my thoughts.

I clamber over roots and stones, keeping an eye out for errant wildlife, until I reach the large, flat rock known as the Druid Stone. The year I turned fifteen and started to embrace the spookiness of the moor, I came here with Mark O'Dowd on the summer solstice, and we sat on the altar stone and shared a can of strong, chemical-tasting lager. He was my first kiss. I can still see his face when I close my eyes – this sweet, dazed boy with my black lipstick smeared on his mouth.

My plan was to lie down on the stone and bathe in the gentle sounds of distant birdsong and the rain, to try and recapture some of the intense joy and wonder that used to come so readily to me in those days. But it feels wrong somehow, and when I touch the rough surface, my hand comes away sticky and russet red. At first, I think it's some kind of fungus, but as I look closer, the copper tang of fresh blood fills my nostrils. I gag, step back, and wipe my hand on my jeans. My mind jumps straight to all those tales we'd hear as kids about witchcraft and ritual sacrifice. I think of Dad telling me about the murder that supposedly happened here, but that was weeks ago. Any trace would have been washed away by now. Maybe an animal dragged its prey up here to eat. A fox, maybe, or a crow. I look around, spooked, and that's when I see it. A booted foot and a bare leg sticking out from behind a hawthorn bush.

My stomach does that lurch you get on a roller-coaster drop, and my heartbeat is loud and splashy in my own ears. I swallow the panic threatening to claw its way out of my throat and carefully approach. Someone is lying face-down, their top half obscured by the scrub. But as I get closer, I recognise the outfit. It's the woman who left me with her husband less than half an hour ago.

"Hello?" I shout. "Hey! Did you fall?"

There's no reply. I shiver. A big part of me wants to just turn and flee, to forget I was ever here. But I know I won't. I slowly approach and pull back some of the brush to reveal her torso and face. Her hat is missing and her hands are scratched. Her face is a mess. There's a nasty gash in her forehead and there's something misshapen about her head, like maybe some of her skull is crushed. She's unnaturally still and her skin already looks different. Pale and waxy.

"Oh God! Oh shit!" I pull out my phone on reflex before I remember it's dead. "*Fuck!*"

My mind is racing. What was she doing here anyway? She must have got lost trying to find her way back to the path and gone in completely the wrong direction. Maybe she tripped, hit her head on the Druid Stone, and managed to crawl a short distance before she succumbed to her injuries. I should check for sure if she's dead, but I can't bring myself to touch her. What if she's still alive, and I try to move her and make things worse? She's so horribly motionless. I don't know how you could do damage that catastrophic by falling over once. It looks like someone repeatedly smashed her head against something unyielding. I remember my hand on the stone coming away bloody.

I walk off slowly and try to retrace my route back to where I left the asshole husband. I go as fast and as gently as I can, taking care not to fall as I scramble through the woods. It's stopped raining but water is still running off branches and soaking my clothes. When I reach the spot where the man should be sitting, he's not there.

"Hello?" I call. "Hello?"

A wood pigeon bursts into hectic flight nearby, startling me, but there's no sign of the husband. Stubborn idiot probably decided to attempt the walk back after all. I decide to go to the hotel myself. If I meet him on the way, I can help him hobble back. Either way, I need to call the police. An ambulance. Someone. God, that poor woman! I try to blink the image of her ruined face away.

I take a deep breath and walk in the direction of the trail out of the wood. Every now and then I hear what sounds like voices – laughter and whispering – carried on the wind, but when I call out, no one responds.

I try not to dwell on how Dad must have felt the last time he was here. The deep, black melancholia eating him up. The loneliness. The despair. The spectre of his failed marriage blighting even the loveliest view, just as surely as the smashed glass and charred aerosol cans left by people who could never be enchanted by the folklore of the moors.

It's a while before I notice the shift in the light and realise it's getting dark. I grab my phone and check the clock. It's gone 7 p.m. How the hell did that happen? I left the hotel straight after an early lunch, the brisk walk here took no more than thirty minutes, and I've only been in the wood for maybe a couple of hours at most. But somehow it's approaching dusk. And I'm lost. I should have hit the boundary ages ago. It's like I've been going round and around in a spiral back to the heart of the wood. I stop and feel an icy dump of adrenaline course through me when I see the Druid Stone up ahead. The woman, however, is gone.

My breathing becomes shallow. I'm thirsty, too. I didn't bring provisions. I wasn't going to be out for long. I just wanted to say goodbye to the place because I knew deep down there was nothing left for me here now. I wanted to feel cocooned by the soft trees one last time and let the magic in the earth fill me up like I used to when my life was just starting, and my friends seemed immortal, and everything felt possible.

I turn my back to the stone and walk in a straight line away from it. After a few minutes I see him. The snake-bite man. He's grunting and swearing, trying to make his way over the boulders and leaf litter. He is using his hands on the rocks, crawling and hopping, his bad leg dragging behind him. He looks up and sees me.

"You!" he says. "Have you seen my wife?"

I pause, not sure how to explain that I thought she was dead, but now her body seems to have disappeared.

"I... I think she fell," I stammer. "She was unconscious so I came looking for you before I went to fetch help, but you'd moved and then I... I got lost, I think, and when I got back to the Druid Stone, she'd... gone."

The man is looking at me strangely. There's sweat beading on his brow and white foam collecting in the corners of his mouth.

"*Liar*," he shouts. "You've done something to her!"

"No!" I protest. "Of course not! She must have stumbled and—"

"You've done it to get back at me. You didn't want her to get help for me because I destroyed your bloody moss, so you went after her and you did something to her."

"NO!" I shout. Maybe the venom has affected his mind. Could *he* have killed his wife?

The man lunges forward on his hands and one leg, scuttling towards me like some horrid insect.

"You're going to tell me where she is, so help me God!" he says, snarling, as he tries to grab at me.

I leap backwards and he topples over, an animalistic howl escaping his lips as he hits the ground. "I'll kill you, you bitch! Come here! I'll strangle you! I'll bash your brains out!"

I break into a run, concentrate on staying upright, and I don't stop until I find myself back at the altar.

I sink down on the stone, avoiding the sticky blood which still stains the surface – proof at least that I haven't totally lost my mind. The light is dwindling and as I sit and try to make sense of my situation, I hear hushed voices again. Now I'm perfectly still and closer to the ground, I realise they are not coming from around me, but *beneath* me. I drop to my knees and put my ear to the stone. Voices. I can't make out what they're saying, but there are hundreds of them. Maybe thousands. Down here, between the fallen leaves and the rocks, I see a myriad of little fruiting bodies bursting up through the substrate. They're so small and perfectly formed. In the half-light, they seem to move – writhing and growing before my very eyes. Tiny motes hover in the air around them – spores, I think – and I wonder if maybe these mushrooms are psychotropic, because the buried voices are getting louder and I feel the strangest compulsion to join them down in the dirt. It would be so quiet under there. He'd never find me in the earth.

I start to dig where the ground is exposed and less stony. My nails break and tear on the impacted loam. It hurts but it doesn't seem to matter much. A few inches down, I touch something soft and woolly. I scrape and tug it free. A bobble hat. The one that unfortunate woman was wearing earlier today. Impossible! How could it be down here under years of soil and rock? I keep clawing at the ground. And there it is. Hair. Her hair caked with blood not yet fully clotted. Again, impossible! It's like the wood has simply swallowed her up...

The crack of branches snapping draws my attention up to where a monstrous, dark shape is moving towards me. It moves sinuously over the crags and crannies in a caterpillar-tread motion. As it approaches, I can make out the prone form of the snake-bitten man, his pale features almost luminous in the encroaching gloaming. He's being transported through the trees on a huge knot of adders, their bodies rolling over and under each other, carrying him inexorably along on the crest of a dark wave. An ocean of snakes. They slither past where I'm crouched, and I see him struggle for a few seconds then go limp again as the snakes form a band around him, their muscular bodies restricting his movements. They take him to the base of an old mountain ash, which tips backwards, making room for them beneath it, gaping open like a giant, ragged maw. Through the hellmouth and down, down they go, dragging their victim through the dense network of hyphae and roots until he's vanished from sight, gobbled up by the earth.

The wood is waking up.

For a second, I hear my father's voice as clear as day, rising up above the fungal cacophony. I must be losing my grip on reality. Maybe it's the trees. Maybe the spores. Maybe grief. I feel the miles and miles of branching life underneath the moor reaching for me, hungry for me. Things with no mouths or eyes or brains, but capable of communion beyond human comprehension. Complex, primal things that were here long before us, things we cannot name and cannot fully understand so we call them madness, and magic, and piskies, and spirits, and God, and Old Nick. I laugh as the truth dawns on me. They're not just here, in this wood, under this moor. They're everywhere – hiding in plain sight. They've always been here, waiting for us to overstep the mark. We are just a blip on their timeline – a pest to be eradicated. Balance must be restored.

It hits me then; I'm never leaving this wood. It won't let me go. What a fool I was to ever try to leave it. I pull myself up onto the altar stone and roll onto my back. I look up at the sky – it's turning indigo like ink in water, and the clouds are parting for the stars to peep through. Old light from dead stars that probably winked out of existence millions of years before the first man drew breath. It's beautiful. I am so tiny. I am fleeting. I understand why my father did what he did now. He was impatient to escape the flesh and become oakwood again. That's why he sat on the altar stone and washed down a handful of diazepam with two-thirds of a bottle of single malt and let the night take him.

Cold tendrils of fern lick at my wrists, tightening as they creep up around my arms. The Druid Stone hums. I close my eyes and take a few deep green breaths. I see Mark's astonished expression, my lipstick on his face. How far away he seems now. How naïve we were. How human. Woody roots probe at my mouth, forcing their way past my teeth and down my throat. They clasp my neck. I taste and smell mud and it feels apt that the site of my first kiss should be that of my last. The rock under my back feels soft and I let myself sink down to join the voices beneath.

I'm finally awake.

Blessed Mary

Stephen Volk

'I wish of this folly, and of all similar follies, that they find no place anywhere apart from the museum of the historian and the antiquary.'

Rev William Roberts
The Religion of the Dark Ages (1852)

MAM IS GONE. Mam is everywhere. In the badly fitted doors of the kitchen, hanging off when all it would've taken is a screwdriver. In the cooker encrusted with splashes of veg and spuds boiled to oblivion. But that's how they liked it, that generation. Post-war. The make-do-and-mend brigade. State of it, he thinks. Old things of old people. The crap they cling to.

I feel out of place here, she says, looking around at the debris of a life as if standing in a bomb site.

Give it time, he says. How d'you think I feel? I'm English.

Her mother was never a hoarder, but there are decent pieces of furniture, Fifties and repro, nothing worth a jot, all inherited, as they've inherited this, and it'll save them buying new. It didn't have to be showy, after all, just liveable-in. A bolt-hole from London, as they discussed. A bit of rough round the edges adds to the charm, he tells himself, almost persuasively.

First day in primary, she says, picking up a framed photograph. Look at those knees.

As soon as they'd arrived, he'd opened the windows to air the place, but now wants to put the heating on, and feels unassailably smug when he gets the pilot light working first go. He's not used to such manly achievements, and says so. She says, I know.

He picks up the copy of *Radio Times* they bought when they filled up with petrol near Newport. A flick to the page for December 24th tells him that evening they could look forward to Christmas Mass from Ely Cathedral with the Choir of King's College, followed at 7:30 by *It's Cliff Richard* with guest stars Olivia Newton-John, Labi Siffre and The Flirtations.

Let's go to the pub, he says.

* * *

Leaving the house, he can smell the earth in the air. Wet. Tangy. He almost likes it, but he'd like a cigarette more. The only pub in town is called The Hendre and it's all downhill. Used to take five minutes when she was in juniors. He says he's surprised she doesn't have calves like a prop forward.

Turn you on, would it?

Might do.

* * *

He's surprised when she slows down as it hoves into view.

What if I see someone I know?

You won't. You've been away seven years.

Some regulars have been coming here for seventy.

Then you'll get a rapturous welcome. The wanderer returns from the sea.

No, I won't.

Come on, what's the worst that can happen? A half of shit shandy?

I'm not drinking, remember?

* * *

As if he could forget – with that eight-and-a-half month bulge sticking out in front of her. Due date looming. Straight in for a check-up when they get back. Whole point of the holiday. Last taste of freedom. Last few days of sprog-free living. He wants to enjoy every second of it. Wants *her* to enjoy every second of it, more to the point.

❋ ❋ ❋

There's no harpist in the corner. What they get is a jukebox playing 'Coz I Luv You' by Slade. The bar isn't busy. Amongst the brown suits, corduroy jackets, and blazers, a smattering of Welsh miners, or ex-miners, he suspects. Their beaten bones and ground-down constitutions make him feel guilty about his own life of fresh air and invoices above ground.

There's a red dragon flag on the wall behind the counter. He wonders if it's a signal of nationalist fervour. The IRA's in the news. Rioting in Ulster. Rubber bullets. *Brits out.* Earlier in the year three off-duty squaddies were lured to a pub and shot. He thinks about what kind of look he'd get if he wandered into a Belfast bar. But the Welsh are apathetical.

More interested in singing and rugby. He shoves his prejudices back in their box, but, honestly, thinks himself hardly an invader. Hardly foreign. Doesn't look it and doesn't sound it. Who is he kidding?

He orders two drinks, convivially, and crisps. Feeling conspicuous as soon as he opens his gob. Oh, and twenty Bensons, please. Ta.

Diolch, the landlord says. Adding, Thanks, pointedly.

He zigzags to the table where his wife sits, catching the eyes looking her over. Couple of long hairs, a few Jason King moustaches, but most of them look like they've never seen flares before, let alone denim dungarees. Let alone a heavily pregnant woman in denim dungarees in a pub.

He knows the reason she's nervous coming back, of course. She'd left under a cloud, but she had to get over it, if they'd have any hope of carving a future here. Spending time in this place, away from the grind of the big city, whenever they could. Kid in tow. Maybe two. Who knows?

The crisp packet is empty and so is his pint glass when revelry booms on the night air. He wonders why drunks are making a racket outside when there's plenty of room within. He hears a noise like two sticks being hit together, then accordion music, which generates a rumble of anticipation. Noses press to the window. The landlord bolts the pub door. A cheer goes up. Fists banging the table in rhythm. Expectation.

Here we go, she says, her eyes becoming strangely blank and focusing on a soggy beer mat as she drains her bitter lemon. The voice from outside is a tremulous tenor, the stuff of Eisteddfodau:

> *Wel dyma ni'n dwad*
> *Gyfeillion diniwad*
> *I ofyn am gennad*
> *I ofyn am gennad*
> *I ofyn am gennad i ganu!*

He raises his eyebrows.

Any idea what's going on?

Bit of madness, she says.

Bit of gibberish, more like.

He flinches and almost leaves his seat when he hears a swish at the window. Sees an old-fashioned broom clawing at the glass. A cascade of laughter greets his discomfort.

What was that?

Tradition, she murmurs.

A loud rapping assaults the door as he remembers it's Christmas Eve, when all sorts of tomfoolery abounds, just like New Year. Mystery plays. Mumming. St. George versus the Devil, with St. Nicholas saving the day. Which he recalls from when he was a child, once upon a time. But these calls from outside, echoed by responses from within, are in Welsh, and he doesn't understand a bloody word.

What are they saying?

Don't ask me. You're looking at O-Level Welsh, failed.

Soon the chanted responses are over, the doors of the pub fling open and costumed men burst in, coloured ribbons and rosettes attached to their clothes, all wearing gabardine macs and flat caps, the leader with a sash around his waist, gesturing a horsewhip at customers with menacing theatricality. The squeezebox player follows, rendering a peripatetic 'Sosban Fach'. After him, a frantic if not manic duo, one with a false, beaked nose, who carries eagerly snapping tongs, the other dressed as a woman in pigtails and a shawl, with padded breasts and a broom made from twigs, which scrapes the floor before being shoved in people's faces, to the regulars' cackling delight. All the visitors' faces are blanked out with greasepaint – white, brown, and black.

He looks at his wife but she doesn't meet his eyes, because then comes the horse-headed thing, led by a man in a top hat tugging a rein attached to its bridle. In from the dark it whinnies and shakes, that big skull of a horse on a pole, painted white, the white of bone. The back of it being attached to a white sheet which drapes down to cover the person underneath, who manipulates the head. He knows that. He knows it is a man, not a horse. Not a thing, even as the light catches its beer bottle caps for roving eyes, it is a feller shrouded in white linen, a bloke with a streaming mane of colours and a holly and ivy crown. He knows that. Rigged with a mouth that can open and close like a puppet's.

Clack. Clack. Clack.

The effigy runs around neighing in man-voice, snapping its jaws, creating havoc, the leader chap pretending to restrain it, while the accordion sails, jitters and wails, contributing to an air of dangerous mischief.

What the hell's that?

His wife isn't looking.

Diolch yn fawr, boys! calls the landlord.

Rattling a plastic bucket under customers' chins, the performers collect money. He gets it now. Takes out a quid. The man with the pigtails and bosom doffs his cap, tweaks his tits, then clutches his genitals. The Englishman pretends to be amused. Making sure his wife can see he isn't.

The horse's head slurps at a man's beer, picking up the glass in its teeth and spilling it down its front. Laughter, gritty and gruff, cuts the air. It guzzles, then lets the invisible liquid warble down its throat, before diving to nip another man's crotch.

Clack. Clack. Clack.

When the horse skull glides to their table, creeping up on a new, unsuspecting victim, his wife visibly stiffens. The pub is clapping, turning to watch as the white bone head nuzzles against the Englishman's shoulder, then it swims over to rub against his wife's cheek, circling her head, clack-clacking, before descending to her chest. She swipes it away from her. Not forcefully, but firmly. It looks perplexed, tilting its head this way, then that.

Let's go.

You're all right, her husband says quietly. Only a bit of fun.

No. Let's go. Now.

* * *

The house is still cold. He puts the electric fire on. All four bars. They watch the end of *The Onedin Line*, neither of them concentrating. He wants a Scotch and the *Ghost Story for Christmas*. She doesn't. In bed, to take her mind off, he does his best imitation of Dylan Thomas.

Captain Curlew curled up in his beddy-byes wrapped like a Swiss roll, dreaming of jam, Belisha beacons, and Gossamer Beynon, who blew hot and cold, if his luck was in.

She turns her back.

Nice as bacon, he says. And twice as tasty.

Your Welsh accent is shit.

English, see.

* * *

Christmas morning he opens champagne. One won't do any harm. Merry Christmas.

Merry Christmas, she says.

It's warming up now. I got more wood. Put more logs on. My arms hurt a bit, to be truthful.

Honest to God. You.

* * *

The presents sit under the artificial tree they crammed into the back seat of the car. Woolworths. Silver-wrapped chocolates and everything. Her present is a dress.

If you don't like it, I can take it back. I kept the receipt.

I love it, she says. Open yours.

He carefully unwraps an expensive fountain pen, Montblanc, and diary.

You'll have plenty to put in it.

I know I will.

They kiss under the plastic mistletoe.

* * *

Still, he feels her tension, and knows where it's coming from – the past. At nineteen she got pregnant. Didn't want to marry her boyfriend. Didn't even want to tell him. Got a train to London. Scraped together money for an abortion. He doesn't know how she did that, and has never asked. All she said was, she told her ex what she'd done by phone. No intention of going home any time soon, or ever. Nothing there for her except her mother's disappointment. The shame she'd feel when she looked into the faces of people who knew. So she became a secretary, then an assistant art buyer at an ad agency. He was an illustration studio rep. They met two, three times a week regarding work. Then two, three times a week outside work. Six months later she asked him to move in, as it was the Logical Next Step. Six months after that he asked her if she wanted to get married, so they did. Soon after that – pregnant.

This time she'd done things in the right order.

This time things were going to work out.

* * *

It was him.

He looks puzzled.

The Mari Lwyd, she says. The hobby-horse thing. The hooded figure. The one in the pub.

She means her ex.

You can't know that.

I can. The way it was moving. The way it was lingering. You must have noticed. The thing went straight to you. Then straight to me.

How could you possibly know that?

I do. I'm telling you.

Her voice rises an octave and he doesn't want her to get upset, so changes the subject. There's another present under the tree. You can open that. I've had mine.

Oh, fuck off.

Merry Christmas, he calls after her as she goes out into the garden. He makes two coffees, knowing it won't mix well with the Buck's Fizz. The garden is a wreck. Hedges down, fencing strewn. Plants and weeds overgrown. But he doesn't want to be negative.

Lick and a polish. Be right as rain in no time.

What is the point?

She returns inside, as if not wanting to be near him. He follows, wanting to be near her.

Are we going to talk about this?

Are we? I don't know. I've got a headache. I'm going to bed.

* * *

Pointless trying to reason with her. Hormones are incendiary. Instead he gets the turkey prepared. Stuffing. Sausages. Roasties. Doesn't know where they are going to put it all. There'll be enough to feed the five thousand.

He wants to call his mum but there's no working phone. The line has been disconnected due to her mother's unpaid bills. No one rings me anyway, she'd complained. Ever the martyr. Making her daughter feel guilty for fleeing to London. To a life. What a betrayal that was.

He'd warned his own mum and dad he wouldn't be able to call and wish them happy Christmas on the day, and had visited the Midlands to exchange presents a week earlier. He was given a book token, and an overdue birthday card with a racing car on it, as if he was eight years old. They'd moved to Dudley. A bungalow, which he was told all the young, successful people were doing now.

* * *

If your ex was partial to dressing up with the local folk dancers, I'd say that was even more reason to completely forget about the bugger.

You don't understand about the Mari Lwyd.

No, I don't. I've never heard of it, to be honest. What is it, some quaint old, bonkers Welsh custom?

Don't be a patronising sod.

I'm not. I want to know. Tell me, he says, refilling his glass of wine. It's an expensive bottle and he intends to enjoy it, even if she's sticking to water.

It's not unique to here. It's enacted all over South Wales in various forms. Penhafod has its own take on it, but basically the hobby-horse goes from house to house begging, I suppose you'd call it.

He stabs some turkey from the platter with a fork. Offers it her. She frowns like it's potentially toxic.

When we used to hear the music and saw she was out, it would petrify us.

She?

Yes, her. The bedsheet mare. My cousin and I would run inside shouting, *The Mari Lwyd, the Mari Lwyd is coming!* and shut all the doors and windows and hide under our beds until she was gone.

Christ. You saw that as a nipper?

Not full on. I'd hear the knocking and the *pwnco* – that's the to-and-fro of the poetry – and hear the clacking jaws. Hear my dad invite them in for grub and a snifter. They were all his mates.

Even so, that must've been terrifying.

It was. You don't come from Penhafod unless you have recurring dreams of the bloody thing. I did.

Most we have in Coventry is Lady Godiva and Peeping Tom, and I thought that was bloody weird. He hopes she might smile, but she doesn't. She's hardly made a dent in her food and the gravy is getting cold.

It's always happened at Christmas. The idea is, a bunch of men accompany the horse on its travels. One carrying the head, the leader who's called the 'Sergeant', the 'Merryman' who makes the music, and two 'Punch and Judy' types. They knock the door and call on you to let the Mari Lwyd in. Doing it through song. You're expected to deny them entry in verse, and the two sides battle it out till the mare is allowed in and confers luck on the household for the coming year. In return for food and drink.

Blimey.

189

Grey mare… That's what it means. Mari Lwyd.

Why would you try to keep it out, if it bestows good luck?

I didn't write the script. Sorry if the legend makes no fucking sense.

He sighs.

Anyway the host always loses and the mare is let in. This horse of the underworld who's been clacking and causing mischief since the Dark Ages, apparently.

You know a lot about it.

It was part of my childhood. All our childhoods. His childhood, too.

Your ex.

Yes, my ex. His dad was the Mari Lwyd when we were kids and I'm damn certain sure his son's the current one. Why wouldn't he be?

Do you know for a fact he still lives here, even?

Where else would he be?

Maybe he's got out of this shit hole, like you did?

No. I know he hasn't done.

How do you know?

I know, all right?

* * *

He asks if she is going to finish her meal and she shakes her head. Says under her breath she's sorry. He says it doesn't matter. Scrapes her leftovers into the bin, knowing the sight of him doing that will make her feel guilty. He tries not to be pissed off. His glass needs topping up again. An inch left in the bottle, then not.

Look, I can't see why you're so worried, he says. First of all we're halfway up a fucking great hill. They won't be bothered coming up here. Why would they?

You know why. Unless you're completely stupid.

Second of all, you said yourself it's an innocent Christmas ritual from time immemorial. Just a way of giving handouts to the poor. Like carol singing. You're not terrified of carol singers coming to the door, are you?

Don't make me out to be—

Well, what were they doing in the pub that was so bad?

You know what they were doing. You saw what *he* was doing.

No. I didn't. Just tell me. What are you afraid of?

It goes on all the way from Christmas Eve to Twelfth Night. That's what I'm afraid of. I'm afraid of them coming here. I'm afraid of *him* coming here.

So what?

So *what?* Her eyes burn at him. You'd let him in?

No, of course not. That idiot isn't coming anywhere near you or our baby. He can fuck off.

Can he, though?

Yes. I'll make him.

What if you can't?

What do you mean, what if I can't?

Nothing, she says, getting up out of her chair. One of the rickety dining chairs that had been in the house since she was born. The chairs had seemed huge when she was five, not a thought of boys or babies in her head. I'm going for a lie down.

You've just got up.

I'm eight and a half months pregnant. I'm tired. Believe it or not. And I can do what I like.

* * *

He leaves it a tactful hour, marinating in his own juices, then goes up to see how she is. The bedroom is even colder than downstairs. They brought new bedding, but the dust is embedded, just like the memories.

Can I get you anything? Are you feeling rough? There's nothing wrong? Should I call a doctor?

She shakes her head, eyes red-rimmed from tears. Clearly doesn't want to talk. Not to him anyway.

Just relax, is all I'm saying.

He leans over and kisses her on the forehead. She is warm. He places his hand on her bump and she holds it there.

When I first came to London I spent a whole day in the British Museum trying to find out where it came from, but nobody seems to know.

Not that you were obsessed or anything.

She discards his hand.

I'm interested.

No, you're not.

I am.

She sighs.

Lost in the mists of Celtic mythology, he says. Pagan, I expect.

I don't know. Chapel and Methodism tried to clamp down on it, though, apparently.

'Course they did. Touting superstition of their own. Sign here for the new improved load of bollocks.

Don't.

Sorry. Sorry.

I don't know if she's pre-Christian at all. One story says she symbolises a grey mare who was turfed out of the stable in Bethlehem to make room for the baby Jesus. They say the mare wandered, but could find no resting place, and ended up giving birth to her foal in the desert, all alone.

Yeah, well – oh, God, he says, suddenly sniffing the acrid smell of burning. Oh, shit.

* * *

He opens the oven door to the blackened husks. A rolling ball of smoke billows out, clinging to the ceiling and hanging over the room like a storm cloud. There was no timer but he thought he'd remember. *Well, you know what thought did*, as his mum used to say. Salvageable they are not. Useful as cannon balls, possibly.

Confession, she says when she comes downstairs to the sorry sight. I've never liked Christmas pudding.

She opens her arms wide and he walks into them gratefully. She wraps him up.

It'll be all right, he says.

What will?
Everything.

* * *

She keeps on her dressing gown. The dress he bought her for Christmas lies draped over the back of the moth-eaten settee. He wants her to try it on, but doesn't dare ask. That is the way the day is going. He does the washing up, squeezing the last fart out of the Fairy Liquid, and she does the drying with the worn tea towel with the scorch mark on it. Then they sit watching *The Two Ronnies* and *The Morecambe & Wise Christmas Special* with Glenda Jackson, André Previn, and Shirley Bassey.

Fireworks illuminate the sky outside. He opens the curtains and watches as they pop and light up the garden in reds and greens. Somebody's birthday, he jokes, given it is Christmas.

Funny man.

Come and watch. He holds out his hand.

She shakes her head, the big ball of her belly confining her to the upholstery. Stretched out on the settee like a beached porpoise, feet up on one of the arms. He kneels and counts her little piggies then kisses them one by one. Runs his tongue over her foot the way a dog would lick. She twitches at the sensation, recoiling slightly, affecting annoyance but liking it really.

When another firework bangs, she jerks.

Nothing's going to happen. You're being ridiculous.

Another descending sprawl drenches the garden in silver glittering stars.

Close the curtains. Please. Close the curtains.

On sufferance, he does.

I can hear voices, she says.

You can't.

I can. Outside.

You can't.

He thinks at first it is the wind but then with a gnawing wave of nausea discerns it to be the wheezing lungs of the accordion. She struggles to bend up, elbows under her, panting.

Right. Don't overreact. Don't panic. This is—

Fuck, she gasps. Shit… No, no, *please*.

He can hear Judy sweeping at windows and doors. Brushing and footsteps circulating the house. Punch is banging the door with his fire iron.

196

Wel dyma ni'n dwad
Gyfeillion diniwad
I ofyn am gennad I ganu

Fuck… What are they saying?

I don't know, she blurts.

You're Welsh.

I told you. O-Level. Failed.

Os oes gennych atebion
Wel, dewch a nhw'n union
I ateb prydyddion y gwylie

They want a response, she says.

Well we can't give one, can we?

Help me!

I can't. How can I?

The knocking gets louder. More insistent. He feels his scrotum wither. Now he can hear Judy's broom beyond the curtains, in the garden. The twig-ends scratching.

Shit!

He walks towards the front door. She grabs him by the wrist.

What are you doing?

Letting them in.

You're joking.

What else can I do?

No! For fuck's sake—

It's a yuletide ritual. It's a fucking wassail. They're not terrorists. They're not the IRA. They're fucking Morris Men. I'll talk to them perfectly reasonably and they'll go away.

No they won't. I know they won't. *He* won't. Please don't do this.

He hears womanly laughing by the non-woman Judy-thing. The scraping melody of the out-of-tune accordion. 'Men of Harlech' now – taking the piss. The hammering tongs threaten to splinter the front door.

If you damage this property, I swear—

But splinter it they do. And she is moaning, pregnant, gabbling, rocking, pregnant, barefoot, freaking out.

Right, you shits, he starts shouting now, addressing them through the woodwork. You're frightening my wife now! I'm being reasonable, but I'm not having it. This is private property and this is beyond a joke. I want you to fuck off please!

She, sobbing, bleating, cowering, lets out a low, low, groan.

Shit, shit, shit…

Go upstairs. I'll deal with this, he says – thinking, you're English, mate. You can't deal with anything. I said go fucking upstairs.

She doesn't. Instead snatches a carving knife. Fear bleaching her skin.

> *Nid ewn ni ar gered*
> *Heb dorri ein syched*
> *Heb dorri ein syched – nos henno*

He wonders what they are spouting. Whether it is even part of the call and response now, or just jibes and taunts. A hymn. Or prayer. Something pagan. Primal. Paleolithic. Megalithic.

> *Nid yfwn o'r ffynnon*
> *I oeri ein calon*
> *I fagu clefydon – y gwylie*

Panic chokes his voice. I don't know what you're saying. I don't know what you want. If you want money, I'll give you money.

She, hyperventilating. Fingers splayed over the

dome belly. Cramps as the door splits, shedding the now-dangling Chubb.

Please. Please don't do this, he calls out. For Christ's sake, don't do this.

Rhyw bump o wyr hawddgar,
Rhai goray y ddaear
Yn canu mewn gwir air
Yn canu mewn gwir air
Yn cany mewn gwir air am gwrw

His eyes are drawn to the fireworks going off in the sky above the garden, the smash of glass, the figure with the pigtails and broom leaping into the room, bringing in bushes, holly, ivy, draped in the curtains, sending the Woolworths Christmas tree flying, baubles cracking. Then he/she is clambering over the settee, over his wife's new dress, staining it with clodges of dirt.

The front door swings ajar, creaking like Mam's death rattle, coming apart with the fire iron and feet and horse's hooves. The Merryman with his music. Sergeant with his horsewhip. Punch in his whiteface and nose. A riot of sashes, ribbons, leather.

Clothes smeared with moss and leaves, they grab the Englishman, force his arms behind his back. The Sergeant wears a miner's helmet. The light of its lamp blinds him.

> *Mae Mari Lwyd lawen*
> *Yn dod I'ch ty'n rhonden*
> *A chanu yw ei diben, mi dybiaf*

Merryman and Punch stand to attention either side of the door. All four men of twilight making way for the Mari Lwyd.

The hobby-horse enters, not at a gallop but perusing the scene created in its honour. The horse's skull, white and shimmering as the moon. Ghost-white cape hanging. No sign of the puppet master within except for the movement he makes. To say dancing would be a blasphemy.

It comes right up to his face and gazes into his soul. Eyes dead. Jaws munching.

Clack. Clack. Clack.

Clubbed by fire iron and horsewhip, he bends as they use the reins to tie him. Unable to protect himself, let alone others. Hearing his wife's screaming, he sees his glasses fall, bloodstained, to the carpet. With the second scream sees the black lace-up boots of the Mari Lwyd tread on the lenses. Crush them. Crack them. Then, with the third scream, sees no more.

* * *

Blood fills his eyes. Smears his vision.

Her wrists are tied to the bed head. She isn't wearing the dressing gown anymore. The electric fire is on, so that is good. All four bars, to keep her warm. Straw is strewn over the carpet. He can smell the heady aroma of a barn.

The miner's lamp scans the room like a lighthouse beacon as the Sergeant struggles to hold the carving knife steady because it's in his hand now, not hers, and the wide, clean, blade glints, pressing under her chin as she writhes. She is a good writher.

Red-faced. Veins in her neck like wires.

Punch and Judy hold her knees apart and high, hooked over one shoulder apiece. Punch making pincer-snaps between her legs with his iron tongs, nosing at her exposed vagina with his pink, plastic proboscis while the flat caps in their gabardine coats giggle. Those of the pit.

Her husband sees his own face in the mirror hanging above the bed, the chin of the grey mare skull of the Mari Lwyd resting on the top of his head. Flats of the hands of the man under the bedsheet behind him boxing his cheeks firmly so he cannot look away as she gives birth.

Amniotic sac, white bubble, feet first, it comes out, wet and inevitable, hoofed legs going on forever, then the head – long, long head, see – joints knuckle-like and slippery, then the sac bursts, or they break it with their fingers. Pull the stick-legs. Ease the thing out into its joyous birthday.

The foal shines with a silvery, moon-begotten film.

He's beautiful, his wife coos in her radiant sweat, looking down between her thighs at the bundle with bottle-top eyes.

He is glorious, she says.

The Great White

Benjamin Spada

YOU HAVE TO pay your dues. Doesn't matter what line of work you're in, doesn't matter how far back the debt goes, a man has a responsibility to settle what's owed. This rule of honor is non-negotiable. It's as unbreakable a law as gravity. If it weren't, then maybe I wouldn't be burning my very well-earned leave days to help out an old friend. A 'hunting trip' he called it. The problem was, if he was calling for my help then there was something very wrong going on.

I'd been driving through the night to make the six-hundred-mile trip from San Diego to Truckee in one go, and the hours were getting to me. I forced back a yawn as I rolled down the window to let the icy mountain air buffet the truck's cabin. My thermos still half-full of hot coffee and the chilling wind worked together to give me a boost. I gulped down more of the coffee, relishing the combined hot and cold sensations. I told myself that the gooseflesh rippling across my forearm was because of the temperature; I told myself I wasn't afraid of what my friend was getting me into. I said a lot of things to myself the rest of the way. I even believed half of them.

By the time I arrived at our meeting spot there was enough caffeine coursing through my veins to send me into cardiac arrest. I pulled into the parking lot of a 24-hour diner and killed the engine. For the next two minutes I just sat in my truck, not wanting to get out of my seat. Finally, I grabbed my .45 from the glovebox, stowed it in the holster on my hip, and headed for the door.

My boots crunched over the salted parking lot as the little heat I'd had from the truck's cabin was quickly sapped away by the mountain air. It was so much thinner up here. I stuck my hands in my pockets and shouldered my way inside the diner. The man I was meeting, Jim Blakes, waited at a booth in the back corner.

"Look who it is: big old Cole West."

"You're looking big yourself, Blakes," I said, pointing at the paunch he'd developed since hanging up his uniform.

"It's good to see you, Cole," said Blakes, offering a handshake.

"Been too long."

We shook, and I slid into the seat opposite him.

"What's it been, six, seven years?"

Blakes had retired eight years ago, and since then looked like he'd completely abandoned the close-cut military look for that of a certified mountain man. His beard went to his chest, and without any mandated PT sessions his belly threatened to knock the table over as he scooted back in his seat.

"Eight years," I answered. "Albania. But you already knew that." I waved down the waitress to order a cup of coffee, but thought better of it and asked for hot water instead. I needed to dilute the deluge of caffeine I'd already guzzled down on my way here.

Blakes shifted uneasily in his seat. Clearly, he didn't know how this conversation was supposed to go. I owed Blakes my life, plain and simple. When a brother-in-arms calls in a no-questions-asked favor like that? You show up. But the request wasn't what

206

was twisting me up. It was how scared Blakes sounded when he called me. We'd walked through the fire together, he and I, and he hadn't even flinched then. So what had got him shaking now?

"I'm not a hunter," I said as I took a sip of the hot water. "But you are. Matter of fact I seem to remember you not being able to shut up about it. Deer. Bear. Cougars. Been around the world, done it all. So why in the hell would you need me?"

Blakes forced a smile. "I seem to recall you hunting certain things just fine."

I set my cup on the table and met his eyes. "People aren't animals, Jim."

For some reason that made him chuckle. It was an empty little laugh. If anything, it only made me more uncomfortable. Just as I was about to speak up again Blakes cut me off.

"It's funny, you look around here and you forget that once upon a time this was the *frontier*. Covered wagons and oxen on the Oregon Trail, headed for California and the promise of a better life. All these winter resorts, Starbucks on every corner, and generous cell service will have you forgetting what people went through out here. But all that bullshit's just a covering. A thin layer of paint. The wilderness? It's still there… Waiting just past the trees. Hiding just up the mountains. Hungering just beyond the tourist trails."

Part of me wondered if my old comrade had been up here in the mountains for too long. Or maybe the demons of our past deeds had done more damage than I knew. There was a spookiness in his eyes. Things swirling around in those windows of his soul. Shadowy things. Not one of them matched the empty smile on his face.

"A lot of things can go wrong out there in the dark, Cole. Lot more people go missing during hunting season than you'd think. Lose their way, maybe. Run afoul of a bear, some. Not much investigating gets done when they don't have a body, even less when it looks like an animal attack."

"Blakes," I said, with just enough of an edge to cut him off, "tell me what I'm doing here."

He nodded to himself as he fidgeted about in his seat. His anxiety only made mine grow. It was like a black spot in my gut that sucked up all the warmth in me. Blakes cast his eyes to the windows. The thick darkness outside was impenetrable.

"There's something out there that's been hunting people," Blakes finally answered. "You said you've never gone hunting, not for any animals anyway. And that's just fine. Because the thing out there? It isn't one either."

My hand moved with a mind of its own to my holstered pistol. "What is it, Blakes?"

He never took his eyes off the window. I tried not to notice the tremor running through his hands atop the table. The twitch in his throat as he attempted to speak, but choked on the words. My own pulse quickened as Blakes let the moment hang. He let it, until he finally broke the silence.

"It's a wendigo."

* * *

When you've faced as many things as I have, survived the encounters I've been thrown into, and pulled the trigger as often as me, you tend to keep an open mind. An old friend luring me in with tall tales of monsters in the dark set me on my heels, though. Whether or not he was crazy didn't matter: Blakes truly believed it. I should've gotten out of that diner right then and there. Should've left Blakes to whatever paranoid mania he'd fallen prey to up here in the mountains. Maybe called some of those fellows in the nice white clothes to hook Blakes up with a lease to a comfy padded white room.

A man settles what's owed...

Instead, I asked him to tell me more. I wasn't a psychologist, but entertaining the ramblings of a crazy person might not be the smartest thing. The idea was I could gauge whether or not he was a danger to me, too. If he was grounded enough to recognize that I was still a friend. And still human.

It was right as I considered waving the waitress over and ordering some food when my friend let loose with the details. I'd known that Blakes' father was a forest ranger, and that he'd taught a younger Blakes everything he knew about being an outdoorsman, but I didn't know that he'd died out in the woods outside of Tahoe, too. Eaten. Blakes recounted how torn up the body had been when they'd found it. Torn to shreds, and despite weeks of searching afterwards his fellow rangers never found the suspected bear.

That had been twenty years ago. That same winter had claimed a pair of hunters going after bighorn sheep, a professor from the University of California, Davis, working on an environmental survey, and a couple who'd decided to take their honeymoon among nature. Every one of them was mauled with a savagery that baffled the rangers. The distance between the victims was similarly abnormal, as a black bear claiming territory over such a large area was already an odd occurrence. No amount of hunting for the beast amounted to anything.

Before I could stomach the grisly fate of those helpless souls, Blakes slid a stack of printed photographs across the table. I thought for a moment these would be crime scene pictures from the attacks, but then I looked closer. The bodies didn't match the previous descriptions. I saw a severed foot that should've fit a shoe smaller than my fist. Another picture featured an arm ripped off at the shoulder, and in the dead fingers was clutched a cracked, broken iPhone.

They didn't have iPhones twenty years ago…

"Ten years," said Blakes. His finger tapped a timestamp in the corner of one. "Ten years to the day, Cole. Every year I take a trip up to the mountains, it always made me feel closer to my dad. But exactly ten years after he died, it happened again. Right up there in that same wilderness."

"Blakes, you might be on to something but there's a million—"

I stopped talking dead in my tracks as he pulled out a stack of folders this time. Each looking older than the last. His hands gripped their edges so tightly it was as if he was afraid their contents would lash out at me.

"Thirty years ago."

He slapped one in front of me. A newspaper clipping detailing how an entire Boy Scouts troop on an excursion had gone missing. Nothing but bloody sleeping bags were found. Not even so much as a finger or toe left behind.

"Forty years."

Slap. This one contained aged black and white photos of a group of hunters surrounding a bear that had supposedly slaughtered a family on a camping trip.

"Fifty. Sixty. Seventy. Eighty. Ninety. On and on, every ten years this happens. Animal attacks. Missing persons. People lost and just never heard from again. It's all the same thing."

"This... wendigo?"

Blakes pursed his lips and nodded. It was as if he couldn't bring himself to name the creature out loud more than once. I found myself looking out the window at the same exact spot Blakes had been staring at earlier. This diner was like a last bastion of civilization, and the darkness of the forgotten frontier was lurking just outside. Could there be... was there something out there in the night? I thought of the last time I'd been alone in the wilderness, and how oppressive the vast open world can be. I remembered that feeling of somebody... some*thing*... watching you just behind the trees.

I stacked the folders atop each other, straightened them, and pushed them back across the table to Blakes, He sipped his coffee. I drummed my fingertips on the tabletop. Minutes ago I was scared of indulging in Blakes' delusions. Now? I was getting more than a little scared at the possibility he *wasn't* crazy.

I thought next, whatever thing had torn all those people up, supernatural or not, it was going to be big. Monstrous. It had ripped a grown man limb from limb. Cracked bones as if they were twigs. The .45 caliber pistol at my hip now seemed like a hunk of stupidly useless metal. I pulled my eyes from the darkness outside the window and turned to meet Blakes' gaze. He was looking for a sign, something that said whether or not I was willing to go down this mad road with him.

"Okay," I said. "How do we kill it?"

* * *

I didn't know the rules to things like this. With stuff like vampires it seemed like Hollywood had vastly conflicting solutions for how to put 'em down. Sunlight, crucifixes, garlic, wooden stakes, silver stakes, and never mind the fact that in Bram Stoker's *Dracula* they managed to kill him with just good old sharp knives. Yeah, I read the book once upon a time and the only thing I remembered was old Drac being allergic to Bowie knives in the chest.

Which is why I was so pleased when Blakes told me what wendigos' weakness was: fire. Seemed much simpler and straightforward. Neither Blakes nor I happened to pack our flamethrowers, so we'd have to make do. Blakes, the accomplished hunter, opened the door to his truck cab to show what he'd brought along.

"Take your pick," he said.

There was a large-bored black lever-action rifle, a bolt-action with woodland camo paint, and two shotguns. One compact pump-action Mossberg with a pistol-grip and a semi-auto, both 12-gauges.

"The legends say anything about how fast they are?"

"Fast."

I opted for the lever-action; it was chambered for heavy .500 S&W rounds which packed plenty of stopping power. I figured we were going to need every bit of it. Blakes snatched up the bolt-action and explained it was loaded with .300 Winchester Magnum, the rifle called a '110 Bear Hunter' by Savage Arms. The name was comforting.

"It's always fire," Blakes told me. "That much is consistent. I don't know if gunfire counts, but these are some pretty heavy rounds. They'll drop it, then we'll burn what's left." He raised his chin at the red cans of gas in the bed of the truck.

We stood outside his truck for a long while, both hesitant to make a move which would pull us from the moment and past the point of no return, then Blakes gave me one last look.

"Cole, you didn't have to—"

"Let's go," I said and walked around the truck to climb into the passenger seat. There were a lot of uncertainties ahead. Whether the rifles would be enough to even make the monster flinch. Whether the gasoline could finish the job. Never mind the strong possibility neither of us would even make it back. But being here, going through this with him to the end? There were no questions there.

Blakes hauled himself into the driver's seat and gave me a knowing nod. There were certain things that were just understood when two men knowingly walked into the lion's den. No words were needed.

It didn't take long to leave the illusions of civilization behind. Just a few minutes of driving and a couple turns off the main road and the streetlights and Starbucks disappeared. Not long afterwards even the asphalt gave way to an unpaved dirt road. Blakes white-knuckled the steering wheel as the truck bucked along the harsher terrain. I tried to steal a glimpse at the tree-line, but the dark just beyond my window was solid as a wall.

"How much time till we get there?"

"A little while. Why? Thinking of resting your eyes?"

"No, figured if we've got the time then you can give me the long version of everything."

He bit his lip and considered things for a second. I gave him all the time he needed to open up. It seemed like he'd spent such a long while gathering all this information, but had yet to figure out how to share it with someone else in a way that didn't sound batshit insane.

"Algonquin. Cree. Saulteaux. Naskapi. Innu. They all shared the same folklore about it. Slight variances here and there, but they all believed in the wendigo. They aren't born: they're created. You take two old Native Americans a couple hundred years ago, and say they're out hunting for the village in the winter. But then the snows come in. Come in hard. They get lost, stranded in the whiteout. Those two hole up in a cave, try to wait it out. But it doesn't let up. Eventually, they're going to get hungry. Eventually one of them will get hungry enough to see their friend as nothing more than meat."

My stomach recoiled at the thought.

"Killing your own is a grave enough sin, but consuming their flesh? It's an affront against all the gods in all of nature. A cannibal gets cursed into becoming a wendigo. A *twisted* inhuman thing. They get paler the longer they live; their skin desiccated and stretched tight over starved bones. Lips cracked and turned bloody red from living alone in the cold. Some say they grow antlers, but others say it's just because they stretch and grow tall and their head reaches the naked tree branches. That's the other thing: every time they feed, they grow. It's part of the curse. They grow, but their skin doesn't. Whenever they eat, they'll get bigger and more starved, so they'll be forever hungry."

That last part struck a chord with me. Paler, bigger, and hungrier every time it killed. And going off Blakes' research it had been doing that for a long, long time.

"Couldn't have brought any more firepower?" I asked, eyeing the small arsenal in the back and wondering if maybe we should've brought a bazooka instead.

Blakes smiled, reached under his seat, and tossed a couple boxes of shells into my lap. "We'll take the shotguns, too. I'll let you take the semi-auto."

I clicked the truck dome light on and read the label on the box. Dragon's Breath. Incendiary shells. *Now* we had some firepower for however big this son of a bitch was.

As if reading my mind, Blakes spoke up again.

"This wendigo… it's special, Cole. A Great White Wendigo. It's been killing for a long time," he said. "I backtracked it through all the years. 1847. That's when its curse started, and not too far away from here."

"You know where it came from?"

"Cole: I know its name. Franklin Graves, of the Donner Party."

* * *

We were well off the edge of the map now. Deep in our own personal heart of darkness, except this one was a dizzying canvas of pitch-black shadows and swirling snow. We left the warmth of Blakes' truck and he guided us up into the mountain where he'd already staged a hide. There was some canvas-covered firewood, and within minutes he had a fire roaring.

"It'll be drawn to the fire," Blakes explained and squatted on his haunches. "That, and it'll probably recognize my smell. Remembers it, from my dad."

He warmed his hands, then pulled a small leather journal from his jacket. He read by the fire for just a second, then stowed the book back inside his pocket.

"Anything else in there you wanna share?" I asked.

Blakes prodded the fire with a long, narrow branch; its cracked end was glowing red hot. He used it like a fire-poker to stoke the flames. The wood answered with a burst of embers. "There's plenty of things that go bump in the night, Cole. Let's just focus on this one for now."

"Blakes, I'm here with you. But there could be—"

A dry twig cracked around the perimeter. All my senses went alert as I shouldered the lever-action. The shotgun I had for backup was still slung across my back and I felt its weight pull against me as I rose to my feet. Smells came to my nostrils: first the pleasant scent of the campfire and crackling wood, but that was soon overpowered by the stench of old meat, like a rotten steak left too long in the freezer. My eyes scanned the tree-line. Looking for something out of place.

Blakes lit a match, and then dropped it at the edge of the clearing. We'd laid a ring of gasoline around us and it quickly lit up into a knee-high wall of fire.

Sparks from the campfire behind me and snowflakes dancing in the air played tricks on my eyes. Everything looked to be moving. But then, I saw something. I saw it because of how still it was. It wasn't a human-like silhouette I saw. No, it wasn't even a whole body. What I thought were two snow-covered tree trunks were merely legs. I wasn't looking high enough.

Slowly, I aimed the rifle higher in the trees. The Great White Wendigo was there, towering over us. Tall as a two-story building. Blakes said a wendigo grew paler and bigger the older it was, and this one had been hunting since the 1800s. Its dry skin had long since turned chalk white; it ripped across its elbows, hands, knees and feet, where its bones had stretched too far for it to take. The cold had stripped its lips entirely away to blackened gums; the mouth behind was filled with long yellow, cracked teeth large enough to tear a grown man in half.

And then those claws, each a foot long in length, reached for me.

"Shoot!" Blakes roared and snapped me back from the grip of terror.

I scrambled away as its claws raked the ground where I'd stood. Instinct took over and, in a heartbeat, I'd fired three rounds. The heavy .500 bullets punched silver-dollar-sized holes through the monster's torso, the butt-stock of the lever-action punching back my own shoulder each time. Still, the creature stood. It didn't even bleed. I half-expected a monstrous roar, but instead it was utterly silent as its mouth hung open. The only sound that came from it was a horrible grumbling, and I realized then that its stomach was growling.

Blakes' own rifle uttered a deafening boom. A grisly but bloodless wound ripped across its chest. I forced myself to slow down, to think rather than fear, because nothing we'd done had slowed it. It stepped over our ring of fire, its exposed skinless elbows and knees glistening red in the light.

There.

"Joints!" I screamed. I emptied the remaining four rounds into its left knee. There was a sharp crack, and the beast stumbled. Blakes followed suit, side-stepping a wide sweep of its claws, before putting a devastating round through its elbow. The arm fell limp by its side. The wendigo's head reared back in a silent scream.

It whirled with a backhanded slash – faster than I expected – and I was tossed through the air. A frozen tree trunk stopped me in my tracks. The claws had torn into my leg, preventing me from getting up again. Blakes saw me go down. He looked my way, and in that instant the wendigo sheared through both his rifle and his chest with one mighty swipe. Blakes fell, and the creature turned back to me.

It loped along like a hobbled animal. A black tongue licked at its lipless gums hungrily. I struggled to reach around for my shotgun as my leg went numb. Blood loss or cold? It didn't matter. I aimed the weapon, silently praying the Dragon's Breath would work.

I pulled the trigger. A belch of sparks and flame caught the wendigo in the face. Once more it writhed in an inaudible scream. Still, it crawled. I fired again and the fiery burst blasted the monster's chest. It wasn't enough.

The wendigo's claws encircled me in a one-handed grasp. Its charred face loomed near, close enough for me to see the blackness of its eyes. Close enough for me to not recognize an ounce of humanity in them.

Close enough to see those eyes go wide as Blakes came up behind it and speared one of the flaming branches from the campfire through its heart. The effect was instant. It dropped me into the snow and its good arm flailed about. The glowing red tip of the wood pierced through the front, and fire spread outward from the branch until the beast was fully enveloped.

An instant later the flames, and the monster, were gone. All that remained was a very human skeleton. The curse of the wendigo had been cleansed by fire. Blakes fell once more to the ground as his lifeblood poured from him. I managed to limp over and cradled his head in my arms.

"You got him," I said. "You did it, Blakes."

"Said it... yourself. I was always... the better hunter..." He smiled with blood-slicked lips. I looked to his wounds. They were mortal.

"We've gotta get you up," I said. He simply shook his head, and then reached into his jacket pocket. He retrieved the leatherbound journal and placed it into my hand.

"There's other things out there..." he said. "Things going bump in the night." He gave me that same sad little grin. "You still owe me one, Cole."

Jim Blakes died smiling. I held him for a while longer after I felt his soul depart. Then I patched myself up as best I could while the fire died down to embers. Every miserable step as I limped back to Blakes' truck was agony. His journal shook in my hand. A part of me thought I'd be better off leaving it behind in the snow. Still, Blakes had a point. I came all this way to pay him back for saving my life, and instead he'd saved it again. Which meant I had no choice. I placed the journal in my pocket, ready to see what secrets it held, ready to go wherever it took me.

A man settles what's owed...

The Marsh-Widow's Bargain

H.R. Laurence

TERIM had been strong and young when he died, and so it was no surprise that the Corpse-Witch came for his body after it had been lying only a day in the grave-water.

Eshae had known the witch would come, and all night after the priests had laid her son's weighted lich in the burial place she had lain amongst the floating corpse-markers, quiet as driftwood, waiting patient while the sun went down and the swamplights began to shine. Her arms were spread against the soft pulse of the marsh, and her skin was wrinkled by the time the second sun rose after midnight.

For an hour it made its progress through the night sky, and its pale green light cast faint shadows from the tall implacable reeds which gossiped together in the low breeze. Eshae's face was just above the lap of the water, and the shadows moved across her; the water brushed her face as though the very marsh sought to restore the tears she had wept, long and bitter, in the days since the hunting men brought Terim back to her.

He must have gone poaching at the very edge of the marsh, where the Jarl's prize buffalo grazed, for the arrow in his back had the yellow fletching of the Jarl's watchmen. The hunters said he had been alive when they found him, though barely, his breath and blood expended on fleeing through the marsh. Eshae had laid him on her table and washed the muddy water from his corpse. *All this for a buffalo calf*, she had thought. *He had my foolishness, as much as he had my eyes.*

She moved not an inch. Then the second sun waned, and the shadows became still again in the blue moonlight. She heard the sly whisper of the Corpse-Witch's punt, moving through the marshwater.

Kekrow the Corpse-Witch was hunched like a crane, thin arms tense at the pushing-pole, his narrow eyes straining in his narrow face for the fresh corpse-marker. He saw it, and Eshae heard his low, satisfied grunt as he brought the punt near with deft strokes of the pole. Then he shrugged his great dark cloak from his thin shoulders, and for a moment stood stick-thin, white and naked in the small-hour gloom. A sharp knife in the shape of a claw gleamed in his wiry hand. It caught the light as he dived from the punt and disappeared into the murk.

Eshae had tied her own knife about her neck. It hung in the water beneath her, like the weights from Terim's linen-wrapped corpse. The rich or well-liked dead might have armed men in skiffs to guard their bodies until the grave-waters had done their work. But a fatherless poacher-boy had no such assurance.

As the ripples from Kekrow's impact rocked her, Eshae lifted her arm, and with her hand in the shape of a spoon she bit through the water and slowly hauled herself toward the punt. She trusted the disturbed marsh not to betray her presence. Her hand found the trailing tether-line of Kekrow's punt. She coiled it about her arm, and lay still again.

A white thing bobbed to the surface. It was not her son, Eshae told herself, though it would look like him – Terim's bandages had yet to decay, and beneath them he would be untouched by the marsh-fish. A moment later, Kekrow emerged, near-as-pale as the white linen of the corpse-wrapping. He coughed for breath, put his bony shoulder beneath what-had-been-Terim, and manoeuvred the corpse towards the punt.

Eshae's right wrist was wrapped around the tether-line. In her strong left hand she held her knife; clutched it. Here would be the place to kill him, were it not the vilest sacrilege to spill blood in the grave-water. Eshae had no great regard for the gods, nor they for her, but she had enough grief to burden her without provoking their enmity. Their good will might make all the difference this night.

With a soft wet thud, Terim fell across the rear of the punt – and Eshae caught herself, would have shaken her head if she didn't need to be still. It was not Terim anymore – he couldn't smile at her words, nor grunt at her admonitions; would feel neither love nor resentment. What had once been his head lolled across the stern of the boat. Despite herself, Eshae gazed up at him.

My boy, she thought. *If we had been less foolish.*

Kekrow had wrapped himself in his cloak; he took the punt-pole and struck out from the grave-water. Soon, the boat was gliding slowly down one of the many channels through the marsh. Eshae heard the Corpse-Witch curse to himself, wondering why his punt was sluggish. She held it lightly, her breath soft. A flotilla of nocturnal snakebirds swam past, long necks bobbing above the water, casting beady-eyed glances at the woman pulled behind the punt. But they uttered no cries to betray her. In the reeds to either side of the water-way nightjars called and warblers sang, and from time to time the Corpse-Witch made low raucous caws like that of a harrier, to startle the singing birds into silence, before chuckling to himself. When that happened, Eshae held her breath until the birds resumed their singing. But it was only Kekrow's dark humour, showing itself anew.

They emerged from the high reeds about the grave-water into the great, flat expanse of the marsh. The lights of Salt Village upon its patchwork of mud-islands were close; distant were those of Bog-Oak Village, built into the squat trees. Somewhere between the two was the dark reed-hut that Eshae the widow had shared with Terim her son, and whichever men of the two villages chose to come bearing fish or coin.

And somewhere beyond was the stilt-mounted house of Kekrow the Corpse-Witch, festooned with the bone fetishes and shrunken heads of his trade; the bone-pierced noses of slain warriors and the long hair of sacrificed girls. The villages brought Kekrow their offerings and their captives – fewer now, in the recent years of peace. And so it was to be expected if, from time to time, the occasional unloved occupant of the grave-water were to disappear, and the Corpse-Witch all of a sudden were to have charms and true sooths for the season ahead.

And perhaps that was well enough, Eshae thought, but it would not be her boy's body that gave them those sooths. She looked up at Terim's linen-wrapped head, hanging from the punt. His big, foolish, lovely head; it had been a day of agony giving birth to him. Seventeen years had passed since that day. She clutched the knife to her breast. Her right arm was numb now with the strain of hanging on. It seemed a small miracle that Kekrow had noticed nothing, but the marsh was loud, and the water busy with small fish and swimming snakes.

On they went, the Corpse-Witch sweating and straining at his pole. Soon the village-lights were half-lost behind tall bulrushes. Here Kekrow began to glance nervously from side to side; he made no more calls to taunt the night birds. They were in the deep-reeds, and in the deep-reeds and dark-marsh went he they called Leopard-of-the-Water, Hunter-of-the-Marsh, Cat-from-Under, with his gaping mouth and his plaintive cry and his great appetite for mortal men. His eyes were greener than the second sun, and his teeth sharper than spears.

Eshae's arm ached. She looked at the sky, and at the banks of papyrus-sedge rolling past, and thought of nothing as she had long trained herself to do when she lay on her back. And at last the mace-reeds receded and she saw Kekrow's stilted house amongst them.

The punt stopped. Now was time. A rough jetty of packed and woven reeds extended into the water, and Kekrow's boat rested against it, and the thin Corpse-Witch leant down across the body of Terim for the tether-line.

Eshae had lain too long in the water. When she came out of it, knife in hand, war-cry on her lips, she was too slow – Kekrow's small eyes went huge with fear as he saw her lunge and he fell back, the knife biting his leg with half the force she'd intended. He shrieked like a stuck buffalo regardless; fell sprawling across Terim's body. Eshae hauled herself half onto the rocking punt, but Kekrow caught her wrist as she swung the bloodied blade up again. She lost her grip on the boat; he over-balanced as he tried to wrest the knife away, and fell and bore her down into the murky marsh.

They thrashed there, and rolled, Kekrow's thin, strong hands gripping her knife-arm by the wrist. Eshae rolled atop to tread him down, and tried to surface. They were beneath the punt. Blank pain seared her head as she struck it crown-first. Kekrow's hand took her throat. She had lost the knife and now he could grapple without fear of her blade. She clawed at him, and scored his chest, and tried to find his eyes to gouge. His elbow found her nose first.

She must have shouted her hate then, for all of a sudden her lungs were full of water. And then she realised she was drowning, and the murky world spun and darkened and spun, and—

* * *

She woke bound, her wrists tied with cord above her head to the wooden wall of Kekrow's hut.

"Ahk," she said. She was still dripping wet, and some of the wetness was warm blood from her broken nose; her face was full of pain.

Kekrow's hut was round and small, and every inch of it was cluttered or hanging with the tools of his foul trade; with tanned hides and steam-cleaned bones and dried or mummified debris, or sharp blades, or piled stinking bandages. It must have smelt foul, though all Eshae could smell was her own blood. A reed-stuffed sleeping mat lay in the corner of the room; a low table at its centre. Upon that lay the bandage-wreathed shape of Terim, marsh-water seeping through the slatted surface.

Beside the corpse sat Kekrow, his leg outstretched as he wrapped a length of filthy linen about the wound she had made, tighter and tighter. He saw that she was awake, and scowled as he tied off the bandage. He flexed the leg to test it, and then with a slight wince of pain sat back on his heels and touched his nail-clawed face.

"You and I, Eshae," he said. "We have lived beyond the villages many-a-year, and had no cause for conflict."

"It's my son," said Eshae.

The Corpse-Witch shrugged. "They are all someone's son," he said. "Or else someone's daughter. And who will do without their prophecies for the season ahead? You could have paid me to leave the body; you could have brought me a different one."

He inched closer, hissing with pain as he put weight on his damaged leg. Eshae held his gaze when he peered at her, eyes scouring close. He could not see what he sought, and turned away.

"Play the martyr if you like," Kekrow said. "You've bought my wares before. Do you think no mother's son went beneath the knife to make them?"

Eshae spat.

"What do I care for them?" she said. "Mine is different."

"No different to me," said Kekrow, and spat likewise, and stretched, then took one of the sickles from his wall and laid it on his table. "I'll not suffer this, Eshae – two years it's been since I prophesied from a body still living. Such prophecies have rare strength – I think the villages will pay me well for them."

He took a whetstone and ran the sickle-blade along it. Eshae watched, fear souring in her belly. She would not show it.

"They might miss me," she said. "They might burn your hut and find themselves a new witch – one who won't meddle with their favourite widow."

But she knew as well as he that there was no such prospect. She was growing older, and her slim frame had become wiry. Few men brought her fish now.

"I think not," said Kekrow. "We outsiders are left to settle our own affairs; a little comfort for our station, don't you think? The village men won't miss you. It's been a long while since they last saw you on the tavern-island, squeezing drinks from every man and spinning yarns."

Eshae smiled, thinking of the tavern. He was right. It had been a long time; the place had stopped bringing her joy long before Terim died. She flexed her wrist against the cord binding it.

"I'll tell you a yarn now," she said. "If you've time to hear it."

Kekrow shrugged, sneering.

"I need you alive for the sorcery," he said. "Talk if it will bring you solace."

He was serving himself, as ever. The words of a doomed woman might be valuable; they might be taken, twisted, and made to serve any number of rituals. They might offer power over some notable man of the marsh. They were all Eshae could offer to be remembered by, and they would be worth hearing.

She spoke quick even so, in case Kekrow changed his mind.

"I was half a girl," she said. "On the side of the cold stream, hunting for marsh-pike. The sun was low, and I was alone, my coracle barely above the water. Even so, I steered it deep into the reeds when I heard."

She paused, and saw the faintest lift of Kekrow's head, arrested as soon as he realised it; and she knew then that she had him.

"It was the cry of a babe," she said. "Lost and faint – so faint! It sounded half-starved. Some poor child, abandoned in the marsh. My heart swelled for it. I forgot all the tales I had been told – all the warnings friends might have given. I took my paddle and struck out into the deep-reeds."

Eshae shook her head at her old foolishness. "You have guessed, of course, what awaited me."

"You found Hunter-of-the-Marsh," Kekrow said, the ghost of a sneer in his voice. "Calling in the reeds, his voice disguised, to lure tender-hearted maidens."

She smiled, bitter.

"I was no maiden," she said, and gestured with her bound arm at Terim's wrapped body. "I was big with this one."

The memory of it came up at her all of a sudden; she felt herself crease, felt the sorrow surge sudden in her breast like an encircled army seeking to break free. She held it, hard as a wall of shield-men, and coughed to stop her sob. When she lifted her head, Kekrow was looking at her with strange uncertainty in his green eyes.

"So you saw him," he said. "And he chose not to rend you in two. Maybe that's true. What of it? Such things happen, from time to time. It is his prerogative to show mercy once in a while."

Eshae laughed. Kekrow flinched; she heard as clear as he the harsh, bitter carelessness in her voice.

"No," she said. "He showed no mercy. I bribed him."

"You did not," said Kekrow, not looking. Eshae leant into the cords until they bit her wrists; until Kekrow's curiosity forced his head to turn.

"I did," she insisted. "I was a coward. I wanted to live. And I was a double-coward – for I sought to have the babe and sell it too."

She remembered it as clear as day – the helpless stammer she had uttered, the words which had once seemed clever.

Let me go, she had said. *And if my boy goes before me* – she had known even then that it would be a boy – *I will put no charm in his bandages. He will be for you, Leopard-of-the-Water, should he go before me.*

Kekrow's face was a-twist with scorn. She could read his thoughts clear as day: it had been a pathetic bargain – at once a blatant attempt to cheat Cat-from-Under, and a cowardly acquiescence to his reign. Better to go into his vast mouth than strike such bargains – to wager with the gods that you wouldn't see your first-born's death? No natural mother would strike such a bargain.

"I am no natural mother," said Eshae, and Kekrow started.

"No," he said, after a moment. "You know too well what men are thinking, and you say it."

Eshae grinned at him.

"Aye," she said. "Some men like that."

He scoffed and looked away.

"It was cowardly," said Eshae. "But I thought I'd had the best of it, once he'd lived a year. All that year I feared he'd die – I feared every fever, every restless night. But he lived! I began to think he always would…"

"You should not have," said Kekrow. "Cat-from-Under knows his due."

Eshae looked him in the eye. And he read something else there, and understood it for the first time.

"You lie," he said.

Eshae shook her head. "No," she said. "I only meant to lame you outside, and take the body from you."

There was a high whistle in the reeds beyond the hut; too high, surely, for the faint breeze which had been blowing while they made their approach.

"You lie," said Kekrow again, but the catch in his voice proved him the liar. Eshae's bonds were tight and wouldn't loosen; she sat back in them and waited.

"I'd no wish to deprive the villages of their Corpse-Witch," she said. "But this corpse is promised elsewhere. There are no charms in his bandages, Kekrow – no shaman spoke over his body. He was promised before he was born, and Leopard-of-the-Water comes for what is owed."

"He cannot enter," said Kekrow, as though to himself. "He cannot enter, unless invited—"

"He was promised," said Eshae, simply. "What more invitation does he need?"

The howling in the reeds had become a shriek; it was not wind. Kekrow cursed, and cast about in the clutter of the hut for the charms and sorcerous weapons of his profession.

"A promise is strong magic," Eshae continued. "A mother promising her son – what charm will overcome that?"

"Quiet!" Kekrow gasped. He knew that she spoke truth. From beneath his mat of reeds he took a staff bedecked in woven hair-charms and studded with finger bones, and even as he did the wind-which-was-not-wind flung open the door of the hut.

There without was Leopard-of-the-Water, the Hunter-of-the-Marsh, the Cat-from-Under, his long body slick with slime and his six webbed paws spread upon the surface of the water, his great mouth open. The teeth within gleamed, and between them his clammy tentacles writhed and flexed and twisted.

Kekrow made a hoarse noise of terror. He flung up his staff. Through the door came Leopard-of-the-Water. A great purple tongue caressed his yellow lips. He looked on the brandished staff, and his tentacles flicked out and plucked it from Kekrow's hand. It became splinters between the huge teeth. Leopard-of-the-Water hawked hair-charms from his mouth, and Kekrow the Corpse-Witch fell quailing to the floor.

The Hunter-of-the-Marsh paid him no heed. The burning green eyes looked on Eshae, and looked on

Terim's promised body, and looked again at Eshae, narrowing with fury.

Eshae smiled at him. The tears were running freely now, and blood from her nose, and from her wrists where the cords had cut into them.

"I broke the bargain," she said. She had woven a dozen charms into Terim's bandages; had the shaman-priests speak a double service over his corpse. Cat-from-Under could not touch her son, no more than she could eat Kekrow's iron sickle.

"I broke the bargain," she said again. "But I would not cheat you, great one – I have brought the Corpse-Witch of two villages in his place."

Kekrow made a strangled noise of outrage and terror as the green eyes swung back to regard him. Eshae leant forward in her bonds.

"Isn't he worth more than a poacher-boy?" she asked.

The Corpse-Witch tried to gasp out some words, some counter-offer, some prayer. He had barely uttered a syllable before the tentacles took him, wrapping about his waist and ankles and throat. He thrashed a moment in their grasp, and then was borne into the vast maw; he cried out once, became wet crunch, and then nothing.

Eshae sat back. Leopard-of-the-Water had every right to kill her now, to make her torment stretch long into the night. Perhaps, she thought, the village men would come in the morning and find the ruin of the hut and what remained of she and Kekrow, would take the linen-wrapped body back to the grave-water to bury it there once again. There would be little left of Eshae to go to grave-water, but Terim's soul would swim through the marsh to the sea. She hoped that would be so.

But there was another, more audacious, hope in her breast. A tiny one; one with little prospect of success. She smiled up at Leopard-of-the-Water regardless.

"Wasn't that a tasty morsel?" Eshae asked. "Won't you let me bring you another?"

Good Boy

Alison Littlewood

OUR NEIGHBOUR is one of those people known as, for want of a better phrase, a *grumpy old sod*. Our houses are a pair at the end of a lane, nothing but fields around them and backing onto a river, but despite our proximity, the most I've managed to raise from him in the years we've been here is a gruff "How do?"

I'm in the garden, having a cheeky cigarette – I gave up nine years ago, when I met Helen, but it doesn't always stick. She won't be happy, but I'm relishing the smoke combined with the night scents and cold air of a bitter November, at least until a sound disturbs me. An inarticulate shout rises from the other side of the fence, then a sputter of words.

"*Gerroutonit…*"

I drop the cigarette and hurry across the grass, thinking of prowlers and thieves, and peer over the fence. The first thing I see is not my neighbour but a giant pair of eyes, glowing red, and a black shape, menacing and huge. I blink – the nicotine must have addled my senses – but Mr. Roper snaps into view. He's standing in front of that shadow, and he has a stick raised in his hand. The perspective is all off, though, because the thing he's attacking – *a dog*, my mind tells me, *he's attacking a dog* – is taller than he is, wider than he is, and way more bloody terrifying than he is.

Roper strikes. I swear his stick passes straight through the dog like it's made of smoke, then the beast leaps away and there's an almighty splash. I peer towards the river, which I know to be wide and fast and deep. I can't see the thing any longer though, can't hear it struggle against the current.

A grunt draws my gaze to Mr. Roper. He's limping away, towards the house – the limp isn't new, he's had it for as long as I remember – and he swears, then his door slams and everything is still. I stand there, not sure if I really saw what I thought I did, and an owl hoots and the river flows silently on and my heartbeat begins to slow.

The dog surely wasn't that big.

There's no way its eyes glowed.

But I do know one thing: that dog is gone. The riverbanks are steep, it won't be getting out again, and I think *poor dog* and *you bastard*, all at once.

That's when I hear a rustling under the bushes.

Another moment and the sound comes again, too loud for a squirrel or a bird. It's on Roper's side of the fence but there's a gap where it nears the river, where the ground is too treacherous to sink posts. I feel the earth turn to mud beneath my feet as I edge around it and approach the bushes.

It takes me a moment to make out the shape beneath them. Then two eyes snap open and I see it: black fluff. An uncertain shape, hunched into the ground. And eyes; those eyes.

Not a dog, hiding in the grumpy old sod's garden. A puppy.

Her puppy. The dog that isn't coming back.

* * *

"Dan, it's bloody huge!"

Helen isn't happy. She hasn't said *It's not staying*, even if that's what she means. But then, that tone is in her voice so often these days. Sometimes, it's easier not to listen.

I find myself talking to the dog, not my wife. "You're not that big, are you? No, you're not." I fondle the little fellow's ears. Well, not *little*, but still. They're about the size of dinner plates. So are his paws.

"He'll get bigger." She folds her arms across her chest.

"Oh – well, yes, you will. You're a baby, aren't you? But not *too* big. You're maybe a Newfoundland, or something. Are you? Are you a Newfie, fella?"

"*Dan.* You can't keep him." At last, my wife gets to the point. "He belongs to someone."

And I'm caught. I was just thinking about how I work from home for most of the week, and Helen often does two days; we could tag-team, we could happily have a dog – but she's right, isn't she? Of course he belongs to someone. He must. He's beautiful.

I sigh. "I'll take him to the vet tomorrow," I say. "Get him checked for a microchip. That'll have the owner's details."

She isn't satisfied. "He stinks."

I bite down my retort. The puppy leans into my hand as I fondle his shaggy fur, and he starts to make a sound: it's not really like a dog, more like a cat purring, a *big* cat, and I realise there *is* a smell. But with all that fur, and him out in the wild… there's little wonder if he's gathered all the scents of November to himself: earth; dead leaves; musk. Bonfires and fireworks; smoke and saltpetre and sulphur.

* * *

The vet scans the dog, then scans him again. There's no microchip. She says I could advertise for his owner. Report finding him to the dog warden at the council, maybe the RSPCA, see if anyone's looking. The warden could find him a place at a rescue centre, she says, though if they can't rehome him, he might end up being put down.

I tell her no way in hell.

The owner gets seven days to claim him, she says. After that, I could get him chipped myself, register him with my own details. She says that yes, he could be a Newfie, maybe. She looks him uncertainly up and down.

She sells me a sack of puppy food – large breed – for forty quid.

* * *

Back home, I fill our biggest plastic bowl with the kibble. The dog sits in front of it and peers down his nose as if he doesn't know what it is. I think of his mum, ripped from him too soon and so suddenly, and my heart breaks a little.

I open the fridge and his head turns. I end up sitting on the floor, hand feeding him the roast chicken we were going to have for dinner. His mouth is snappy, his teeth very white and sharp. His gums are red and healthy. He finishes the lot and I give him the plate to lick. When he's done, he sits on his rounded puppy haunches and looks expectantly at me.

Helen's voice comes from the doorway. "Is that our din—" She swoops in, snatches up the plate, and I hardly see what happens. The dog lashes out with his paw. Helen snatches back her arm, lets out a hiss of pain. "*Jesus!*"

The dog jumps back, cowering at the sound of her voice, or perhaps in shock at what he's done. Blood drips from between Helen's fingers, wrapped around her wrist.

"Let me see, love." I reach for her, but she pulls away. "It can't be that bad. He's only a puppy. They scratch, it happens, it's noth—"

"Thanks," she snaps. "Thanks a lot." She stalks off to the bathroom and I hear running water, then Helen rummaging in the cabinet.

I look at the dog. He looks at me. "Don't worry," I find myself saying. "She'll get over it." He tilts his head, not understanding a word, or understanding all too well but not quite agreeing, and I can't help smiling.

"You need a name," I say softly. "If you're staying for a bit." I wonder for a moment, and it comes to me, and it's odd but it fits somehow. "Gary," I say. "How about it, boy? I'll call you Gary."

This time, it looks like he concurs.

* * *

"His eyes are red."

It's as if Helen's never left off. This time I don't even bother answering. Dogs' eyes are reflective. They have a structure in them like a cat's, to help them see in low light, and sometimes, their eyes seem to shine. Mostly they look greenish, but the colour varies, doesn't it? I

249

almost think it can. Or maybe there's something in his genes, just a little awry. Albino dogs have pink eyes, don't they? Or are they light blue? I don't know. I don't care either. There's nothing wrong with my boy, my *good boy*, and I tell him so.

Helen's eyes glitter down at the pair of us, a little too bright. I find myself thinking that at least the dog has an excuse.

* * *

I do what Helen wants. I put an advert in the local shop window, add Gary to the 'found dogs' register at the council, inform the RSPCA. I do it all, then sit and watch my phone and pray it won't ring. *Seven days*. That's all we need.

Helen watches Gary with doubt on her face, but I tell myself she'll grow to love him. Once she knows he can actually be ours, she'll allow herself to love him.

* * *

The next morning, when I wake, Helen is sitting up in bed, rubbing her wrist. The skin looks pink; she's making it sore. I reach out and catch her hand.

Her head snaps towards me and she says, "How can you sleep? I can't sleep. All I can hear is that damned dog, all night. Making those sounds. Crying."

"He cries? Aw, poor boy. I thought he'd settled in just fine." I frown. Gary's sleeping in the kitchen. Maybe he shouldn't be.

"No – not that kind of crying." She takes a shaky breath. "It's not right, Dan. He doesn't whimper or whine like a dog. It sounds like *real* crying. Like a baby, crying, all – bloody – night."

I stare in dismay. I'm not entirely sure it's Gary we're talking about any longer, that her feelings are anything to do with the dog. For a moment, I don't speak. I sense the distance that has opened between us, that has been there for a while, a crack opening wider and wider, since our last attempt; our last failure.

I stroke her arm. "You were having a dream, love. Of course he doesn't *cry*. That would be weird." Even as I speak, I tell myself it wouldn't be, not really. Even if Gary does make some odd sounds sometimes, it's not that strange. I've seen the videos that do the rounds on Facebook: hounds grumbling and muttering;

huskies yowling in conversation; the terrier who says 'sausages'. Nothing's impossible, not with dogs. Not with my good boy.

"Dan, that dog *attacked* me, and you don't even—"

"*Helen.* He's just a puppy." I throw the covers back. "He's alone and defenceless, and – I'm going to check on him."

I walk downstairs and into the kitchen and stare at Gary's dog bed, which is empty. I stare at the collar I bought for him, lying next to it. I stare at the kitchen door, which is wide open, and at the dead leaves scattered across the floor, twitching and rattling in the breeze that's blowing inside.

Fury floods through me as I grab my trainers and rush outside. It's barely light, but I can already see there's nothing moving in the garden; only the wind twitching the trees' bare branches.

The river.

I stride across the grass, yelling Gary's name. There's no sign of life in the garden, not even a bird singing. It's as if the place has been abandoned and I finish up staring down into the river. It flows full and fast and dangerous, its surface opaque and brown, its skin puckered like old gravy.

No. He wouldn't have gone in there. He wouldn't have followed his mother. He's got me.

I glance around at Mr. Roper's house to see if the old man is watching, dour-faced, from a window, and see a furry mound heaped on his doorstep.

Gary. I lope towards my dog, my *boy*, who doesn't seem to be hurt; he's simply lying there, his head on his paws, staring at Roper's door with a mournful expression in his eyes. I touch his side and feel the heat in him, the *life*, and relief fills me up. When I pull on his neck, he rises and pads at my heels back towards our house.

Halfway there, he pauses. He lowers his head to sniff something in the grass and I see what he's found: a poker. The memory comes, Mr Roper striking out at Gary's mum, not with a stick as I'd assumed, but with cold, hard iron.

Bastard, I think again, and Gary lets out a soft *huff*, as if casting off all thought of Roper, as if Roper isn't even worth his time any longer, and we return to our kitchen, where Helen stands in the doorway.

This time, I speak first. "Did you open the door?"

She flinches, no doubt hearing the other questions behind the one I've voiced. *Did you leave him out there on purpose? Did you take off his collar? Did you leave him to the mercies of Mr.-bloody-Roper?* But she can't or won't answer. She looks at me for a long moment before stalking inside and away, up the stairs.

Another image rises: a picture of how things might one day be. The cracks between us opening so wide, they become a chasm. Helen gone, the house empty. Living here alone.

No: Helen will be alone. I'll have Gary.

And I realise that today's the day. I can adopt him. I'd meant to discuss it with my wife, but I know now that I'm not going to.

Gary is my boy. My good boy. *Mine.*

* * *

The next day, I notice there's a van and a couple of cars parked outside Mr. Roper's house. Among them must be a doctor's car, a coroner's van, because the next thing I see is a surprisingly small form being carried out on a stretcher.

I step outside and ask what happened. The old man's son is there, terse but dry-eyed. He says his dad died during the night. I give him my commiserations. I can't quite bring myself to say it's terribly sad.

I go into our back garden and light up a cigarette, a more frequent occurrence now than it used to be. Gary is outside too. I think he must be teething. He's ignored all the chew toys I bought for him, but he must have found something to his liking; I can hear him, gnaw, gnaw, gnawing, somewhere in the bushes.

* * *

A few days later, we attend the funeral. We feel like we should; so few people are there. I notice taped-off areas around some of the gravestones.

"Been dug up," I hear someone say. "Right mess, big 'oles, all ower. They dunt know where t' bones have gone."

It's odd, but I don't think much more about it. It's not our problem. I'm more concerned that Helen keeps on opening the back door for Gary during the night, then forgetting she's done it. Still, I'm not so worried for Gary now. Roper is gone, and anyway, my boy keeps on growing. He's bigger every day. He's as tall as my thigh; my hip; my waist. His fur grows denser and blacker. He still carries that smell: musk. Meat. Brimstone. Burning.

* * *

"You treat that dog like a child," my wife complains.

I don't treat him like a child. I treat him like my boy: there's a difference, but I don't say so.

Gary sleeps in the lounge now. He's too big for the kitchen anyway. He pads around, so heavy I can hear each step, softened with fur so that it sounds like he's walking through mud. I get used to it. Sometimes I hear it where it can't even be. It'll come from the hall, when he's actually snoozing on the sofa. Or I'll hear him padding softly at my heels, only to see him in front of me, in the kitchen, awaiting his dinner.

He's hungry. Always so very hungry. He still won't eat kibble, though, and who can blame him? I buy him choice cuts from the butcher's.

My wife complains that I'm too soft on him.

My wife complains.

* * *

"My wrist still hasn't bloody healed," she says one night. We're sitting side by side in the half dark, watching television.

She thrusts her arm under my nose. Light flickers and I make out a dark line. Is the skin around it raised and reddened? But then, Helen keeps scratching at it. Irritating it. Worrying at it with her nails, something she just – can't – let – go.

"Well if you stop fussing with it, love."

"It's a sign," she says.

Gary, a black shape in the corner of the room, raises his head. Two eyes gleam.

"I heard stories, when I was a kid," Helen says. Her voice is guttural, as if clogged with something. "Black Shuck. The Barghest. Skriker. Padfoot. Legendary dogs. Not like real dogs. Not *right*."

"Jesus, Hels. What are they supposed to be, then? Why don't you tell me?"

She pauses before she says, "They're all pretty much the same. Some kind of black dog."

I look over at Gary. "Well, yes," I say, my voice laced with sarcasm.

"Will you *listen*, Dan? I looked them up. They're huge, for starters. Bigger than a regular dog. They have red eyes."

257

"Well, dogs can be big," I say. "Dogs have eyes. Sometimes they're red. Blah blah."

But Helen won't stop. She says that such dogs aren't natural. She says they're connected with the Devil, with death, with places of burial. She says they stink of brimstone and leave scorch marks behind them. Just about every English county has its own story, she says, and sometimes the details are different but the gist is pretty much the same. They howl at anyone who's about to die. Or they lie down on their doorstep. Sometimes, they're the ones who *make* them die.

"Gabble Ratchets," she says. "Some say those ones are the spirits of unbaptised children." She pauses again. "Why did you call him Gary? It's not a dog's name. Why did you do that?"

For heaven's sake. I open my mouth to tell her she's being stupid, ridiculous, but she jumps in again.

"If you speak to one, it gives it power over you. How much power do you think it would have over you if you *named* it, Dan? What if you *gave* it power over you? What then? Maybe that's why I can see all this and you can't."

Once again, she holds out her arm. She must have been scratching again, scratching it even as she talked about unnatural dogs, *Devil* dogs, because her skin is broken. Blood runs from it, drips to the sofa. "This is what happens if you get in their way," she says. "They leave wounds that won't heal, that never heal."

Her voice breaks over the words. And I sense again that thing that lies between us, a dark fissure, leading to – what? I don't want to see; it's too raw, still bleeding. I reach for her hand, miss it in the half dark, and then she is gone, her footsteps stamping up the stairs, away from me; away from us both.

* * *

That night, Helen removes herself to the spare room. She says she's sick, that her wrist is making her sick. I want to tell her that it's the other way around. It's Helen who's making her wrist worse, with her mind, her words, her constant *picking*. Her thoughts are poisoning her; poisoning *us*.

But I don't say that. I lie down in our bed alone and try not to think of the empty space next to me. I wonder if Helen's asleep.

After a while, the door scrapes open. I blink, seeing only darkness, then a weight sinks into the mattress at the end of the bed.

After a minute or two, I make it out. The shadow is tall, as tall as a child might be; perhaps even taller than that. Its weight tilts the whole mattress towards it. Fear laps at my senses and I have to remind myself that it's *Gary*, only a dog, only my boy. He's come looking for some love, for comfort, or to offer it, and at last, I find I can push myself up. I reach for him and my fingertips meet with fur as soft as cobwebs, as fine as a baby's hair. I lean into him and he is solid and warm and *there*. I wrap my arms around him and bury my face in his neck and hold on tight.

* * *

The next day, Helen won't get out of bed. She won't take a shower, though there's a smell in the room; a musty, unpleasant smell. Her face looks pale, but then, she won't let me open the curtains either.

"It's gone bad," she says. "There's rot in it. It's spreading. I told you. The wound won't heal."

"Of course it will," I say. "Of course. If you'd stop scratching it, Helen. If you'd only."

"We need help, Dan. *I* need help. A doctor."

It comes to me then that *black dog* is also a term for depression. Maybe that's what's wrong with my wife.

Maybe a doctor really could help, even if it's not in the way she thinks. Maybe he could prescribe something to help her.

Something that would help us both.

* * *

The doctor arrives late in the afternoon. The first thing he does when he walks in is make a fuss of Gary, exclaiming over his size, ruffling his long fur. "Gary, is it? Good boy, Gary. Hmm? I always talk to the family dog first. Show I'm a friend. Saves no end of bother." He winks.

Gary makes a low growling noise deep in his chest. I hope it's just his purr, but he doesn't move, keeps on staring out of the window, his glowing eyes reflected in the glass. The doctor sees them too. He stares at them; for a long time, he stares.

When he turns back to me, his expression has changed; grown vague, unfocused. "Now, the, erm – the patient? There *is* a patient, hmm?" Absent-mindedly, he pats Gary. "Good... er—" he says, as if he's forgotten the rest.

"Good *boy*," I say to Gary.

The doctor nods. "Good – yes. Good."

He goes up to see Helen. He isn't long. He emerges from our spare room, still with that puzzled expression on his face, that distracted air. His words are clear enough, however. "Fine," he says. "Yes, fine. That's it. No real problems, not at all."

"Does she need anything for her wrist? Something else, maybe?"

"Oh, her – no, all's fine. Good, in fact. Yes, *good*." He puts on his coat as he speaks, picks up his bag, holds it across his chest like a shield. He's still saying it as he walks out the door. "Good. Good."

I nod. I nod at Gary, since he's the only one left. "Good," I echo, for want of anything else. "Good boy."

* * *

Gary grows to a size I can only describe as magnificent. When he stretches out to sleep on my bed, I curl into his side like a child. When he stands next to me, his haunches are level with my shoulders. His teeth are as long as my fingers. His eyes smoulder and gleam.

One evening, he lies down across the step in our open doorway, facing not towards the house but

262

away, into the autumn dark, and his nose twitches.

He is waiting. I do not know what for, only that something will happen. I can sense it. I don't want anything to change. I want to drag him back inside, to close the door against the night, but I already know I won't be able to move him.

Gary. I form the name on my tongue, but it doesn't seem to fit him any longer, not quite.

Outside, in the garden, two red eyes open in the dark.

No, I think. But no matter how I wish them away, they do not fade. They only gaze steadily at us; at *him*.

Gary's mother makes no sound. She doesn't move. I can barely make her out, but I know it is she. Her son rises to his feet. He walks towards her and he does not look back at me. He pads across the garden, and each step leaves a pawprint scorched into the earth.

I do not know where she has been. Whether she has been healing, or hiding, or something else. Perhaps she was only waiting until he was grown. Until he was ready, or she was.

When he reaches her, she doesn't paw at him or lick his ears or anything else. They simply turn, together, and with a single leap, they have cleared the river and are gone. I peer out, across the fields, but cannot see a trace of them at all.

I want to fall to my knees. I want to tilt back my head and howl my loss to the moon, but I don't. I only gaze after them for a very long time.

* * *

When I go back inside, it is different.

The smell of burning is stronger, I realise. It isn't like I'd thought, though; not soft like November but acrid in the back of my throat.

The walls and doors are gouged with deep scratches. Plaster and wood alike have crumbled under their force.

The carpet is full of scorch holes. One, by Gary's bed, smoulders still, though there is no fire. I stamp on it until it dulls.

I stare at the coffee table, the first thing that Helen and I bought together. We'd had a new flat and no bed, no furniture, and that was what we chose: a coffee table. Now it is heaped with cigarette butts and covered in burns.

The table is by the sofa, where Helen and I had wrapped ourselves in each other so many times, talking of our lives; our jobs; our hopes. Of the child we would one day have, running around our feet, kicking a ball around the garden. We had spoken of where that would take us; everything we would do. How happy we would be. How much we would love him. How much we already loved each other.

How much power do you think it would have over you if you named *it, Dan? What if you* gave *it power over you? What then?*

I go upstairs, rubbing at my eyes, and pause on the landing. The smell is stronger here. I glance into my bedroom to see that the sheets are filthy, covered in muddy pawprints and bits of dead leaves, patched wet with drool.

No, not *my* bedroom: *ours.*

How long is it since I last saw Helen? How long since I looked at her face, into her eyes? Spoke to her? *Listened?*

I turn towards the spare room. And it comes to me that there's another smell, an unfamiliar one, beneath the charring; another *stink*. I breathe it in. There's that hint of mulch and earth, of musk, of bonfires and fireworks, but that isn't all. This new scent is hard to identify. It is sweeter than the rest, but not *good*-sweet. It's not a wholesome smell. It's like festering; like rot; like poison. Like something spreading from a wound, one that won't heal; that perhaps will never heal.

This time, when I open my mouth, a sound emerges. It is an odd sound: not quite a howl, not a whine nor a whimper. It is not quite like crying, yet it is all of them at once, and that smell floods in, it is on my tongue and all around me, something that won't be denied. It creeps from under the door of the spare room, where inside, my wife sleeps.

Where my wife surely sleeps.

The Finest Creation of an Artful God

B. Zelkovich

THE FIRST TIME I see the woman in the woods behind my house, it's foggy and bitter cold. The mist carries a whiff of salt and seaweed and something dead. A message from the ocean, reminding me that I haven't made it out to say hello in far too long.

I haven't left the property in far too long.

The fog clings to everything – my skin, my clothes, my eyelashes – dampening all of me. It obscures everything. Sight, sound, and with the message from the Pacific, even smell. It leaves me feeling clumsy, a newborn tottering through the unknown.

So when I finally see the woman in the woods, I start hard enough that the horse nearest me spooks a little. That catches the woman's attention. She turns her head, her eyes passing right over me and to the chestnut mare to my right.

The woman looks at that horse like she is the finest creation of an artful god.

The mare is pretty enough, with a delicate face and a fine, long neck, but she's Grade – she's not the finest anything in the eyes of anyone.

Nevertheless, this woman's eyes are glued to the mare as if she's never seen something so magical as an eight-year-old, paperless, mix-breed horse who's spent the winter supplementing her hay with ragged coastal grass.

For a split-second I consider catching my father's stud horse and showing him off. Parading the stallion, with his gleaming golden coat, past the fence like this woman's the judge at an in-hand competition. She's not.

She's the impossible woman in the woods behind my house.

In the time it takes me to imagine such foolishness, she vanishes. She vanishes and I spin around like an idiot, scouring the field and wondering if I made the whole thing up.

I didn't, I decide. But even if I had, the horses still need bringing in and I'm running out of daylight.

The second and third times I see the woman in the woods are much the same. She stands at the edge of the trees, swallowed up in fog, and stares at my little herd of has-beens. Her eyes glaze over me, a tree for all she cares, and glues onto whichever horse stands closest to the fence.

And each time her wonder looks a little less awed and a little more starved. She catalogs the horses' every step, the lines of muscle as they ripple shoulder and flank, and licks her lips.

She's pinched and thin, though she's so covered in fabric it's hard to tell at first. She's draped in shawls and scarves and skirts, and those are covered in pine needles and spruce tips. Detritus from nights spent lying in the woods.

I want to offer her food. Shelter. Warmth. It's been so long since anyone has visited me, since anyone but me has walked these fields, but I see the gleam in her eye go from longing to craving and I keep my distance. Because there should not be a woman in the woods behind my house.

I start leaving little things on the fence posts anyway. Things the horses aren't liable to eat. A thick cut of jerky. A hardboiled egg. Leftover bacon slices from breakfast. She takes them. I know she does because I've seen her thin, ghostly arm reach out of the fog to snatch them.

The horses don't go to that side of the field anymore. Even in the light of day.

I've lived here long enough to know that not all the forest's creatures are benevolent. The occasional deer hopping the fence to forage with the horses, or even the raccoons that pilfer my compost bin are one thing. But the bear that's too big, too smart, and lived too long? The woman who shouldn't be? They are another thing entirely.

The fourth time I see the woman in the woods behind my house is different.

The wind is ripping, bullying the trees and riling the horses. Horses go crazy in the wind, like all that sound in their ears leaves them suddenly deaf and frightened, even if nothing else has changed. I bring them in one by one, careful not to get trampled. All that wind has banished the fog, and in the late afternoon sun I see her, leaning over the fence, hand outstretched.

She looks bereft, like I've robbed her of something vital, of something exquisite, by taking the horses to the barn ahead of schedule. The wind pulls at her, shawls and scarves whipping behind her towards the wood.

As if it wants to haul her back.

That's when the rain comes, heavy and freezing. It might even be hail, I'm not paying too close attention. All I know is I see that woman, the impossible woman in the woods behind my house, get drenched and pelted with the mountain's fiercest winter rage, and I can't stand it.

"Come on!" I shout over the storm.

She looks at me, *really* looks at me, for the first time. Her face is softer than I remembered, rounder, like maybe the offerings I've left are doing some good. I hope so. I hope to high, stormy heaven that I've earned some good will.

I've lived in these woods long enough to know that not all its creatures are benevolent. I've lived on this mountain long enough to know when a storm isn't just the weather, but a warning. I've lived in this beautiful, quietly magical world long enough to know when something is dangerous.

Still, I wave her toward the house. And as she comes running up the field I wonder just what kind of predator I've invited into my home.

She reaches us a little too fast and without breathing heavy for the effort. My father's stallion shudders beneath my hand and tugs at the lead. He dances away from the woman, keeping an eye on her at all times, then whinnies toward the barn.

We set off without a word, but I make sure never to turn my back on the woman. I consider leaving her in the barn, letting her ride out the storm with the horses, but they won't settle with her there. She watches them all like they're a spread at a buffet – each item more tempting than the last.

The horses kick at their stall doors and snort their displeasure, so I turn out the light and lead the woman up to the house.

It's small. Only one bedroom, a bathroom, and an open living space with a kitchen tucked up against one wall. It was crowded once, when I had my father to care for, and for a while it felt empty after his passing. In the years since then I've filled the crevices and found solace in solitude. It is enough.

But now, standing in my living room with an impossible woman, it feels a bit cramped.

I clear my throat. "I'll stoke the fire. Make yourself comfortable." I don't look at her as I add a couple logs to the wood stove. When I turn back to her she's sat with her back against the front of the sofa, her legs crossed beneath her. She wears gray leggings beneath her skirts and a pair of tired work boots.

In this light she looks shockingly human.

"Can I get you something to drink?" I head to the kitchen, expecting a request for water or maybe tea to fight the cold.

"Gin."

I glance at her. She doesn't quite smile, but humor glints in her eyes. If I look into them too long they shift from green to gold to yellow to orange and then back again.

They're beautiful.

I frown. "I don't have any mixers—"

"Just gin's fine." Her voice is low and breathy, like wind in the trees. It's rough like pinecones and sweet as sap. It's music, if you're willing to hear it.

I take the bottle from the top of the fridge and pour her a glass, then pour whisky for myself. I sit across from her, back against my father's recliner, while she sips her drink and sighs. I want to ask what she is, what she's doing in the woods behind my house, but figure that'd be rude.

"What's your name?"

She cocks her head at me, like she's never been asked something so ridiculous before. She licks her lips, and I don't like how much I like the sight.

"Juniper." She smiles. Her teeth are white and sharp, but I can't seem to find the sense to be afraid. "I know your name, Theodora." Her grin is wicked, but still I don't feel the threat.

"Theo," I correct. "And how do you know that?"

She laughs and it is sweet as Timothy hay. "The wood and mountain know you. Even the ocean knows you, in places."

I snort and sip at my whisky. "Don't know what I did to get so popular."

She frowns. "You listen. So few listen these days. And you tithe." She reaches into her skirt pockets – it takes all my strength not to flinch – and reveals a hardboiled egg.

I shrug. "Only seems polite. You looked hungry." I wonder which part of nature she belongs to. Not the ocean, for sure. She could be kin with the mountain, but I'd expect sharper angles, a face hard as granite.

"I am hungry."

"Is that why you stare at my horses? You want to eat them?"

She doesn't blush, but I think maybe she can't. "Just a taste!" She glances at me and bites her lip. "You have much I would like to taste, Theo."

That sends a coil of heat up my spine. The sensation is so unfamiliar that it startles me and I go still. It's been so long.

She shoots back the last of her gin and crawls toward me. "You're so lonely, Theo. All alone at the top of the mountain."

I've lived on this mountain a long time. I know a bargain when I hear one and I know that making bargains with nature is a losing game. But she's right.

I am so lonely.

I sip my whisky and make a show out of considering her. She's beautiful, in a feral, definitely-not-human sort of way. She's as likely to eat me as she is to fuck me. And somehow that only makes the offer all the more tempting.

"What's the price?"

She barks out a little laugh. "It's not so much. A night with you would be fun." She runs a finger up my chest, the point of her nail coming to rest at the base of my throat. It's sharper than it should be.

And when did she get close enough to touch?

The storm hammers at the roof, the sound ratcheting up as I hold her gaze. Hail, for sure now.

"I want to taste all of you, Theo." She looks at my lips a moment too long. A moment that says exactly what part of me she'd like to taste first. She sits back, giving me space. "And I'll take the palomino stud."

"No." The word cracks from me, sharp as a crop on flank. The stallion is the last colt from my father's mare. I would sooner die than sacrifice that horse to some woodland she-devil. I clear my throat. "You can't have him."

She pouts, a fingertip tapping at her chin as she weighs her options. "Fine. If I get to taste all of you, I'll take the chestnut mare."

I still don't know exactly what she means by 'take,' but I'm more worried about 'taste.' I say as much.

She laughs. "Has it been so long that I need be explicit?"

It probably has, if we're being honest. But there's only so much honesty something like her can bear.

"Indulge me."

She rolls her eyes. "My tongue. Your skin. Any and all of it... and if things get heated and there's a little blood, well…" She shrugs.

That should be a deal-breaker. I should say no. I absolutely should say no and tell her to leave. But it's dark out, the storm is still wailing, and this close I can smell her. Spruce and loam and peat. She smells like the woods in the dark after the rain. She smells like a place I could get lost.

I think I want to get lost.

"What do I get?"

She laughs. "You're getting me and my tongue and sweet relief."

I snort. I'm not giving some forest creature my blood and my mare because she thinks she's Casanova.

"Not just physical relief, Theo," she chides. "Relief from the monotony. Relief from the memories burying you here. I'll give you a thrill, a risk, a night so sublime it will be your final thought upon your death."

I raise a brow at her. "Is that because you're going to kill me before we're through?"

Another laugh, breathy and wild as eagle's wings. "No, Theo. I promise you, you will be whole when I leave your home."

This is a bad idea. I know it. The mountain and ocean and sky know it, and have told me as much. But

I look up into shimmering autumn eyes, green then gold then yellow then orange, and I know what I'm going to say. After all, if not all the forest's creatures are benevolent, then they can't all be malevolent either.

"Okay."

Her smile is voracious, vicious, sharp. I should feel fear, but in that moment, all I think is that I hope she swallows me whole.

* * *

Looking back on that night, she might have. There are moments I can't remember, like I was blackout drunk. Pockets of nothing that I think I'm better not knowing. Other moments are impossibly clear. The feel of her nails in my hair, gentle until I didn't want them to be. The heat of her breath on my neck, the sting of her teeth when she bit me. And she did bite me. A lot.

I loved every minute of it. I remember the sight of her, swaying above me like she was made of branches in a storm. And I remember the taste of her – sharp cedar and sweet apple, heavy with the musk of dirt. I think I took the forest incarnate to bed.

But it's afterward that I'll never forget.

She stayed with me until the morning, until the storm moved on and there was peace on the mountaintop again. She cuddled me and ran her claws through my hair and hummed me a tune so old the house shivered with her voice. When her eyes met mine, there was that look again, the one she'd only ever had for the horses.

She looked at me like I was the finest creation of an artful god.

That wasn't part of the deal. We didn't negotiate aftercare or tenderness, but I didn't complain. No one had ever looked at me like that. I think I'd sacrifice plenty of livestock to be looked at like that again.

When sunlight cast across my bed she stood to dress. I watched, rapt, while she navigated skirts and shawls, and so much fabric she was swallowed in it.

I think she would have left just like that, without a word. Maybe it would have been better if she had, but I opened my fool mouth.

"Will I see you again?"

She laughed, but it wasn't mean. "Oh sweet, lonesome Theo. You don't want that."

"Why not?"

She stepped back to the bed and leaned over me to brush her lips across my jaw, featherlight with the promise of fangs beneath. "Because I do not think you would survive another night with me."

Deep down, somewhere I didn't like to think too much about, I figured that meeting my demise in her arms wouldn't be half bad. Maybe even thought it would be preferable to the long, dark, and lonely nights I'd known before.

She pulled back, putting distance between us, and sighed. "Besides, the mountain would never forgive me." She sniffed and wound a ratty scarf around her shoulders. "He's protective of you."

I watched her and tried not to succumb to the sudden fear crawling in my gut as she gathered her things.

"I don't want to be alone again." Such a confession I never thought to speak. I'd been alone and strong all these years. I chose this life of solitude, because hard as it was, it was easier than wanting something I could never have. There was no love for me, beyond this life I'd built.

But one night with the forest laid me low and left me wanting.

She smiled, sharp and sweet and unsettling. "Silly Theo. Friend of the ocean, sibling to the sky, child of the mountain, and beloved of the wood – and still you think you're alone!" She gave me an admonishing look. "You are not so unlovable as you think, Theo."

She took my hand and hauled me naked from the bed. I pressed against her, hungry for more of anything she'd give. With her hand pressed against my heart and her mouth on mine, I breathed her in for the last time.

Juniper pulled back sharply, pushed against my chest to separate us, her pupils wide and teeth sharp. "Enough!" The house shook with the force of her voice, then she took a deep breath and swept the hair back from her face. "Enough, Theo. I am still owed a horse."

I still think back on that moment and wonder which one of us was ever truly in danger? What tragedy did she divert us from by sheer force of will? I'll never know.

I dressed in silence and led her out to the barn. Of all the horses, only the chestnut mare remained calm. My father's stud horse raged, kicking and snorting so much I thought he might actually break loose, but the stall held.

Juniper's hand on my elbow stopped me when I reached for the mare's halter.

"That won't be necessary." She turned hungry eyes on the mare. "She has accepted her fate." And sure enough, when the stall door swung open, the horse went calm and easy after Juniper, as if she hadn't feared the woman the day before.

We made our way down toward the wood, stopping once we reached the fence at the edge of my field. Juniper stopped to look at me, the horse pausing in step with her.

"Don't look for me, Theo," she said. "I've taken what's mine and given more than I should." She looked at her feet. "Let that be enough."

In the cool morning mist, the memory of her hands sent spirals of heat up my spine. I didn't think I could ever get enough. But I've lived on this mountain a long time. I know a warning when I hear one. Even when I think it was more for her than for me.

So I watched her walk away, my horse following at her shoulder, until they were swallowed up in mist and spruce.

That day was clear and unseasonably warm, and no matter how much I wanted to languish in the memory of the night before, I had chores to do. I was busy mucking stalls when I fully understood Juniper's gift.

I'd shucked my coat and had worked up enough sweat to tie my flannel around my hips. I felt it before I saw it – something splitting the skin on my collarbone, clambering up and out of me.

It hurt. Enough that I dropped my shovel and cursed, snatching at my chest. I almost crushed the delicate petals that sprouted along my clavicle. There, blooming up from where she had last touched me, were three velvety soft purple petals.

A Pacific trillium, wrinkled, wet and new.

I should have been scared. I should have worried what this meant – what kind of person has a flower growing out of their bones? But all the space in my fool head was consumed with Juniper, the woman in the woods behind my house, and the gift she'd given me. A forget-me-not for the wood's beloved.

A blessing and a curse to carry her with me, remembering and wanting and knowing this was the most I'd ever have. And it was more than I'd ever hoped for. A fragile bud to cherish and loathe, knowing Juniper had made good on her threat. On her promise.

I would think of that night we shared every single day, until it was all I had left.

I shuddered at the realization, part terror and part desire, but still I couldn't find the sense to feel fear. I was too enamored for sense.

That would come later.

That night I sipped whisky by the fire, lost in memory. My hand kept reaching up to my collarbone – to the flower, so I could stroke its petals. They were so soft, and I somehow managed to feel not just through my fingertips, but through the flower itself. The touch was soothing.

Until I heard a horse scream in the dark, too faint to have come from the barn. It came from the wood. The sound curdled the whisky in my guts, knowing I'd bartered a horse's life to numb the ache of loneliness for one night. Knowing that whatever the mare's fate, it was terrible enough to shatter the bewitched calm Juniper had cast over her.

My grip on the flower tightened, all that sensible fear and disgust crashing over me. I made to rip the thing out of me, root and all, but the pain was flash-fire in my bones. When I pulled my hand away, my palm was sticky with blood.

I rushed to the bathroom, to the mirror, and bore witness to the true cost of my desperation.

The trillium petals were creased and wilted from my grip, but they were whole. Impossibly whole. The skin around the flower was torn, furrowed like soil after weeding, and blood trickled from the ruined flesh.

I pulled, gingerly, at the flower, and hissed with sick fascination as I watched it stretch the skin of my collarbone. But it did not come free. I felt the tug deep in my bone, the roots twined so deep they'd ossified to become part of me.

I knew then that I had sealed my own fate. I was the forest's beloved, and she had taken me as surely as she had taken my mare. Only my death would be slower. Years of springtime blooms sprouting from my bones. An endless reminder until it was my only memory.

Until it was the final thought upon my death.

The Third Curse

Helen Grant

THE FIRST CURSE, the one people sometimes call a gift, is seeing. Like any respectable curse, it runs in families. It runs particularly fiercely through the MacNeills, who have been seeing things for as long as anyone can remember, and longer.

The second curse is going, which follows naturally from the first. If you are walking home at night, alone in the velvet dark and the glittering cold, you may see something beckoning to you from the dim recesses of a copse or a ruined house. Should you go? Probably not. But to go at all, you must first see.

The third curse, the fatal one, is remembering. Many years ago – not scores of years, but actual *centuries* – a young man named Farquhar MacNeill went with the fairies. It seemed to him that he was only a little time in their company before a chance utterance, words of blessing, recalled him to himself. But when he tried to return to his father's house, not a stone remained; there was nothing but a patch of nettles. Upon enquiring about, he at last realised that many generations had passed in the seemingly short time he had been away. The shock was so great that upon that very instant his bones crumbled into dust, leaving nothing but a handful of grey ashes that dispersed with the wind.

Be warned: seeing is bad enough; going with what you have seen is worse; but the most dreadful thing of all is remembering.

1747

James MacNeill is a handsome young man with dark hair, high cheekbones, and green eyes that have something of a faraway look to them; like all the MacNeills he sees further into things than other people do. He is clad in a full-skirted coat and embroidered waistcoat with knee breeches and a tricorn hat – dressed perhaps rather too finely for his current situation: he is leaning against a tree in the Bois de Boulogne, his stockings and buckled shoes spattered with mud. At this moment he wears an expression of irritable discontent that has nothing to do with the mire underfoot.

Everything is wrong. He meant to do great things – to be a hero in a worthy cause. He did not mean to be here, in France, licking his wounds after a defeat that took barely an hour. So many men dead, or ignominiously dispersed. As for the Pretender – a sullen voice at the back of James' mind tells him that the man was not worth it; for all his handsome, swaggering looks he is too fond of the bottle and forever chasing skirts. And James himself has barely a *sou* to his name, and cannot live on credit forever.

"No," he says to himself, "the entire venture was a disaster."

With these preoccupying thoughts it is some time before he realises that he has been gazing at one particular spot in the undergrowth, and even then it is hard to say what has caught his eye. A faint line seems to run to it from close to where he stands, vanishing into the straggling plants under the trees, but it is barely a rabbit track – not even that, perhaps. There is no reason to follow it, but after a swift glance over his shoulder he does exactly that, brushing against wildflowers which leave a sprinkling of yellow pollen like gold dust on his legs.

The forest is never truly silent: birds cry in the treetops; small creatures scurry through the undergrowth with tiny snaps and rustles; the wind sighs and hisses among the leaves and stalks. Nor is it ever still. Among the swaying plants and dipping branches James sees a more definite movement – something slender, smooth and pale, gleaming in the sunlight slanting down through the canopy of trees. It might be a sapling stripped of its bark by deer, moving with the breeze. James thinks of pearlescent skin, of slim, feminine limbs weaving in a sensuous dance. He swallows, and tries to step carefully, silently, getting nearer without giving his presence away. The air is humid and warmer than he thought; the coat and waistcoat feel too heavy, too constrictive. James doffs the tricorn hat; it falls unheeded to the grass. He thinks of removing his coat, and before he knows what he is doing he has shrugged it off; he leaves it hanging on a branch. His shoes follow, in spite of their fine buckles, and then his stockings, and now he feels the rich earth under his bare feet. Damp and clinging, it oozes luxuriantly between his toes.

James steps into a small clearing, and there she sits. Eyes less penetrating than his might see nothing but the play of dark and light, yellow blossoms for hair, green sward for her robe. She smiles at him and her eyes are the blue of speedwell flowers. The hand that she holds out to him is as pale and slender as a young shoot. Her touch is cool, her skin smooth. James has never seen anyone so strange, nor so beautiful.

"My Queen," he says.

He lifts her hand to his lips and kisses it softly. And forgets.

He forgets the Prince whom he has followed to France, and his own mean lodgings, and his debts. He forgets the land of his birth, and the cool mist that hangs over the purple heather, the grey bulk of the mountains, the gush of the river over the stones, and the rough track that leads to home. When the young woman rises, James goes with her willingly; when the earth opens to reveal a narrow tunnel threaded through with tree roots, he does not falter. He follows her down, and down, to the place where the Sithichean live, the Fées, the Little People. He leaves behind him a tricorn with a silver trim, a coat hanging from a tree, and shoes and stockings scattered along an almost invisible path. The shoes, stockings and coat are eventually found by a vagrant, who takes them gratefully; the tricorn moulders where it lies.

James' new love and her people welcome him kindly, although there is always a hint of sly amusement in their behaviour towards him, as though he is a child, not understanding everything. Their language is not a problem to him: it seems to grow like a seed in his brain, flourishing rapidly. He joins in their revels, weaving his way with increasing confidence through their complicated dances. He drinks from acorn cupules and feasts on mallow fruit, finding it wonderfully satisfying. When she permits it, he makes love to his strange lady, though her diminutive form makes him feel like a bear playing with a young leveret. She laughs at him, but he doesn't care, so long as she lets him love her.

Time passes drowsily here. There is no real sense of the past, only a kind of eternal present; there is flow, but it does not flow onwards, it rounds upon itself – an endless whirlpool. Dancing, drinking, feasting, loving.

Gradually, however, James begins to perceive that something is changing. Glances that were friendly, if suffused with sly humour, have become grave and speculative. The revels that hitherto seemed to continue unabated are sometimes interrupted by arrivals and departures, small commotions from which he is subtly excluded. His lady rebuffs him more often than not, and he sees something new in her gaze – a reassessing, even a slight repulsion.

In the midst of a feast there is a sudden uproar. One has returned, where half a dozen were expected. The one who has come back is borne into the midst of the others and laid upon the earthen floor.

At first James cannot tell what it is. It looks like a magpie, he thinks, until he sees that the black feathers are burnt; the plumage was originally white. It is not even all bird. It was horribly seared in the transition from Sithiche to dove or perhaps from dove to Sithiche; James sees charred and twisted limbs and one dreadful, beseeching eye.

What has done this? James does not know, but suddenly the others are close around him, and their chattering is so swift and so angry that he cannot make anything out. He knows what they are saying, though: they are blaming *him*. He protests in vain; he calls for his lady love.

They draw back, parting to allow her to approach through the press of bodies. James has never seen her look so beautiful, so queenly. So cold. She comes closer, her chin raised, her gaze averted. When she is so close that he could put out a hand and touch her, she turns her head, looking away. He sees that she is refusing to know him anymore. He is heartbroken, and also afraid, because there are many of them and only one of him, and he is angry, because of the injustice. What has he done?

He opens his mouth.

"By God—"

And with the uttering of those words James remembers.

He finds himself in the dark, alone. Disoriented, he looks up, and sees stars. He is no longer underground, in the domain of the Sithichean; he is in the world of men. The ground is cold under his bare feet. Clad lightly in knee breeches and a shirt, he shivers, wondering where his coat is – his shoes, his hat. He left them here, a little time ago, but it will be hopeless looking for them in the dark. At first light he'll come back and search. He begins to walk, wincing when he treads on things – stones, jagged sticks.

After a time, to his surprise, James feels a smooth solid surface under his feet.

A pavement, he concludes, but he cannot think where that might be. He only remembers dirt tracks.

There are lights in the distance – a great many of them. There must be some grand event taking place for there to be so many lamps burning.

Extravagance. There'll be no more of that for him. He wonders whether he could go home – under an assumed name, perhaps. He imagines himself walking the drovers' road that leads to his village – he remembers the purple heather and grey cloud hanging low over the mountains and the sweet scent of damp air. He walks on.

James' eyes are acclimatising to the dark, and he is getting closer to the lights. A deep furrow appears between his brows. He recognises nothing of this place. When he followed his lady love – a few days ago, he thinks – he was in woodland. This is more like a park. There are stretches of lawn, kept as neatly as any Lord's gardens, ponds, even buildings. How did he come to be here?

At last he reaches a set of great iron gates. He stands there, barefoot, hugging himself against the cold, and stares.

There are *machines* out there, moving up and down the wide avenue. They are plainly visible by the light of the streetlamps, which are brighter than anything he has seen before. James stares and stares. The curiously dressed people who hurry past do not seem at all surprised by the machines; indeed they barely notice them. Among these people are men in dull blue uniforms and helmets, carrying some type of musket. Soldiers. One of the machines passes close to him, and he sees that there are more of the soldiers inside it, staring ahead, grim-faced.

James puts his hands over his face. Although he is prepared to believe that there are untold wonders in other parts of the world, he has never conceived of anything like this. Is he dreaming? He takes his hands away, and it is all just as before: the machines, the lights, the soldiers.

Eventually he plucks up courage and accosts a passer-by.

"Monsieur?"

The man eyes him disdainfully. James knows how he must look: half-clad, unshaven, barefoot. But he is lucky; the man gives him a second's consideration rather than shaking him off immediately.

"C'est où, le Bois de Boulogne?"

The man's eyebrows go up. He gestures.

"C'est ici, M'sieur."

He hurries away before James can ask anything else. As for James, he stares at the iron gates, and then he turns back to the avenue with its bizarre horseless carriages. It is beginning to occur to him that the question is not so much *where* he is, as *when*.

* * *

The following afternoon, James is picked up by soldiers because he is making a commotion in the street – enough of one that not even the well-bred Parisians can ignore it. He is cold, dirty, thirsty and desperately hungry. Seemingly he is also unbalanced, since he keeps shouting in peculiarly accented French that he wants to go back.

The soldiers take James to their headquarters, where a bored officer looks him up and down and asks him questions. He listens to James' halting replies and shakes his head; either James has misunderstood the questions or he is a mental patient, escaped from confinement. Something occurs to him.

"Monsieur, vous êtes anglais?"

"Non," says James indignantly. "Je suis écossais."

The officer shrugs. It is the same thing as far as he is concerned. He tells the soldiers to feed James and then hand him over to the British.

* * *

James finds himself in front of another officer, flanked by more soldiers. The uniforms are khaki this time, and the language is English, but so far as he can tell, the questions are the same. The replies he gives them are the same, too. He keeps saying he wants to go back.

The officer regards him stonily. James represents a problem. He is clearly British, and clearly of enlistment age, but he has no uniform and no identification of any kind. The things he is expressing so incoherently suggest delusions, but what would a British mental patient be doing in France? More probably he is feigning madness, and his uniform and identity tags are hidden in some French barn or cellar.

A *deserter*, decides the officer. The court-martial is arranged for the following morning. It takes very little time to find James guilty. He is taken out shortly afterwards, and executed by firing squad. It is June, 1915.

Remembering – that is the fatal thing.

2024

James MacNeill has a direct descendant, though he died unmarried; a local girl, perceiving her condition, capitulated to the urgent marriage proposals of a widowed farmer. The farmer gained a pretty wife, and the girl kept her good name, but the bairn was James', and its offspring were his kin.

James' descendant bears the name of Lewis Munro, but he has the MacNeill sight. He also has the MacNeill looks – dark hair and green eyes, handsome enough to tempt anyone. Handsome enough to tempt the Sithichean.

Lewis lives and works in Glasgow. He has a desk job in a futuristic modern building, a dazzling construction of glass and metal with not so much as a single spider plant to spoil its clean lines. His flat, on the eighth floor of a block, well above the height of any city trees, has no window boxes or hanging baskets – not even a single succulent in a pot. Lewis doesn't *dislike* the natural world. Far from it; sometimes at weekends he goes for long walks in the countryside, or tackles a Munro. But he cannot live in it, and especially not work in it. Too distracting.

Sometimes, when he is sitting on a plastic chair on his unadorned balcony, sipping a cold one and watching the traffic passing far below, he wonders whether there is something wrong with him. He doesn't feel anxious, or depressed. He just sees things – things other people don't see. Something rough-skinned and grey and ancient, blending with the rock it is slumbering on. Something spindle-limbed which moves among wind-tossed branches. Amber eyes blinking lazily in a dark crevice furred with moss. Most of the time these things are not alarming, but if other people saw him reacting to them, they'd be tapping their brows significantly, and who could blame them? *They* don't see these things.

The city is safe. There is something aseptic about the acres of concrete and tarmac, the gravel and paving stones, the glass and steel. Even the grass visible in a plot far below Lewis' flat is made of green plastic. If anything eldritch lives here, it is distinctly human in nature.

One Sunday in August, however, the city becomes unpleasant. It is hot – one of the hottest days on record, they say – and the streets become grimy kilns, stinking of exhaust fumes and sweaty bodies. Lewis takes a train to the coast, enduring the journey for the sake of the relief at the end. There is a place he knows, where the tourists and the loud groups with cool boxes full of beer and the families with screaming kids don't go. He sits on a flat rock with the sea breeze in his hair and looks out over the water.

He's been there a while when he realises he's not alone. There's a girl sitting not far off, perched on another rock with her knees drawn up. She is small and slender and very, very blonde, her hair almost white, and she is wearing a dress in a daringly unfashionable shade of green. Her feet, he sees, are bare. She looks at him, and smiles.

Lewis, who is used to making human connections through a device, by swiping left and right, does not think of approaching her. That would be too weirdly organic. He nods once, and then turns back to the ocean.

When he looks up again, she is right beside him, and he almost jumps. Still, it does not occur to him that she is one of the things he sometimes sees. She's a girl, after all.

"Hello," he says cautiously.

"You *see*," she says. She has a curious accent that Lewis can't place. He has the strangest feeling that she didn't address him in English at all, but he understood her perfectly well. Her eyes are very blue – bluer than any Lewis has seen before, blue as speedwells. Lewis can't seem to look away from them.

"I'm sorry?" he says.

"You *see*. You can see *me*, can't you?"

He nods slowly, baffled.

She puts her head on one side, flaxen locks falling fetchingly across her face. "Some say we shouldn't talk to you any more."

"To me?"

"To your kind." She pushes back the wayward tendrils. "You're destructive. Selfish. *Greedy*."

Lewis raises his eyebrows. "Thanks very much."

"Silly. I don't mean you personally." She laughs, and

it hurts his ears a little; it's like a wet finger run around the rim of a wine glass. Then she stops. "I think there's still good in you."

"Me personally?" says Lewis drily. "Or my kind?"

"Either," she says. "Is there good in *you*?"

"I hope so," he says. The conversation is surreal; he can't quite take it seriously. And what does she mean by 'his kind'? Men?

For a little while she stands by him, looking out to sea in silence. Her chin lifts and he sees her gaze following a gannet as it dives into the water, then bobs exuberantly to the surface.

She turns to him and says: "Do you want to kiss me?"

Lewis stares at her. "Er…"

"Do you?" she persists. She is even closer than before. Those blue eyes are all Lewis can see. They are fringed with fair lashes, which he has always thought unattractive before, but which look exquisite on her. He can smell damp grass, dog roses, woodsmoke.

"Uh…" Put on the spot, he says: "I suppose…"

She smiles impishly, leans in and presses her lips to his. And Lewis forgets.

* * *

Work, flats, income tax, social media, drinking on a Friday night, swiping left and right: all of it is a lot easier to forget than you'd think. The lure of the old runs like a deep current under the surface of things.

On the way down into a place that feels more like home than the eighth-floor flat in the city ever did, Lewis somehow mislays his keys and his wallet and even his expensive trainers. The cool earth is very pleasant under his bare feet and also he is more interested in drawing that blue gaze back to himself than he is in unimportant things like where he left his bank cards. She pulls him along with one slender hand and he asks her what her name is, laughing, but he can't reproduce the answer; it sounds like a flock of birds taking flight, or the wind over the waves.

He is received kindly by the others like her. There is food and drink, and yes, loving, and there is even work, although it is never tedious nor long lasting; Lewis is simply bigger and stronger than the rest of them, and can tackle tasks that it would take half a dozen of them to do. There is a vague feeling in the back of Lewis' mind that he used to be somewhere else, somewhere that he probably ought to go back to at some point, but he hasn't been here very long at all; a day or two, or perhaps three. Time has a curious, slippery quality down here; he seems to live the same moment over and over again, rather than going forward.

He sits with his back to a tree root, his head back and his eyes half-closed, thinking languorously about his love, about the long limbs under the green she always wears. Then he opens his eyes and she is there in front of him. So are the rest of them. Their faces are stony.

"Hello," says Lewis, looking uneasily from one to the other.

They don't have a leader, exactly, but the older ones are held in high respect, and one of them steps forward now.

"You must go," he says, and there is no room for compromise on that wrinkled face.

"What?" says Lewis. He looks at his love, and she shakes her head, her face icy.

"You must go," she says.

"Why?" He doesn't want to go; he can't even remember what he'd be going back to.

Silently, they hold things out to him: the withered remains of plants, the body of an animal that is mostly bones and fur, a handful of dust.

"I didn't do that," protests Lewis.

"Your kind did," says the old one. He pauses. "So you must go."

Lewis looks at them, at their cold expressions, and he feels a slow, sluggish dread. "I don't want to go," he says.

"You must."

He hasn't uttered any chance words of blessing, or any holy name, which would break their hold over him and make him remember – which would take him instantly back to the world he knew before. He doesn't use those words – never has. When they lay hands on him and try to drag him away, Lewis employs all other kinds of curses, but not those. He tries to fight them off, with some success at first. In the end it takes about a dozen of them to subdue him. They hurt him as little as possible, but they are absolutely inexorable. Because he won't stop swinging his arms, they tie his hands together, and then they haul him by main force, out through a ragged opening in the earthen wall, and along a tunnel which slopes up, and up, towards the surface.

"Stop," says Lewis. "Don't."

They say nothing.

The tunnel opens into a crevice and Lewis feels air moving against his face. The air smells wrong; it smells of death.

The Sithichean push him out. He stumbles, and then he turns, but already the crevice has closed. There is no way back down, nothing but bare rock.

Lewis draws a breath, and begins to cough. The air sears his bare skin, his throat, his lungs. He turns away from the rock and looks around him. Everything is dead. Under his feet is grey dust. Out of the thick, poisonous mist loom the naked black branches of trees. Nothing blooms on them; nothing sings or flutters. He sees a flattened thing that might once have run or scampered; it's hard to tell.

Lewis drops to his hands and knees, but this isn't the kind of smoke you can get underneath; it's everywhere. He coughs and coughs, and does his best to crawl, trying to get away, but there is nowhere to escape to. The air is corrosive; he can feel it. He knows that very soon he will be dead too.

In his extremis he chokes the word out.

"God—" he says.

With that word, he remembers – at least in the last moments before he dies. He remembers the city, his flat, his job. He remembers 2024.

But he'll never know what year it is now.

The Lights Under Rachel

Kathryn Healy

THE OLD MAN found me while I was bent over a plate of 'Big Jimmy's Jambalaya,' wolfing it down despite its blasphemy towards the good name of Creole cooking. Not that I had expected anything authentic from a tourist trap seafood chain like Big Jimmy's Bait 'N' Bite, but it was too late for any other restaurants to seat me and I was starving from my day of travel. I looked up from my overcooked rice as the man slid into the seat across from me and gave me a warm smile through his scraggly white beard.

"Sorry to bother you, ma'am, but did I hear you ask the waitress about a ferry to Rachel?"

I nodded and wiped my mouth. "Yes," I said. "I was told there'd be a ferry out to the island, but I wasn't sure where to find it."

"You just did," said the man. "Name's Clyde, I'm the ferryman. The bride asked me to come pick you up, so I figured I'd keep an eye out for the most lost-looking person I could find. The out-of-towners usually come through here first," he said, looking around at the restaurant's tacky nautical interior. A ceiling fan protruded from the eye of a hurricane mural, and I frowned. Topical.

I turned back to the man. "Thank you, I was starting to think I would die here. I'm Kaleisha Hill, Amy – I mean, Clover's sister."

"Her sister?" Clyde asked with a quirk of an eyebrow.

I shifted in my seat, knowing exactly what he was thinking: Amy and I didn't look anything alike. She was a little white girl, and I was not. I was Jamaican, displaced by the first of the big hurricanes and evacuated to America with the other 'rescued' children, and then never given back. "Foster sister," I said, terse.

The man nodded, and I relaxed a little. "Well," he said, standing up and pointing over the deck railing to where an old wooden fishing boat was pulled halfway ashore. "The boat's ready to leave when you are." I stood up immediately at that, slapping a twenty-dollar bill on the table and not bothering to collect my leftovers.

* * *

Twenty minutes later, I found myself in Clyde's 'ferry,' bobbing along on the waves as the coastline disappeared behind me, and a small rocky island emerged from the fog. "I'm not too late, am I?" I asked Clyde. "I know the invitation said to arrive yesterday, but my flight was delayed by the storm."

"You haven't missed much," Clyde said. "Everyone else is already here, but Clover postponed the rehearsal until you arrived. She's excited to see you!" He tossed a grin over his shoulder at me, and I smiled back. "How long have you and the bride known each other?"

I sighed. "About fifteen years. She came to live with my foster family in New Orleans when we were teenagers."

"Oh, yeah? What was teenage Clover like?"

"Weird, honestly," I said with a laugh. "My parents put so much energy into trying to wrangle her that I flew under the radar. She wasn't a bad kid, but she'd always end up running with bad crowds and getting in trouble. She'd go through different phases and cycle through friend groups and name changes. When I met her she was going by Amy, and then Lilith during her

Goth phase. Apparently, she's Clover now. My theory is that her constant reinvention likely came from a desperation to fit in somewhere."

Clyde said, "I hope she feels like she fits in with us. She's certainly popular amongst the other Rachel girls."

I smiled at that. "I'm glad. She and I lost touch for a while after I went to college. I guess without me around to help, she was too much for my parents and they rotated her out to some other family, and I could never track her down. A few years later I found her online and she seemed to be doing well. Like, she had been selling Mary Kay and going to wellness retreats in Joshua Tree. Not my kind of thing, but whatever makes her happy."

"That sounds like her," said Clyde with a chuckle.

"Eventually, she announced that she was 'going off the grid' and deactivated all her social media, and that was the last I heard from her until her wedding invite came in the mail. Normally, I wouldn't trek all the way out here, but I wanted to check on her. Make sure she's okay." I paused, and Clyde remained silent. "How long have you known her, Clyde?"

"About a year. She joined Lightspring Ministries last summer. She's a sweet girl, and I'm happy that she's joining the family."

"You're related to the groom?"

"We all are," Clyde said. "Everybody on Rachel." I blinked. He couldn't mean that literally, not even Amy would get involved with incest. I turned my gaze back to the island. It was looming in front of us now, all jagged cliffs and foamy grey waves. Along the shoreline was a cluster of small buildings, and a path snaked its way up the cliffside towards a large manor house. The red stripe spiraling up the nearby lighthouse was the only color to the dreary scene, and I found myself smiling despite it. I preferred the sunny island from my childhood, but I could see how Amy could make this place her home. The sixteen-year-old, eyeliner-caked Lilith that I had to chaperone to metal concerts would have adored this place.

The sun had nearly set and, up on the island's cliffs, the lighthouse clicked on. It arced its beam across the ocean, dazzling me for a moment as it swept over our boat. A ghost of the light remained burned into my vision, stark yellow against the murky sea. It undulated slightly with the motion of the waves, its glow pulsing like a heartbeat. I shut my eyes as the lighthouse beam swept over us again, and when I opened them the patch of light was gone.

* * *

We reached the dock a few moments later, and Clyde offered a hand to help me step out onto the planks. No sooner had my feet touched solid ground than they were nearly knocked out from under me. A blonde woman in a white dress had launched herself at me, and though it had been many years since I'd last seen Amy, I'd know her hugs anywhere. "Kaleisha!" she cried, and I flung my arms around her and squeezed, relieved to hold her again after so long.

"Oh, God, Am— Am I glad to see you!" I corrected myself, narrowly avoiding calling her by her old name, and pushed my sister to arm's length so I could get a look at her. She was beaming, her cheeks rosy and eyes shining. This was the happiest I had ever seen her, and despite having no idea what 'Lightspring' was, I decided that it had to be a good thing for making her so happy. Over her shoulder I could see a row of five similar-looking women in pale dresses, all giving me identical smiles. "Hello," I called to them, and gave Clover a quizzical look.

My sister stepped back from me and motioned to the other girls, as if suddenly remembering they were there.

"Oh, these are my other bridesmaids. They're all sisters of the groom," she said. That explained how similar they looked. The incest thought crossed my mind again, and I forced it away. "Come on," Clover said, taking my carry-on bag from me. "Let me show you up to your room."

I shrugged at the other girls, as if to say, "I guess I'll learn your names later," but they just gave me the same unwavering smiles, so I turned to catch up to Clover as she made her way up the rocky footpath towards the manor house.

"I'm sorry you ran into so much trouble getting here," Clover said.

"No, I'm sorry for being late. Thank you for waiting for me," I said.

"Of course! Lightspring weddings only work if the entire party is present."

I should have asked then and there what exactly 'Lightspring' was, but something made me hesitate. Maybe it was the posse of girls trailing us silently up the hill, or the cold, foggy atmosphere getting to me, but I didn't want to let on that I was an outsider here. As if it wasn't already obvious enough.

"We've been getting so many hurricanes lately, I wasn't surprised that you were delayed," Clover said as we stepped into the shadow of the old house. She pushed the wooden door open and I peered over her head into the dim interior beyond. "We used to have a bridge, but a while back a storm knocked it out. The state tried to fix it, but since Rachel is private property they had to ask us for permission and we said, 'no, thank you'."

"Rachel's private property?" I asked.

Clover nodded. "Yep. We're not an incorporated town, so we don't show up on most maps. The island's always been owned by the Rachel family, and then after a few generations the village cropped up and now here we are!"

Clover shut the door behind me, barring the other women from coming inside. I imagined them all walking forwards until their faces touched the wooden slats, moving their legs stiffly in place like wind-up toys. I shivered. There was the sound of a match being struck, and then a candle glowed to life in Clover's hands.

"Beeswax candle. I make them with the wax from our beehives out back," she said. "We grow all our own food, make all our own clothes, that sort of thing. We have Clyde's boat if we really need to get to the mainland, but for the most part we have everything we need on the island already."

"But do you have a 'Big Jimmy's Bait 'N' Bite'?" I said, earning a laugh from Clover as she headed up the winding stairs ahead of me, the candle flame guiding our way. "Do you not have electricity?" I asked.

"Nope! I don't even think the electric company knows we're out here!" Clover was laughing, but something about that made me feel like I had been swallowed up by a black hole. Spooked, I hurried up the next step so I could walk beside her.

Clover led me into a guestroom and used her candle to light a few lamps. "Take a look at this," she said, and waltzed over to a closet door, opening it to display what hung inside. It was a white dress, not unlike the ones the other bridesmaids had been wearing. "It's vintage," she told me.

"I can tell."

"Do you like it? It's a Rachel family heirloom."

"I do," I lied. "So, when do I get to meet the groom?"

"Tomorrow!" Clover was grinning. "It's a Lightspring tradition that the couple stay separated leading up to their wedding. Luckily, we don't need him for tonight's rehearsal. We're going to want to start that before it gets too late, by the way, so…" She trailed off and tilted her chin towards the dress.

"Oh, sure. Give me a second to change."

Clover smiled and ducked out of the room. I pulled out my phone to check the time, but was met with only the low battery symbol. I looked for a wall outlet before remembering the lack of electricity. "Stupid cultists," I said. I was being facetious, but as I put on the white dress and stared at myself in the cloudy mirror, I began to wonder if Clover was out of her depth, and pulling me down with her.

* * *

A little while later I was standing barefoot on the cold sand, the moon barely visible through the gathering clouds. Thunder rumbled somewhere in the distance, but nobody seemed to care. The other girls and I were standing in a semi-circle around a stone archway that framed a table and two chairs. Clover was hovering next to Clyde, looking over his shoulder as he flipped through a large book. It had no title, and appeared to be hand-bound. Likely another Lightspring relic of some sort. I looked around at the other bridesmaids, but they were all watching Clover with that same smile from before. None of them had spoken a word since I'd got there, and even Clover seemed a little put off by them. The thought made me nervous, and I was glad that I had come. If Clover was uncomfortable, or being forced to do something she didn't want to do, maybe I could find a way to get her out.

"Okay ladies, I think we're ready to begin," Clyde said.

"Is there anything specific I should do?" I asked.

Clover smiled at me. "You can choose a girl to be my rehearsal stand-in, if you like."

"You don't want to rehearse your own role?" I asked.

Clyde said, "She can only do her job once, during the real ceremony."

"Okay," I replied, and then stared at the girls around me. They were all watching me, their faces devoid of emotion. I pointed to one at random, and she ducked her head and approached the table, taking a seat. There was another clap of thunder, and I jumped.

Clyde placed a pair of bifocals on his nose and tilted his head back to read from the book. I could barely hear him at first over the thunder and the waves, but gradually I realized that it didn't matter. Though his lips were forming words, there was no sound coming from them. Was he just mouthing words, pretending to read a sermon? I glanced at the others, but they were predictably stoic. Behind Clyde, Clover looked giddy, her eyes fixed on the seated girl in the center of the semi-circle.

There was a crash of thunder just above us, and I yelled as a bright light flashed, blinding me. I couldn't see, but something smelled awful, like burnt meat. I blinked, trying to regain my vision, and I heard Clover say, "It worked. It actually worked." She sounded more awestruck than excited. Finally, I was able to make out my hands in front of my face, and when I turned to look at the table I had to clap them to my mouth to stop myself from vomiting.

The girl that had sat at the table – the one I had *chosen* to sit at the table – was now nothing but a charred skeleton. She had been struck by lightning. I was panting even before the realization had fully settled. My entire body spasming, I sank into the sand, grabbing fistfuls of it and letting it run between my fingers. There was a low rumble of thunder, and then the sky opened up. The sudden cold rain against my skin snapped me out of my shock. I screamed, crawling across the sand towards my sister, who recoiled as if *I* were the thing to be feared. "What did you do?" I cried, grasping at her skirts. "She's dead!"

"Of course she's dead," said Clyde, stepping in front of me and shoving Clover behind him. "That's exactly what we want! It means that everything's in order for tomorrow's ceremony, and the groom will accept his bride without issue."

I looked back and forth between Clyde and Clover. He seemed annoyed at my outburst, but Clover wouldn't meet my gaze. I stood up, clasping Clover's rain-soaked shoulders and shaking her. "Is that going to happen to you? Is that what we were rehearsing for, for that to happen to *you*?"

She still wouldn't look at me, and with a motion from Clyde I was pulled off of her by the remaining bridesmaids. "Put her in the lighthouse if she's going to be difficult," Clyde said, and took Clover by the hand. He led her back towards the house as the other girls dragged me away towards the red-striped lighthouse. "Let me go!" I screamed as I thrashed my arms, but the girls ignored me, wordlessly obeying orders. "What is wrong with you?" I yelled. "Are you just waiting around for your turn to be microwaved, as well?" To my surprise, a girl at the front of the pack laughed. The sound stopped me dead in my tracks. It wasn't a light laugh, but a bitter one. One that said, "What is anyone going to do about it at this point?" All the fight left me then, and I stared at the back of her head, defeated, allowing them to escort me the rest of the way to the lighthouse.

* * *

Clover came to me the next morning, bringing some oatmeal. I didn't even attempt to eat it, I just watched her from the corner I had designated myself to after I had been locked in. My fingernails were broken from trying to pry the door open, and my fingertips were more splinter than flesh. "Are you okay?" Clover asked. She was in her wedding gown, a silver tiara holding her veil in place. Under any other circumstances I would have cried at how beautiful she looked, but I could tell she, too, had barely slept.

"Are you?" I asked her. My mania had passed, replaced by a dull, hopeless dread.

She tried to smile, but it faltered, and she put her face in her hands. "I thought I was," she said. "Before you showed up, I was so happy to have been chosen as the bride. Everyone had told me what an honor it was, especially for someone so new. But since you've been here, that feeling has cracked, and now I'm just scared."

"Amy," I said, deliberately using her old name, the one she always went back to when her phases ended. "Lightspring is a cult. Not in the way that Mary Kay had been a cult, but an actual fucking cult. Isn't it?"

Amy hung her head. "I just wanted to belong somewhere," she muttered.

"You can belong somewhere normal! Go tell them you don't want to be the bride anymore, I'm sure one of those creepy girls would be thrilled to take your place. You're coming home with me."

"I can't," Amy said. "There's no way Clyde would take us back to the mainland. Besides, it's already too late. We woke up the groom last night and now it won't rest until I do what I was chosen to do."

"What does that mean? Who's the groom?" I asked.

Clover was silent for a moment. "There's something that lives under this island," she began, and I remembered the glow I had seen from the boat the evening before. "Something that will get out unless it's fed, and if that thing gets out…" She trailed off, shaking her head. "That would be it. For everyone. Backing out now would be pointless. The groom would just come after me and devour anything else in its way. I'm the only one who can hold it off now, so I'm going to do my job, whether I want to or not. You can choose to either watch from up here, or you can be there with me when it happens." She paused, her eyes red, and when she spoke again her voice was shaking. "I would be less scared if you were there."

I leaned back, letting my head knock against the wall. "Were you happy, Amy? Ever?"

"Yes," she said. "Growing up I was, with you. I was happy while I was traveling. I was even happy hocking lipstick. But I'm not sure I would know how to go back to normal. I think knowing that thing is out there would drive me insane. I'd honestly rather just get the whole thing over with."

I closed my eyes for a long time, and when I opened them again a few tears escaped down my face. I stood up and went to my sister, folding her into a hug. "I'll go with you," I said. "If that's what you want."

* * *

We walked hand in hand down to the beach, where Clyde and the rest of the girls were already waiting around the table. The charred body from the night before had been removed, and fresh flowers had been arranged in a vase on the tabletop. Each bridesmaid held a matching bouquet, and I was handed one as I entered the circle. Clyde pulled a chair out for Amy, and she flashed him a smile that betrayed nothing of our conversation. I stared at her, trying to burn her serene expression into my memory.

Clyde swept his gaze across us, lingering on me for an extra beat, before putting on his glasses and taking up the book from the night before. I closed my eyes, picturing my sister's calm smile. I would be there for Amy, but I would not watch it happen. I assumed Clyde was reading, but I still couldn't hear anything. I braced myself for a lightning strike to slash through the silence, but nothing happened. There was no thunderclap, no bright light, nothing. I opened my eyes.

Everybody was looking out towards the ocean, and I followed their collective gaze across the beach. That was when I heard the hum. It was constant, yet barely audible, like walking into a room with a TV on. I looked around for the source of it, and spotted the underwater glow that I had seen beneath the island. It ran along the perimeter of the water, reaching further up the shore with each break of the wave, like branching fingers of light stretching towards us. I couldn't look away, but I didn't really want to. The light was breathtaking. Its glow was warm and inviting, and I wanted desperately to run to it and let it envelop me. Was this what Amy had been so afraid of? There was nothing to be frightened of here, only beauty and glory and peace.

I could hear a man's voice droning unintelligible verse, and something was happening in my peripheral vision, but I ignored it. There was something large, a great black shape dragging itself out of the water, but why should I care about a great black shape when the tendrils of light were creeping towards me? Finally,

finally, something was paying attention to me, finally something *wanted* me. The light was like fireworks, like molten lava, like liquid gold. It was so close to me now, and I held my breath as it closed the gap between us.

Then it was gone, the hum falling silent as Clyde finished his sermon. There was nothing on the sand, nothing in the water, nothing reaching out to touch me. There was nobody at the table. Amy had disappeared, taken by the light, or the shadow, or both, and she hadn't even made a sound. For a moment, it was as if the whole world had stopped turning, and then everyone in the circle seemed to relax at once. Clyde snapped his book shut and gave us all proud smiles like a coach applauding a little league team. He tossed me a wink, but then something I was holding caught his eye.

The only thing in my hands was the bouquet that all the bridesmaids had. I looked over at my neighbor's, but it was gone. All the flowers were gone, except for mine. I was the only bridesmaid holding a bouquet. "You know what that means," Clyde said. "You're next." The scent of the flowers wafted up to me, intoxicating, and I felt warmth bloom throughout my body. Amy may have gone, but she had done her job valiantly, and now I would do the same. My turn, finally. I brought the flowers to my nose and inhaled deeply, and then I looked at Clyde with a grin.

"I accept."

Pilgrimage of the Hummingbird

V. Castro

I SQUEEZED my eyes shut at the pain blooming from the space between my breasts. The needle had made the outline and now been dipped in indigo. The sharp point brushed against my skin in tight points to create what would be feathers. A hummingbird, the small creature that signified the god Huitzilopochtli. I had only one other small tattoo that I'd got in Brooklyn six years before. However, instead of sitting in a chair with music playing out of speakers and people chatting, sipping on Starbucks, I lay on a sisal mat with a Curandera making the small creation without any stencil. The only sound was our breathing and people working in the distance. Warm sunshine hit my face with my eyes closed. It was the beginning of a new cycle. The world we knew had fallen. It was a world so full of animosity and apathy it failed more humans than it helped.

I was getting a new tattoo because we celebrated rebirth during the winter solstice with a great feast for the gods. Panquetzaliztli. Cataclysm had struck before, just not when humans had phones and social media, or science as we knew it. Bits and pieces survived as ancient texts and archaeological sites that many dismissed as folktales and speculation. We couldn't *be sure* of how these sites were used or if the stories were true. Now there was real proof. And these were not fuzzy images of what might be Bigfoot in the woods. The gods returned, hearing the rumblings of a burning world. The stories of ancient beings were real. We had just forgotten to keep them alive. Magic was needed in the world again. They helped reignite it.

You could judge the feast during Panquetzaliztli, but it was far worse before the Cataclysm, the way humans ate each other with the savagery of starved hyenas. The world was set alight from weeks of falling meteors and the ground burping volcanic ash and magma across the globe. Fire came from above and below. But the gods knew better and sent the bitter cold to cool the soil enough for some of us to escape the destruction before their arrival. I left my home in six feet of snow with a handful of others. None of us looked back as I followed a sporadic radio transmission that said we could travel south-west. We wore as many layers of clothing as our weary, hungry bodies could carry. The climate was stable and pleasant at our destination; some parts of the Earth had been hit harder than others. My journey from the north-east of the US took me to Texas.

When the fires died down, I walked through fields of bodies, all in various states of decay and of all ages. Was it sadder than what I watched day in and day out on the news? Not really, except I couldn't look away. Death and destruction and horror crunched beneath my feet like a morning frost. Not frost, bones. And that initial journey took me months. I began in what should have been summer and arrived in winter. All the plastic ornaments had melted, fairy lights would be permanently dark, and no shopping mall parking lots remained for people to circle while wondering how much would be spent that holiday season.

That was three years ago, my first and only time doing the pilgrimage to the feast at the winter solstice. My last because I stayed. There was nothing left for me in the barren world of ash. And like my ancestors, there were no Apple watches or Pelotons or streaming services any longer. No distractions. For exercise we walked, it didn't matter what time of day. For entertainment we talked to each other. We looked to the sky to guide us. Three happy years I had been in that village. If I was honest with myself, the things of the previous world hadn't made me happy at all.

The winter solstice approached and it was time again to welcome more pilgrims for what we called the Pilgrimage of the Hummingbird. The time had come to feast. We honored the cycles of life and death. And just like a human life, the Earth had come to an end, yet those who survived didn't know how or where to rebuild, so there were more people roaming, searching. A blueprint was needed. Our blue outline was the hummingbird god himself, Huitzilopochtli, and this feast, Panquetzaliztli. His presence was how the village was established. Other pockets of settled survivors gathered at neolithic sites that remained by some miracle. We all had to go back to using the celestial bodies to guide us, like those who came long ago.

The people who arrived in the village we created took the Pilgrimage of the Hummingbird to be consumed. They sacrificed themselves for a greater calling, and some were just plain tired of existing. I once asked a woman in her sixties why she offered her body. She looked me in the eyes, and said, "I've seen everyone pass in my family except for myself. And for years I was the sick one. I can feel the lumps in my breasts growing by the day. Think I'm ready to see what happens next before I can't see anything but pain." I wrapped my arms around her and kissed her on the cheek, wishing I could do more. The flip side of a simple life set back to zero meant there were harsh consequences to not having access to all the technology that had kept humans alive for so long. We salvaged what we could find. Knowing life-giving technology was mostly gone was part of the sacrifice we had to accept, until we somehow rebuilt that part of humanity again. Or miracles were granted by the gods. Sometimes people settled here because they felt at home amongst other like-minded individuals. This part of Texas was once too hot to grow certain vegetation. No longer. Orchards and fields blossomed with life. It was calm. There was a silent healing taking place within the village and on the land. We were too tired of fighting from our previous lives.

* * *

I walked through the camp with my new tattoo aching and on show as preparations were made for the evening celebration at the site where we were building a new Tenochtitlan. Huitzilopochtli's temple was destroyed when the Spanish arrived in the New World, but the pilgrims who stayed in our village were rebuilding it. Something that would have never happened before at the original site. Too many questions about why, about budgets, tourists, disruption to the city. The type of unimportant questions the world always asked about most things. Nothing was sacred or appreciated before the Cataclysm. Nobody gave a fuck now because the previous ways of thinking and existing were gone like the remnants of smoke from a volcano.

What did we feast on once a year? No one suffered a machete to the head or across the throat. We made no spectacle of those we ate. That was not the way. The ones wanting to be made into pies and sauces showered, meditated, and lay in a tranquil hut on a mat with copal burning. Some came with loved ones and others by themselves. But none of them passed alone without a hand holding theirs and blessing them for their sacrifice. One of us injected them with just enough salvaged drugs to send them into a slumber that would take them to the other world, where they would hopefully see loved ones. After, the body was expertly segmented and prepared in a sterile kitchen cleaned after every body. No one ever suffered food poisoning. This was no cheap, corporate-run slaughterhouse with people working for scraps and no health insurance.

The colonizing Christians in the sixteenth century made the original Panquetzaliztli into Las Posadas, a mixture of Christian and pagan beliefs. Another way to force the ancestors to submit. The original feast honored Huitzilopochtli, the blue-skinned god of war, sacrifice, and the sun. They feasted and played games. Statues of their god were made from honey and maize. But most of all, eyes were to the heavens. Of course, paganism was not to be tolerated. But that was before. Every church, as far as I knew, had burned to the ground. Ash can be a fertilizer for something new.

My white cotton dress brushed against the dirt and I felt a swell of pride as I stared at the half-built temple with the sun setting fast behind. Before the modern world ended, I slumped in front of a computer looking at numbers, or at my phone for likes and messages. People bitched and moaned about things of no consequence. They spread hatred with the ease of peanut butter on bread, for others to eat and regurgitate, for someone else to lap up in blind hunger. The misery and terror of not knowing where any of it would lead except a grave left me with a constant sense of malaise. Not anymore.

This was not perfect, but it was a start. You don't have to eat flesh and you don't have to sacrifice yourself. That was the beauty and the horror of this new world. People were forced to make up their own minds. Two nurses with four sacrifices dressed in simple linen clothing and sandals walked past me and nodded. I placed my hand on my heart and nodded back. At the foot of the temple laughing children made dolls and animals out of maize and honey, like centuries before. There were no iPads or gaming devices for them to unwrap. It amazed me that the temple had been demolished during the sixteenth century and now in the twenty-first it was being rebuilt. These children would see it in their lifetime. Who knows what else they would be able to accomplish as survivors.

* * *

For the feast I chose a low-cut dress so my hummingbird tattoo could be on full show. Huitzilopochtli would be at the feast and I wanted him to see it. We hoped the right people at the right time with the right skills would be drawn here as well as those who wanted to nourish their souls by nourishing our bodies.

It was mid-morning and I could smell a fire burning where Huitzilopochtli remained on his own most of the time. Our radiant blue god sat with crossed legs and barefoot, staring at the warring flames. I sat next to him and looked up. It would be a good feast. The sky was usually clear in this part of the world and we could see all the stars that night. It was also a new moon. The sounds of drums beating to the rhythm of a heart would break the silence of the darkness as we feasted.

"What will we do when the temple is rebuilt?" I asked him. His blue face was striking when he turned towards me, his gaze seeing me from the inside out. I wanted to kiss him, but knew better. It would be instant death to my flesh and soul. At least that is what some said. Many people whispered about him, yet few directly interacted with him. There was a fear seeing this blue man standing eight feet tall. And he kept to himself when walking amongst us. He observed, yet only spoke when he felt inclined to lend his magic or hand. I didn't fear anything anymore. What was the point? What did living in that state ever get me but more of the same? He looked at my tattoo.

His thick lips curled to a smile. "Do you consider yourself a priestess? You are a beautiful woman. Humans might find this distracting."

I nodded. "Yes… I would like to become a priestess. Many come to me to lay down what is making their heart heavy. Not sure if people find me distracting… Do *you* feel distracted by my presence?"

He let out a laughter as soft as flitting wings. "I am not human, yet I do find it… of interest. Yes, you are of interest to me. But to answer your question, the temple will be rebuilt and more will come to feast and to share of themselves. Are you prepared?"

I touched his bare chest and ran my fingernails down the length of his torso. "I am prepared for anything. Even sitting next to a god."

"You think yourself worthy?"

I looked him in those eyes with no pupils, only deep-space darkness. "I know I am. Especially after what I survived to get here. I went through war and came out the other side. Could you not see the aftermath of the Cataclysm?"

"I did. And that is why I knew my time to return had come."

I shifted my eyes to his little fire. Its warmth made me feel alive, just as sitting next to this god did. His fingers touched my chin as he moved my face towards his.

"Then take what you want, priestess. I will not harm you. This new world is for you."

I wouldn't die. I knew this. I propped myself up on my knees and kissed him. His lips tasted like honey and blood. His skin was hot like the sun he represented. If I didn't know better I just might erupt into flames. I pulled my mouth from his. "I want something lasting and good."

"Then build it. This is the new cycle. The new dawn after the longest and darkest of days."

I believed him. This village was a testament to the good in humans despite seeing so much of their worst inclinations before the Cataclysm. It had to be possible to create something new infused with magic, beginning with the winter solstice, this feast of flesh. The question that popped into my mind as I continued to look at the flames was, what do we internally sacrifice and what do we feast on to create something new within ourselves and with each other?

He continued to stare at me. "I want you to be by my side during the feast. But you must prove yourself a true warrior priestess first."

I looked into his eyes again, feeling elation at this unexpected statement. "What? Are you sure? And anything. Tell me what to do."

"I am. You see, I am the god of war and when it is near, I feel it. There are those approaching that want what you have built here, and they will take it by force."

I shook my head. "What? Why? I thought we would be beyond that. Haven't people endured enough?"

"Some do not want to learn new lessons and will continue on the path of destruction."

"What do we do? You are the god of war. Can we win? Defeat them?"

"If I am to stay, and protect you, no blood can be shed. And you must learn first to do it for yourselves."

I moved to stand up. "I have to warn the others." As I rose to my feet he touched my hand.

"Do you?"

I stopped and sat back down as my mind raced. What would happen if the entire village was told at once without any other details? It would cause panic. People would want to form some sort of defence. Our thoughts and actions would be sharpened blades before they even arrived. No blood could be shed. "What would you do?" I asked him.

He stood, tall and lean, and extended his hand towards me. I rose to my feet. "This is your test, priestess, as well as theirs. If you can figure out a way, then I will give you whatever you want."

"Will this village be safe as well?"

"Yes, it will be under my protection. No others will have the opportunity to attack and the rest of the gods will respect my authority here. Other places have failed tests and those perished. I have seen that too."

"Why now?" I asked.

"Because we must not repeat the same mistakes... Now, what is it you want?"

I looked at him towering over me. There was nothing I lacked, except a companion. I swallowed hard before speaking. "I want you. You to share my bed and be my companion."

340

He leaned down and smiled. "Now that is something I did not expect. You are a bold one. But I will keep my word if you succeed."

"Thank you. But I must leave now. How long do I have?"

"They will arrive just before the feast."

I nodded and turned to leave. How would I stop those intent on destroying something beautiful without bloodshed? Watching the exuberance of the others as they made preparations for the feast made me sad and a little angry. The joy and gratitude on their faces hurt, knowing it could be taken from them. What would these strangers do? As I passed the building where the bodies were prepared I stopped. Two children squatted on the ground and exchanged homemade sweets. They giggled as they licked them before handing them to each other. The idea, the *vision*, hit me like a spear.

We would meet these travelers just outside the village and share our feast with them. Except they would fall down dead as they took their last bites. If they thought this was a place to be taken, they had another thing coming. I ran to the feast coordinator, Zelda, a woman in her fifties who kept her head shaved to the scalp and wore dangly beaded earrings her granddaughter made her. She sat with others weaving branches together for the long table centerpiece. "Zelda, may I have a word."

She gave me a friendly smile and rose to her bare feet. "Your tattoo is beautiful... How can I help you?"

I glanced at the others, engrossed in chatting while they worked. "Let's talk privately." Her face dropped, seeing I didn't return her look of calm or thank her for the compliment. When we were out of earshot I looked her in the eyes. "We must move the solstice feast to the entrance of the village. Not only must we move it, none of us can partake in it. At least not at the usual time."

She looked at me in confusion. "Can I ask why? This is a huge change. Has anyone else been told about this?"

My eyes darted to see if anyone was close. "No. This is my decision but based on information from *him*." I didn't have to say his name.

She knew and her eyes went large. "Understood. I will gather a few at the temple site to stop their work to move the long table. How do we prevent our people from feasting?"

"We don't. Fruit and vegetables only. The meat will be reserved for our guests. We will tell them when we gather for prayer in front of the temple. I also want the bonfire lit at that same time. Do not repeat anything else."

"Understood."

Zelda had the job of organizing the feast because she knew how to get things done. Her efficiency made it run smoothly every year. She walked back over to the group and excused herself. I ran back to my hut for an essential item for the next phase of my plan.

After, I made my way into the meat preparation room. Mercy and Bert sliced flesh in thin strips, dressed head to toe in white sterile suits and hairnets. They looked up at me. I had only covered my shoes and wore a hairnet. "Whatever you have already prepared, I need you to add an extra ingredient."

I placed the bag on the ground. It was something I had found in one of the surviving surrounding buildings when I first arrived. For some reason I thought we might need it if too many of us had to be in close conditions. If anything survived the apocalypse and was still a nuisance, it would be rats. They were one of the many threats to a scarce food supply. Mercy and Bert looked at the four boxes of rat poison in the bag.

"What?" said Mercy, looking at me in disgust.

I scrambled to clear up any misunderstanding. "It's not for us... there will be unexpected guests for tonight's feast. Believe me when I say they do not come with good intentions. No blood can be spilled. *He* has deemed it."

They looked at each other, then back at me. "You can count on me to do what needs to be done," said Mercy.

"And I," said Bert.

"Thank you. Do not let anyone we know eat that meat. Mercy, can you please be by my side for this? I don't want any accidents."

"Of course. It was only a matter of time before others came and wanted what we have made. I will do anything to preserve it."

"See you in front of the temple at the usual time of day. Just before sunset."

* * *

We all gathered in front of the temple. The entire village whispered about the change of location for the long table. "Please come closer," I said in an even, calm tone. They all did as I asked. "We are expecting travelers. The feast of meat will be offered to them. I ask you... it is imperative you do not taste a morsel. The fruit and vegetables you can eat as much as you like. When they are gone, we will resume the usual feast. Please do not speak of this change. I promise all is well if you listen to me now. *He* has given me these wishes."

The whispers and conversations began when I stopped speaking. Mercy moved next to me. "We must all move to the long table and wait," she said for everyone to hear.

There was suspicion regarding the travelers. We hadn't had any in all the time I had been there. This was a test. I could sense it. Despite my assurances I could also sense the fear, even though the village tried to remain positive and calm.

As if it was pre-written, it happened exactly as Huitzilopochtli foretold. In the distance we could see ten men and women carrying weapons slung across their chest, pistols holstered. The only bags I could see were backpacks. They traveled light. We didn't have any weapons except knives and the poison in their meal. They appeared dirty from travel, their faces hardened from survival on the road. Mercy glanced in my direction. I nodded. We approached to meet them halfway. The man who must have been their leader didn't smile. His eyes studied the village and our numbers. "Hello and welcome," I said.

"This is something else." He peered behind me. "Looks like a feast."

"Yes, it is the winter solstice. You are welcome to join."

He sniffed the air. "Meat?"

I nodded. "You and your group look like you need nourishment. Come and enjoy. You may have our meat as a show of goodwill and peace."

He glanced back at his group that had stopped a few feet away from him. "Hope you're hungry. These kind people have offered us food."

A woman in her forties looked me up and down. Her eyes appeared dead. I didn't want to know what she had seen or done to survive. I didn't judge her, but we would not accept any violence. "How can we trust you?" she said in a flat tone.

Mercy spoke up. "If you prefer to keep your distance, I can bring the food here."

The woman continued to look unamused or ungrateful. She didn't seem to want to make friends. Perhaps she'd already decided we should be enemies. "Where did you get the meat from?" she asked.

Mercy didn't back down. "We raise our own. Here, let me bring you a taste." She turned and walked towards the table. Zelda locked eyes with Mercy and pushed a wheelbarrow towards her with a large pot inside, along with dishes. The rest of the village remained silent with the sun beginning to set. The bonfire's ferocity gained momentum behind the long table. Mercy took the wheelbarrow and pushed it to the travelers. "Have as much as you like."

The leader continued to eye up the village and the forty of us gathered. "You have a good thing going here."

I smiled. "We do. It is as good as the people who live here. We always welcome others."

The meat smelled delicious. His group of ten looked at the pot with greed. Before Mercy could put the wheelbarrow down, they had set upon it. I turned to Zelda and gave her a nod. This was her signal to tell the others to begin eating the fruit and vegetables on the table. Our meat remained in the preparation room. Mercy and I stood there, not wanting to ask too many questions or make sudden movements. The woman kept glancing up at me as she ate mouthfuls of meat. The red sauce stained her smacking lips. My heart began to beat faster the more they ate. It wasn't long until it was gone. The man wiped his mouth with the back of his hand. "Thank you for that. We have been looking for a place to call our own. Start over. This might be it. Can you tell me who the leader is?" The woman's body tensed after he said this, and the others put their bowls in the wheelbarrow. They wanted their hands free.

"Of course." I waited for a beat, praying the poison would kick in. He stepped towards me, scanning the crowd.

"I asked..." He stopped mid-sentence. His chest heaved and his mouth opened. The whites of his eyes were all that could be seen as they rolled back. Foam and blood dribbled down his chin before he fell to the ground, convulsing. The others with him had the same reaction. Those behind me gasped and began to whisper amongst each other as they watched the horror of their deaths unfold. I could hear Zelda calming our people down.

The bodies of the ten guests lay dead on the ground. But their meat, their intent, was poison. It would be an offering and not for consumption. On that night, the longest night of the year, we would burn their carcasses. Their blackened flesh would be the incense of peace.

"You have passed the test. Not a drop of blood spilled. You all acted without question. These travelers will be a suitable offering. I will stay and be your protector. Eventually there will be others, but you have my hand of guidance. If they bring chaos, they will reap chaos."

We all looked to our left. Huitzilopochtli approached, his giant frame almost as high as the fire. The village erupted into cheers. People hugged each other and cried tears of joy. His gaze stopped on me. I walked towards him to claim my gift for following through.

"Do you still want what you asked for?" he asked.

I nodded my head. "I do. You are to be my companion and share my bed on this feast of the solstice."

He smiled. "I shall enjoy consorting with a human. You have proven yourself."

"And you have kept your word."

The fire jumped next to us as the bodies were tossed into the flames. If others like them came again, they would share their fate. Huitzilopochtli extended his hand to me. "Time to feast, then time to give you a night you will never forget."

The Grim

Cavan Scott

1.

BEN DIDN'T KNOW what Noah saw in the woods, only that it scared the boy. He would stop halfway through a sentence, sometimes halfway through a word, to stare between the trees, colour draining from already pale cheeks. Ben couldn't remember when Noah had become so pasty, but wasn't that the point of this trip? To reconnect with a son who had become a stranger.

"Dad, it's started to rain."

And a daughter, too.

"It's okay, Kaylee," Ben said, glancing up at a gunmetal sky barely visible through the mass of skeletal branches. "I don't think it'll come to anything."

Of course, Kaylee reminded him of this failed forecast two hours later when the rain was coming down in sheets and they were struggling to pitch the tents. And by 'they', Ben meant him and Anna, his sister, not the kids. Kaylee's idea of helping was to flap around, not listening to instructions, moaning about the deluge she'd warned was coming. Noah, meanwhile, just stood, getting drenched to the skin, eyes darting this way and that as if he expected something – or someone – to come charging from between the trees.

"At least put your hood up," Anna called across to her nephew as Ben tried to unsuccessfully feed the tent pole through its loop. "Noah? Noah!"

The boy didn't even acknowledge his aunt, long black hair plastered to bloodless skin, dark-rimmed eyes never leaving the shadows.

"He'll be fine when we get this thing up," Ben told her as the half-erected tent strained against the gale. "We'll get them in dry clothes and crack open the hot chocolate. As snug as bugs in the proverbial rug."

The pole snapped in his hand.

2.

Anna had been Ben's rock as he'd attempted to rebuild his life. He knew it was supposed to be the other way around, him looking after a sister four years his junior, but that had never been the case, not even when they were kids. *Especially* when they were kids. Anna was the sensible one, the boring one, and he'd ribbed her mercilessly about it, telling her to get a life, meaning a life like *his*. Not the best advice. He'd been a little shit, in all honesty. To Anna. To Mum and Dad. To just about everyone he knew. Lies. Broken promises. Disappointment after disappointment.

His wife Susie was supposed to change all that. A nice girl. A *beautiful* girl with a dazzling smile and eyes that made him feel that he could stop being the Ben everyone tolerated and become the Ben he wanted to be. And it worked. *Really* worked. The perfect wedding. The stunning house. The steady job. Mum and Dad visiting for Christmas. Anna over for dinner with her girlfriend. So grown up. And that was *before* the kids arrived. Noah wasn't planned. Not exactly an accident, but more of a mishap. Noah with the laughing face. Noah the bundle of joy. Noah the excuse when things started to unravel.

They were tired, that was the excuse. Ratty with each other. Nights away with work became a chance for Ben to let his hair down. To relax. Yes, there were mistakes, but they were easy to cover up. What goes on at teambuilding exercises, stays on teambuilding exercises, even when it follows you home, on nights in anonymous boozers when you say you're working late at the office. Bunk-ups in cheap hotels.

Kaylee was the sticking plaster after Susie had found out about the other women, a second chance that Ben grasped like a drowning man. But the affairs hadn't been the problem, although he didn't want to admit it. Isn't that the way of all alcoholics? They never admit they have a problem until it's too late.

* * *

"I told you we were lost!"

"We are not lost, Kaylee."

"Then where's the car?"

"Not to mention the car *park*?" Anna muttered, earning a glare from Ben.

"Not helpful, Annie."

"Yeah, but a *little* bit funny, right?"

Ben didn't feel like laughing. It wasn't supposed to be like this. The kids. The weather. The tents he'd borrowed from a buddy at work. Tents that were now trashed, poles bent or snapped in two, canvas ripped and ropes impossibly tangled. They should've tested them in Anna's garden, a dry run rather than a failed attempt in the middle of a storm that wasn't supposed to happen. And now, yes, they *were* lost, and they were cold, and it was getting dark and Ben *really* needed a drink.

"Noah! Noah, come on!"

"Don't yell at him, Ben."

"We can't get separated."

"We won't."

"He needs to stay with us!"

Anna's hand found his arm. "Benny."

He stopped, listening to her unspoken advice. To take a moment. Breathe. To calm the hell down. This was why he'd asked her along in the first place, not because Susie didn't trust him to look after the kids (and, let's face it, his ex-wife had *every* right to be sceptical), but because he didn't trust himself. Not yet, six months sober or not.

Anna looked him straight in the eye. Calm. Controlled. "We just need to get our bearings, okay?"

"In the dark, spooky forest."

She nodded. "In the dark, spooky forest full of rabid wolves that want to feast on our intestines. We don't want anything to feast on our intestines, do we?"

He couldn't help but smirk, just a little. "I don't know, Anna. Might be preferable when Eric sees what we've done to his tents."

"Eric's stupid flimsy tents."

"Eric's stupid, flimsy, probably already broken tents."

Suddenly, the rain didn't seem so bad, or the fact that he had no idea where they were wasn't *so* much of a concern. That was his sister's superpower right there, water dripping from her large goofy glasses, gloved fingers squeezing his arm.

"Wait," Kaylee exclaimed, breaking the moment, glaring at them intently with her mother's eyes. "There are *wolves* now?!"

Ben let Anna deal with that one and trudged back to Noah, booted feet slipping on the churned-up mud that once resembled a forest floor.

"Hey, big guy. Sorry I yelled. We just need to keep moving."

Noah didn't look up, his hood still down and collecting water, a usually floppy fringe hanging heavy in front of haunted pale eyes.

"Noah? Noah, are you okay?" The question that had prompted the entire trip, a chance for Ben to be a dad again to a kid who had withdrawn from everyone, not just him. A kid who had lost his best friend.

"Hey. Champ."

Noah jerked his puffer-jacketed arm out of the way as Ben reached for his son.

"Don't."

"Don't what?" Ben tried to put himself in front of the lad's shifting gaze. "Look, I know this isn't exactly ideal, but if we stick together—"

At that, Noah snorted. "Together? Since *when* have we been together?"

Ouch.

"We're going home, okay? We can talk about this then."

"There's nothing to talk about, *Dad*." Ben didn't like the emphasis Noah placed on that word. "I'm here, aren't I? I came on your poxy trip. I'm playing happy families, just like you wanted."

"You don't *look* happy." Ben winced inside at the comment, desperate to take it back. "I mean—"

"I don't care, Dad!" Noah finally looked at his father, the venom in his glare matching the fury in his young voice. "I don't care what you mean! Don't care if you want to make it up to us because you feel guilty or think you can pick up where you left off."

"Noah…"

"Mum didn't want us to come on your trip. *Kaylee* didn't want to come, but Aunt Anna kept on and on, saying how good it would be for us all, only nothing about this is good. Nothing at a—"

And there it was again, Noah breaking off mid-word. Mid-rant this time, eyes wide, mouth open, a strangled cry from the back of the lad's throat as he stared at something behind Ben, something in the trees.

"Noah?" Ben glanced over his shoulder, but there was nothing there, only Anna slip-sliding her way over to check how they were doing. Bad. They were doing really bad, worse when Ben looked back to see his son taking off between the trees.

"Noah? Noah, where are you going? Come back!"

Ben didn't think, just reacted, dumping the tent bag at Anna's feet and yelling at her to look after Kaylee.

He had to find his son.

3.

Are you free? Can I call?

The text had come out of the blue, Ben's stomach lurching. He'd phoned Susie straight back rather than answering, a sudden call from his ex-wife meaning one of only a few, equally distressing scenarios.

"Susie? It's me. What's wrong? Is it the kids? Are they alright?"

"No." She sounded hollow. Exhausted. "I mean, yeah, they're fine. It's Noah. You remember his friend, Eli?"

Elijah Johnson. Noah's best friend since reception. The 'Eli' bit was new, but Ben had only seen them together a few months ago, by chance really, waiting for a bus from work (the new job, that was, at the local DIY warehouse, not the accountancy role of ten years he'd fucked up). The boys had gone past on the number 74, heading back home... no – correction – heading to Susie's place. Same old Elijah, although the bum fluff on the lad's lip had been a surprise. Where had the time gone?

At the bottom of a bottle, Ben. In a pint glass. Between the sheets with Mel from Accounts.

Noah looked the same as always, of course. That cheeky grin. Those sparkling eyes.

God, Ben missed the sparkle in Noah's eyes.

"What about him, Suse?"

"*Susie*." She always hated it when he used his pet name for her, especially now.

"Sorry. Susie. What about Elijah?"

A pause at the other end of the line, a lowering of the voice so no one could hear.

"He's dead, Ben."

Suicide. It was such a damned waste. Fifteen years old, for God's sake. No surprise that Noah would take it hard, retreating into himself. He'd been quiet enough since the split, moody, sullen, while Kaylee went the other way, throwing herself into drama productions at school, bursting into song at the drop of a hat. Defying gravity. Letting it go. Telling everyone who'd listen that the sun would come out tomorrow, all of which only made Noah worse.

"Kaylee. Your brother needs some space. A little peace and quiet!"

That and a constant stream of rows and spats it appeared, punctuated by extended periods of angry metal reverberating from his room.

Suse was at her wits' end when Ben suggested the camping trip, sending in Anna for a charm offensive when she inevitably said no.

"Susie, the kids used to love camping…"

And now Ben had lost Noah. No, he'd run away, but was there really a difference? However you looked at it, Ben had screwed up. Again.

"Noah? Noah!"

Ben found his son at the bottom of a ditch, sobbing like a toddler. He slid down the bank, nearly going arse-over-tit himself.

"Big man?"

Noah was clutching his ankle, the contents of his backpack strewn over the mud.

"It hurts."

"Can you move your foot?" Ben asked, engaging Dad mode. "Wiggle your toes."

Noah sniffed and nodded. "Yeah."

"Can you stand?"

A shake of the head this time.

"Let's give it a go."

"I *can't*!"

"And I can't leave you here. Let me help."

"Ow!"

"That's it. You're doing great."

"It *really* hurts."

"Probably just a sprain. Did you come down the slope?"

"*Obviously*."

"Try to take a step."

A sharp intake of breath.

"Lean on me. That's it. That's it."

Anna and Kaylee came crashing out of the trees above them, Ben's sister almost joining them until Kaylee grabbed her arm to stop her from falling.

"Is he okay?" Anna called down.

"Just a twisted ankle," Ben answered. "You're okay, aren't you, kiddo?"

"I'm sorry, Dad." He sounded so small; rain and tears having washed away the stroppy teen for a moment to reveal the little boy who still lurked inside.

"It's okay. Accidents happen."

"He keeps looking at me. In the shadows. Keeps staring at me."

"Who does, Noah?"

"Make him go away, Dad. Make him stop."

"Ben?"

He looked up at his sister, Kaylee, shivering at the top of the ditch. "We need to get him out of the rain. I don't know, strap it up or something."

"Strap it up," Anna repeated, brain snapping into fixit mode as she scanned the wood for solutions. "Strap it up. Strap it up. Strap it up."

She was still gazing around as Kaylee tugged at her sleeve.

"Auntie Anna. I need a wee. Auntie Anna!"

Anna's teeth flashed as she spotted something through the trees. "Then we may *all* be in luck. Ask and you shall receive."

4.

They should have kept walking the moment they saw the church. It was little more than an oblong box constructed from rough-hewn stones, the wooden roof sagging but seemingly intact. The surrounding graveyard was a riot of weeds and grasses, crooked headstones slowly sinking into the soft ground while the path that led to the entrance was cracked and uneven. It had obviously been a long time since songs of praise were sung within its crumbling walls, and yet the derelict church offered one ray of hope that Anna had spotted between the trees: a light shining dimly through its high, broken windows.

"Is anyone in there?" Ben yelled through the thick oak door as his sister and the kids huddled in the poor excuse for a porch. There was no answer, the door locked from inside. "Hello! Can you let us in?"

"There's probably no one home," Anna reasoned, having scouted around the squat building to see if there was another way in.

"But there's a light," Ben argued, refusing to give up.

"That could have been left on by accident. No one's coming."

Ben pressed his ear against the rough door, but the wood was far too thick to hear anything, especially with the storm hammering above their heads.

"Dad," Kaylee whined. "I need to wee!"

"Then go in the churchyard," Ben told her, slamming his shoulder against the door. THWAM!

"In the rain?"

"It's either that or do it right here in the porch." THWAM!

Still the door wouldn't budge.

"But there are graves!"

"I doubt their occupants will care."

THWAM!

"Dad!"

"I'll take her," Anna said brusquely, holding out a hand to her niece. "Come on. Let's go and find a tree."

"There are enough of them," Ben muttered as they disappeared back into the downpour. Maybe that was the answer. They could find a fallen tree and use it as a… what? He almost laughed at the idea. A battering ram? What did he think this was? The Middle Ages?

"Dad," Noah whimpered from where Ben had perched him on an unsteady bench, his back flat against the porch wall. "Dad, we need to get inside."

"That's what I'm trying to do, Champ."

"We need to get inside *now*!"

"I know!" Ben didn't mean to snap, but Noah hadn't even noticed. Instead, he sat staring out into the darkness, face drained and eyes wide.

"He's out there, Dad. I can feel him, looking at me. Watching me. We need to get inside. Get inside!"

"Woah, woah, woah," Ben shouted as Noah propelled himself off the wooden form, his wounded ankle immediately giving way beneath him. He stumbled, Ben only just catching him in time. "There's no one out there, Noah. Other than your sister piddling beneath a tree."

"Yes, there is!" Noah argued, trying to stand only to cry out in pain. Was he going into shock? Had he hit his head? Christ, could this trip get any worse?

Ben helped him back to the bench. "Who's out there, Noah?" he asked, trying a different tactic; one crisis at a time. "Who's watching you? The person you saw in the trees?"

Noah nodded, looking his dad in the eyes. "It's Eli."

"Elijah? Noah, that's—"

"I *know* it's not possible. I'm not stupid. But that's who it is. I know it is. He's following me. Wants to get me."

"Why would he want to get you?"

"Because I let him down," Noah said, sobbing. "I let him down when he needed me most, when I should've stood up for him. But I teased him, joined in with the others and now he's dead. Dead because of me." The words were coming thick and fast, Noah barely pausing for breath. "I knew it was wrong, but I did it anyway, because I was scared, scared of what the others would say. That they'd think I was like him."

"Like him?"

"That I was *gay*!"

If Noah could have opened the church door with raw emotion it would've been off its hinges by now.

"Eli was gay?"

The boy nodded.

"And the others teased him?"

"They called him a poof. And I pretended to laugh. Because I didn't know what else to say, and he killed himself. Killed himself because I let him down. And now he's here. In the wood. And he wants to kill me too. We have to get away, Dad. Have to get away!"

Again, he launched himself from the bench, panic overtaking him as it had in the wood. This time Ben was ready. He grabbed the boy, holding his son tight as he struggled in his arms; a boy consumed with guilt, a boy who had needed his dad, but his dad had been wallowing in his own mess.

But Ben was here now.

"Dad, Dad, look at this!" Kaylee charged back into the porch, eagerly holding something out in her hand. Anna appeared behind the excited girl, eyes immediately darting to Noah breaking his heart in Ben's embrace.

"Not now, Kaylee," Ben said, indicating for Anna to take her nephew so he could return to the door. She looked at him quizzically, but Ben shook his head as Kaylee babbled on, oblivious to Noah's distress.

"But it's a pig, look. A little wooden pig. I stood on it in the graveyard. Nearly twisted *my* ankle. But it's so cute. Look at it, Daddy. It even has little tusks."

"I said, not now!" Ben barked, a newfound determination welling in his chest. He hadn't been there for Noah when Eli had taken his life, hadn't been there to tell his son that it wasn't his fault. He wasn't about to let him down all over again.

Ben threw himself at the door. THWAM!

He *would* get them into the church.

THWAM!

He'd get them into the church and head back out into the storm.

THWAM!

He'd walk for miles if he had to, until he found the car park or maybe someone's house.

THWAM!

He'd knock on the door and ask for help; to use their internet or make a call. Find out where they were. Ring Susie.

THWAM!

He didn't care what she'd say or think. All that mattered was being there for Noah.

THWAM!

Ben had a sense of Anna calling his name, but it didn't matter. Nothing mattered right now… because the door had moved. Just a bit, but it had definitely moved.

"Help me," he wheezed, exhausted from his efforts, and Anna fell in beside him, Noah too despite his fear. They shoved in unison, feeling the door shift. It wasn't locked; it was just stuck, or maybe something was wedged behind it. But there *was* a light that spilled through the crack. They just needed to push more.

One.

Two.

Three.

5.

Something *was* behind the door. Something was stopping it from opening. Ben had wondered if it was a bookshelf that had toppled over, depositing mouldering hymnals across the floor. Or maybe a beam that had tumbled from the ceiling, but it was neither of those things.

It was a body.

A dead human body.

"Stay out there," Ben barked at the kids, attempting not to gag, not so much from the state of the corpse but the stink of copper and evacuated bowels.

"What is it?" Kaylee asked, hugging the wooden animal she'd found close to her chest as Noah hugged only himself, rocking back and forth.

"Don't come in, baby," Anna said, the colour draining from her face as she saw the cadaver for herself. "Stay with your brother, please."

The body was lit in the dimming glow of a camping lamp that was lying on its side in a sticky pool of blood. Whoever it was, they were young, no more than twenty at most. Acne smothered their pallid skin, strands of long hair draped over sightless eyes and into a lolling mouth. But it wasn't the eyes that Ben was staring at. It was the gaping hole in the kid's stomach, guts tumbling from the body to rest in a glistening heap on the church floor.

"Oh God, there's another one," Anna gasped, ignoring Kaylee's insistent pleas to be let in on the secret of what lay inside the church. Ben followed his sister's gaze to a second corpse on the other side of the dusty nave; this one a girl, her back to them, blood splattered up the white-washed wall in front of her. Most ghoulish of all was the mural that loomed over her. The paint had faded over time, an image of a gigantic skeleton, hourglass in one hand and knife in another. The message of the medieval artist was clear: your time is running out, so make the most of it. Time had definitely run out for the girl lying at its bony feet, jagged vertebrae stretching the grey skin of her broken neck.

This time Ben *was* sick, grabbing hold of an ancient font built to hold holy water that now received the contents of his stomach. Bizarrely, it wasn't the corpse that had sent him over the edge, but the head of the skeleton in the mural: not the human skull you'd expect, but that of an animal. At first glance, it looked like a sheep or a ram, until you realised its curled horns sprouted not from the sides of the skull but from its jaw, like the tusks of a boar.

Ben wiped grit from his mouth with the back of a shaking hand, fighting the primal fear that tore through his mind, telling him to run, to save himself, to abandon everything he'd been fighting so hard to reclaim. But why? What was it about that grinning mural? What was it about this place?

He screwed up his eyes, trying not to retch at the stench of his own vomit, trying not to imagine the touch of a bottle to his lips. When he opened them again, his eyes rested on something tossed behind the font, an object that, like the corpses, had no place in a church, ruined or otherwise. Something that only belonged in the cheap horror films he used to watch with Suse.

He kicked it into the light, a bloodied board printed with the letters of the alphabet above a row of numbers and a solitary word: Goodbye.

"Is that…" For a minute, he thought his sister was going to giggle. "Is that a Ouija board?" He felt like laughing himself, hysteria bubbling in his now purged belly.

"We need to get out of here," he said matter-of-factly.

"And go where?" Anna asked.

"I don't know. Anywhere that isn't here. Find the car. Find shelter. We just need to leave!"

That was when Kaylee screamed.

6.

The kids were through the door before Ben or Anna could stop them. Not that they even noticed the bodies; they were too busy running for the adults, Noah hobbling on his swollen ankle.

"It's Eli," he jabbered, throwing himself into Ben's arms. "Eli's coming for me."

Ben looked into the night through the open door.

"It's not Eli, Noah," he told his son. "Not in the slightest."

The creature was taller than Ben, taller than anyone he'd ever met. Wider too, a lumbering giant of pure muscle racing towards the porch. But that wasn't the scariest thing. That honour was reserved for its head. Like the image on the wall, the thing charging down the path didn't have the head of a human being. It had the head of a giant boar.

"What is it with this place and pigs?" Ben yelled, peeling Noah from him to run for the entrance. Anna was already beside him as the creature reached the porch. They shoved at the door, only to be nearly thrown back as the monster struck the other side with a bellow and a snort.

Kaylee screamed as they slammed the door shut, pushing with preternatural strength neither had possessed five seconds before. The need to survive is a powerful thing. No, more than that. The need to protect.

Ben slid the heavy bolts at the top and bottom of the door into place, locking them in as the creature pounded furiously on the panelled wood. Strong as the latches appeared, they wouldn't hold for long.

"What *is* that?" Anna yelled, but Ben didn't answer. He was looking around for something, *anything*, to barricade the door. The stone font was too heavy to move, and he doubted the corpses would hinder whatever devil was trying to batter its way in. Ben reached instead for the nearest pew.

"Help me!"

Anna did as he asked, Ben catching hold of a carved animal on the end of the warped bench to haul the pew across the door. The squeal of wood against stone matched the wails of the monster outside and, when it was in place, Ben released his grip, realising he had been holding another boar, like the one Kaylee had found in the graveyard.

"We need more," Anna said as the pew rattled with another blow.

"There's no time," Ben said, turning on his heel to look around. "We need another way out."

"There isn't one. I looked, remember?"

When I *was the one trying to break in*, Ben thought. THWAM, THWAM, THWAM, THWAM, THWAM.

But there *was* another way out of the church. Straight ahead. Anna followed his gaze, looking down the littered aisle to the wooden screen that separated the congregation from the altar. And *above* that altar…

"You've got to be joking," Anna breathed as she realised what he was suggesting.

Ben was already running towards the screen. "I'm sure the Almighty will forgive us in the circumstances."

The towering window that had once dominated the chapel was already partially shattered, fragments of the ancient stained glass clinging stubbornly to the lead frames like jagged teeth. All it needed was a little encouragement. Ben snatched up a wooden message board that had once announced hymn numbers to the faithful and flung it, numbers and all, at the window. It arced clumsily in the air before striking the already damaged portrait of the Holy Family. The remaining glass exploded, the lead frame tumbling out into the rain as the monster howled all the louder.

"You didn't want to do that," said a weak voice to his right. "It won't like it."

Another kid, little more than a teenager, slumped on the other side of the oak screen. He was alive, but only just, his skin ashen even in the chancel's gloom, a bloody arm pressed tight against a deep gash in his torso.

"Do you know what that thing is?" Ben asked, pointing towards the door as Kaylee and Anna helped Noah hop up the aisle.

The teen barked a sharp laugh, coughing up blood in the process. "History student. Cursed with knowledge."

Ben wanted to shake the lad but stopped only at the thought of his intestines spilling over the floor like his friend at the door. Instead, he dropped down beside the kid, resting a hand on the boy's neck. His pulse was dangerously faint.

"What is it?" Ben repeated.

Red drool spilt down the teen's chin as he spoke: "Early churches like this needed protectors when they were built. They needed Grims."

"Protectors against what?"

"Attack? Devilry? It was supposed to be the spirit of the first parishioner buried in the churchyard, a kind of spectral watchman, but no one wanted to think of their loved ones being denied their rewards in heaven, so instead the builders slaughtered a hound to act as the Grim. And if they couldn't find a dog…"

Realisation, ridiculous and yet implacable, dawned on Ben as the poor lad choked on his own blood. "If they couldn't find a dog, they sacrificed a pig."

The boy nodded. "Or a boar. I told the others it wasn't a good idea to perform a ritual in an abandoned church. Never been deconsecrated, you see. Still… still protected."

The student opened his bloody hand to reveal a key on a bulky fob.

"You have a car," Ben said.

"A van." The kid nodded at the window. "Through the trees on the other side of the yard. Take it. Get out of here."

"We'll go together," Ben told him, snatching the keys from his sticky palm and standing to face his family as the creature continued to pound on the door. "Anna, you take Noah and Kaylee. I'll bring…"

He looked down at the student.

"Henry," the boy spluttered.

"I'll bring Henry."

"I can't," Anna said, shaking her head. "I mean, *we* can't. What do you expect us to do? Climb on the altar?"

"I've already smashed the window. We're probably going to hell anyway." He glanced down at his terrified children. "That was a joke, like the wolves, but seriously, no one in heaven or on earth is going to care as long as we get to that van."

He grabbed Anna's hand and closed her fingers around the keyring.

"Please!"

They locked eyes for a moment before she finally snapped into action.

"Okay, kids. We're leaving. Out the window."

"But what if it comes around the outside of the church?" Kaylee squealed. A good question. An intelligent question. Kaylee was the clever one, always had been. Ben wished that he'd given her more attention over the years.

"It's not going to come around the outside, sweetheart," Ben said calmly, putting himself between his family and the nave to glare down the aisle. "Because it's already in here."

At the other end of the church, the Grim glared back. In the fading glow of the overturned camping lamp, Ben could make out the coarse hair covering its monumental body. It stood on two legs like a man, but that was where the similarity ended. Clawed hands were curled into fists, gore dripping from its ragged tusks where it had eviscerated Henry and his foolish co-conspirators, its eyes glowing with unearthly fury. The bolts were still thrown, the pew still where they had dragged it, but the Grim was inside all the same. In the church, where it belonged, where they were the invaders.

"I'm sorry, Henry," Ben said, staring down the beast.

The teen shrugged, resigned to his fate. "I told them this was a mistake."

"Yeah," Ben said, grinning with determination. "I know all about mistakes. Go, Anna. I love you. I love you all!"

Ben heard his family clamber onto the altar and out of the window as the Grim threw back its shaggy head and bellowed in outrage. He didn't move as it surged towards him, tusks down low; didn't even flinch.

Susie would never believe any of this, if Anna and the kids got home – when they got home – but Ben didn't care. He was just like this monster. Finally.

Protecting his own.

Pontianak: An Origin Story

Christina Sng

IT RAINS the day my parents sell me to the old man. Tears from the heavens wash my old life away as my mother holds my hand and nods reassuringly at me. Father walks ahead of us, anxious to get to the meeting place.

They convince me it is a good thing. The Master is wealthy and will give me a comfortable life. Unsaid is how he will waive off Father's gambling debts. They think I don't know, but I do.

My stomach sinks when I see the old man. He is older than my father. Balding, bulbous, dressed up in rich clothes, with a cruel glint in his eyes. Despair hollows out my insides. My heart pounds wildly as I clutch my mother's hand. *No!* my gut screams. I look around frantically, but no one is listening.

The old man wears a moon-faced wax mask of pleasantry. Behind it, I sense an undercurrent of malignancy. His eyes narrow too fast and hide his pupils so I cannot read them. I do not trust him nor like him. And my parents want me to marry him? I physically cringe and pull backwards.

My father takes me from my mother and hands me over to the old man. "You will call him Master."

"No!" I shout, reaching for my mother.

My father hits my face with the back of his hand, stunning me. I stagger backwards, clutching my face, now burning.

"Please…" My mother gasps and pleads with him. But he slaps her as well. She cowers, as she always does.

He looms over me angrily. "You are a girl. You were born to be sold. This is all you are good for."

After this demonstration of 'control', he smiles, signalling for the old man to take me.

I look to the sky, begging the gods to take me away instead. But they don't.

Seething with hatred, I turn to my mother, beseeching her to help.

She shakes her head, tears mixing with the rain till I can't tell which are tears and which is rain.

My father grabs her arm and pulls her away, striding off. One blink, and they are gone.

Abandoned by my parents whom I believed loved me, I numbly let them go and follow the old man with the waxed face. As I trudge along down the path behind him, I realise my definition of love has changed. My parents do not love me, and perhaps never have. They have only ever seen me as a commodity, a piece of property, a thing to be traded or sold.

Master, as I am told to call him, says nothing to me. He occasionally turns to stare at me up and down like how my mother regards a fruit before she buys it or how my father considers a card before discarding it. Then, Master smiles, an expression that makes my skin crawl. I brace myself and start putting up walls.

The house is ornate and elaborate, filled with intricately carved objects and uncomfortable furniture. Everything sharp-cornered, even the fabrics. This is a house, not a home.

Master hands me over to two servants, no younger than me, who bow and usher me to my room. They place water and fruit on the table, and leave as quickly as they entered.

A moment to breathe… I collapse onto the bed and feel an acute pain in my heart, the memory of how my father hit me and how my mother let it happen still vivid in my mind. How they gave me away.

I think of my grandfather, who died two years ago. He loved me. Doted on me. Put me first. My wishes and my needs. I realise now this is what real love looks like. Not the lie of a life my parents put me through.

I think of Grandfather's last words as he held my hand on his deathbed. "Never let anyone put out your fire."

I promised him, "I won't."

Stirred by my grandfather's words, I get up to open the door. Locked! I shake the handles but they will not budge. Panicked, I try the window. It cracks an inch but not further. I call out, "Help! Please open the door!"

A couple of servant girls scurry by, glance at me, and run away. I keep crying for help.

A middle-aged woman peers through the gap. Simply dressed, hair in a loose bun, she looks at me with scared but kindly eyes.

"Shh," she says. "If he hears you, he will beat you."

Her eyes dart around anxiously before she rushes away.

That night, they come for me. Servants clothe me in an exquisite dress and tell me to smile because it is my wedding day. I let them. Thinking about my parents has sapped me of all my resolve.

The ceremony is brief but the celebrations loud and alcohol-fuelled. The stink of stale wine hangs in the air like a throng of lingering ghosts, while the sound of drunken cheering bores holes in my head. Mercifully, the servants usher me back to my room and remove my dress. They put me in a white nightgown and tell me to wait for Master.

He staggers in shortly after, reeking of alcohol, his moon face reflected in the light from outside. I back away from him, but he hits me hard across the face and pins me down. In these few minutes, I learn not to scream and hit, my face and body now bloodied and bruised from fighting back. When he is done, he leaves, grunting. I am wracked with a new kind of pain.

Gingerly, I get up and stumble past the pile of drunken guests in the hallway, leaving a trail of blood behind me, out the front door, past the grove of banana trees in the outer garden, and into the river. There, I wash myself clean to feel whole again. Ribbons of dark blood sail away to sea, taking what remains of Master with it.

Then, I let myself sink to the bottom of the river and look up into the sliver of moonlight piercing through the water. Is this what marriage is like? Becoming someone's property and treated like a *thing*? Hate wells in my heart and I cannot breathe. The weight crushing my chest demands I surface.

Air swells in my lungs. The moon watches me as I wade to the river's edge and walk to the banana grove. Amid the tall trees, I feel safe, reminded of my happy childhood climbing such trees. I touch each trunk, as if greeting old friends. They are the only allies I have in this world now.

And then my will crumbles and I collapse to the ground. The soft soil sinks, taking my shape. I press my hands into the earth and beg the gods to take me from this life. But nothing happens. I am all alone, lost and uncertain of how to live.

My grief overflows as I gingerly nurse each of my wounds, heart pounding to be freed from its cage. The hollowness in my gut leaves me curled up and weeping. A soft breeze runs its gentle fingers across my face. The trees whisper to me, *You will survive this. Bring the fire to your enemies*. Soothed, I slowly stand up. A new resolve crystallises in my mind. I will live. I will survive.

The sun peers over the horizon as I walk back to the house, bloodless.

* * *

Over the next few days, I realise I am not the only wife.

First Wife is an elderly relic dressed in elaborate garb, scoffing at anyone who will listen. I encountered her one day when she looked me up and down and retorted, "Such a tiny person. Will she survive giving birth?" Before I could respond, she strode by. Now, whenever I see her, I turn my nose at her and walk away.

Second Wife was the woman at my window.

She is middle-aged, a mouse of a woman who hides in her room most days. Master leaves her alone now as she is neither young, beautiful, nor compliant. She often walks in the garden alone, breathing deeply, clutching her belly as if communing with a lost child.

386

Her eyes resemble fish eyes, glazed and glassy. I think her mind is broken.

Third Wife is made of pure poison. Young, beautiful, and glamorous, she is always well-dressed and groomed, her makeup flawless and hair perfectly coiffed. When she speaks, her voice sounds like she has been gargling with razors. Unlike First Wife, she does not directly insult. Instead, her words manipulate, burrow under your skin, making you doubt yourself.

I am Fourth Wife.

* * *

In many ways, I should thank Third Wife. Master visits her for pleasure, while I am just a birthing machine, visited only when I am fertile. The servants chart my cycle like clockwork. I am also not a pleasant visit. Despite my earlier lesson, I refuse to succumb. I fight back, kicking and screaming, even when he beats me till I am bruised all over. He wins every time.

After each visit, I flee to the grove of banana trees and hide there, wracked with pain, my blood seeping into the soil. Then, I steep myself in the river, washing away every part of him still embedded in my flesh.

Eventually, I become pregnant. Master left me alone even when it was just a rumour, so desperate is he for a son. None of his other wives have given him one.

The servants pamper me for the first time and feed me well. I learn from them that Third Wife is barren and jealous of Master's younger wives, all of whom died under mysterious circumstances and are buried in unmarked graves beneath the banana grove.

After a loud and angry fight between Third Wife and Master, a new girl joins the household. She is around my age, small with frightened eyes, a pale narrow face, and long black hair. I barely meet eyes with her before she is shuffled into her room.

The wedding ceremony the next day is brief but elaborate. That night, I cover my ears to block out the screaming.

In the morning, I wake up to screams of another kind. The servants found the new bride swinging from a tree outside her room. Waif-like in her bloody nightgown, arms limp, long hair covering half her thin, pallid face, she wears an expression of serenity and relief.

Master storms out of the room, disgust painted all over his face. "Stupid girl! I paid so much for her!" He stalks back to his own quarters.

That is all we are to him. Pieces of property to be bought and sold, our parents complicit in this crime.

Rage churns in my stomach as I walk up to the girl. She is even tinier than me. I touch her hand.

She looks down at me, eyes bright and alive. Her lips part, and the rosebud whispers, "Justice" before she goes limp again, hair falling like curtains to shroud her face from the sunlight.

Did I imagine it?

A medicine man pushes me roughly aside to pray over her, to tell her to go to the afterlife and not haunt this house. After he finishes his chanting, he hammers a nail into the back of her head. "So she will return in the next life as an obedient wife," he says, winking at me as he leaves. I am too horrified to respond. The servants collect her body and take her away.

The next few months are discomfortingly idyllic. I eat, exercise, and take care of myself and my unborn child. I do not see Master or the other wives, except for Third Wife who has taken to lingering near me, her eyes darkly envious as she stares at my growing belly, thinking I do not notice.

I spend my days wandering by the river and the banana grove, thinking of my grandfather and Fifth Wife. Most of all, I talk and sing to my child and dream of a better life for us. The banana pups grow, ready for harvest, as do I.

On a cool, windy day, my water breaks, and I stumble, clutching my belly all the way to the house. Servants usher me to my room and lay me down, wiping my face with cool, wetted cloths. Excruciating cramps wrack my body for an entire day. I am exhausted by the time my baby is born, entering the world in a quiet gush out of me.

"It's a boy!" A jubilant chorus resounds in the room. Master appears, nods at his newborn son and exits the room without another word.

My baby returns to me and nurses contently, curled up in the crook of my arms. Looking at him, I feel my life is complete. My heart fills with an abundant, overwhelming love. I know I will do everything in my power to keep him safe and happy always.

* * *

The next few years pass in a blur. My son's first gurgle. His first smile. When he calls me "Mama." His first steps. His long embraces in my arms and running to me, grabbing my legs.

Third Wife scoops him up one day and takes him from me. "He is mine now," she says.

He screams, kicking her, and she smacks him on his bottom, silencing him.

I grab at her, but servants hold me back.

She laughs, walking away with him in her arms, his heartbroken, terrified eyes burning in my mind.

"Let her go. You will still see him in the nursery and he will still know you as his mother," one of the servants whispers in my ear.

That night, Master visits me and I want to die.

"You will give me another son," he says, tearing my tired, beaten body apart.

I search for my son the next day but there is no sign of him in the house. Frantic, I run to the banana grove and to the river. Then, back to the house.

"Who are you looking for?" Second Wife peers out from her window, her eyes harried and dark.

"My son!" I blurt out.

"They take your children away here," Second Wife tells me. "They took my daughter away."

At that moment, Third Wife walks by with my son. He sees me and his eyes brighten. Shaking off her hand, he runs into my open arms. I pick him up and cuddle him.

Second Wife screams and points to Third Wife. "They took my daughter and look what he has done to her!"

The truth dawns on me and I clutch my son, horrified.

Third Wife stares at Second Wife with unadulterated hatred, her shameful secret spilled out for the world to see. Servants passing by stop to watch.

"Lies! They should have killed you years ago for the lies you tell," Third Wife curses at Second Wife.

"What kind of monster are you?" I shout at her. "To damn your own mother to death and to marry your own father!"

Unhinged by the gathering crowd, Third Wife staggers back to her quarters.

I return to Second Wife's window as the crowd dissipates.

"Is this true?" I have to ask.

"Yes," she cries. "First Wife took her from me when she was just a child. She was such a beautiful little girl. He used her till she became barren and brainwashed her to hate me. I was too crippled with grief to ever leave, hoping one day she would acknowledge me as her mother. But I think the shame consumed her and she accepted her own role in this."

I have no words.

Second Wife vanishes for a moment and returns with a small satin pouch, stuffing it into my pocket. "Take this gold and flee with your son. It is too late for me, but not too late for you."

"You!" Master's loud voice booms. He strides to me, eyes bulging. Two servants trail behind him.

He backhands me so hard that I fall to the ground, my child flying from my arms, landing with a loud crack. I see my son in the distance, blood gushing from his head.

He reaches for me, his tiny hand wavering. "I love you, Mama," he says before closing his eyes forever.

"*No!*" I scream.

Master backpedals. He stares at us on the ground, then grabs me by the neck. I turn to look at my son, my hand scrambling for his. His face is the last thing I remember before I die.

* * *

I awake, breathless, choking, soil in my mouth and in my eyes.

Stop. Calm. Think, I command myself.

Holding my breath, I pull my arms toward me, then push upward. The cool breeze curls its fingers around my hands, rising in the air like saplings. On my left, I feel the sturdy trunk of a banana tree. My arms close around it and I slowly pull myself out of the shallow grave.

The image of my son lying in a pool of his own blood returns in vivid colour. Grief grips my heart with an iron fist. Tears flood my eyes, clouding my vision, but I can still see two more mounds beside mine.

Desperate, I scramble to the smaller one and dig. I uncover his face, his hands, and pull his body from the ground. He looks so peaceful, like he is just sleeping. I press him against me, telling him I love him and I always will.

Time stands still. Around me, the blanket of night falls and I fall asleep with it, my son in my arms.

I dream we are by the river together, feet dipped in the cool water. He regales me with stories about adventures with his friends at school and how he loves math and drawing. Time shifts and he is now grown up, telling me about the girl he loves and how they will marry soon and give me many grandchildren to love. Then, we are old and he is holding my hand, telling me what a wonderful life he has led and how happy he has been to have me as his mother, always loving him and protecting him, keeping him safe and alive.

I open my eyes and there he is, a child again, sleeping beside me. But he will never wake up again and live the wonderful life he was meant to live. Because of his father.

A dark cloud engulfs me. Rage fills my heart until it feels it is about to burst.

I leave my son by the banana tree and dig up the adult-sized grave beside his.

Second Wife! Her face is battered and bruised, and in death, she seems more shrunken than she was in life, as if the ground seeped all the vigour out of her when it held her in its cold embrace. But the earth did not kill her. Master did.

I touch my pocket. The gold she gave me is still there.

Second Wife's existence is a cautionary tale. I remind myself to unfreeze and leave this place, not be trapped by my own fear and inertia as she was. However, I will not leave another girl to his mercy.

I hug Second Wife's frail body and rebury her. Beside her, I lay my son to rest, promising she will look after him now.

I stand up and see the two of them hovering above their graves, hand in hand, nodding at me. Behind them, Fifth Wife appears and takes my little boy's other hand. My bare feet feel a charge of electricity as I walk back to the house, my fury fuelling a new kind of fire.

The house is silent, lit only by moonlight. In the kitchen, I light several branches with fire.

Striding to Master's room, I see glimpses of my son and Second Wife waving at me, alongside girls my age in white nightgowns, holding their hands, their long black hair billowing in the wind.

I kick Master's door open and throw the flaming branches at him as he stirs from sleep. He screams, writhing in fire.

Servants arrive and stare in frozen terror at the growing flames engulfing Master, until he is a charred blackened figure, steam rising from the ashes.

They look at me with frightened eyes.

"But you're dead..." one says.

"And I rose from the grave," I reply.

From behind the crowd, I see a few heads nodding. Second Wife's and Fifth Wife's servants.

They were there when Master hit me and my son with the killing blow. *The shallow graves...*

"Tell people this is what happens to evil men," I say. "That the ghost of the banana trees will come for them."

"The Pontianak," one whispers as they part to let me walk through.

I return to the graves to say a final goodbye. I will not go far, just far enough for people to forget what I look like so I may return one day.

Now I have work to do, to instil fear and terror in evil men so that what was done to me and Master's other wives will never happen again. It all begins with a whisper.

The story spreads – of the household where a master had many wives, some of whom were far too young, and one, his own daughter. And how one of his young wives returned from the dead as the Pontianak to bring vengeance to the house.

As it always does with whispers, the Pontianak's origin shifts to one where she is a woman who died in childbirth. She returns to disembowel her cheating husband, only to be tamed by a needle nailed into the back of her neck, whereupon she becomes a 'good' wife again, presumably brought back to life. I know where that story came from.

With time, it evolves. The Pontianak is now a woman who died while giving birth to a stillborn child and returns to take revenge on unsuspecting men. I have no doubt this version will change again as the powerful shape the narrative over the ages.

The story becomes myth and the myth becomes legend.

Wherever I go now, I hear whispers of the Pontianak. If they have not heard of her, I remember to share a whisper I heard from another community about her true story.

Fear shrinks households from multiple wives to four, then two, and finally, one. Laws enact to prevent child marriages. Soon, it is shameful to have more than one wife. Incest is maligned and illegal. My work is finally done.

I return to my son's grave. Dandelions grow atop his mound and wave at me.

In the distance, the old house is now in ruins. Although other communities have cut their banana groves to the ground, this one still stands. Perhaps it is the ghosts who protect it.

I look up to see my little boy standing there with Second Wife holding his hand. Fifth Wife holds the other. They are smiling. He runs to me and embraces me.

Now we will be together forever.

Ghost Land of Giants

Linda D. Addison

You, the land larcenist, looking for treasure
in rocky soil years ago, arriving at first light,
    digging sinking holes, hoping for gold,
    waking us from our long slumber, in
    deep tunnels beneath the valley of sand
    dunes, salt flats, rugged rock formations.

You, tumbled into a cave of the dried bodies
of our ancient ones, followed the caverns,
    touched objects we left for their journey,
    called them *giants* as they towered over your
    bodies, with gold not found, greedy for fame,
    you left to gather others to see your discovery.

This land, our land, of constantly shifting sand,
reburied your uncovered breach, honoring our
      ancestors, leaving only you to search for
      another way down. We opened the ground,
      took you into our deepest caverns, where no one
      heard your screams, to taste you, learn you.

This land, the People's land, chosen for its extremes,
a safer place for our settlements than green land
      near flowing water, we knew you would bring
      wasteful consumption, endless hunger for all
      things, we pass the poem song to our offspring
      of blood actions hidden behind your promises.

As moon rise partners with stars to bring night's
curtain, do not fear People of the Land you can see
      we, the giants, wait in the growing shadows of
      vast canyons, jagged rock walls to chew your bones,
      to decipher the insane animal you are, delivering
      nonstop death to Earth and living beings on it.

About the Authors

Neil Gaiman is the author of such diverse *New York Times* bestsellers as *Norse Mythology, Coraline, The Ocean at the End of the Lane, The Graveyard Book*, and *American Gods*. He is the recipient of the Newbery and Carnegie Medals, and many Hugo, Nebula, World Fantasy, and Will Eisner Awards. Neil has adapted many of his works to television series, including *Good Omens* and *The Sandman*. He is a Goodwill Ambassador for the UN Refugee Agency UNHCR and Professor in the Arts at Bard College.

John Connolly is author of the Charlie Parker mysteries, *The Book of Lost Things*, the Samuel Johnson novels for young adults and, with his partner, Jennifer Ridyard, co-author of the *Chronicles of the Invaders*. John Connolly's debut – *Every Dead Thing* – introduced the character of Private Investigator Charlie Parker, and swiftly launched him right into the front rank of thriller writers. All his subsequent novels have been *Sunday Times* bestsellers, and he has sold more than 8 million copies in English alone. He was the winner of the 2016 CWA Short Story Dagger for '*On the Anatomization of* *an Unknown Man* (1637) by Frans Mier' from *Night Music: Nocturnes Vol 2*. In 2007 he was awarded the *Irish Post* Award for Literature. He was the first non-American writer to win the US Shamus Award and the first Irish writer to win an Edgar Award. *Books To Die For*, which he edited with Declan Burke, was the winner of the 2013 Anthony, Agatha and Macavity Awards for Best Non-Fiction work. John writes regularly for newspapers, hosts a radio show on RTE and divides his time between Dublin and Portland, Maine.

Jen Williams is an award-winning author from London. Her Copper Cat and Winnowing Flame trilogies have been nominated for British Fantasy Awards several times, with *The Ninth Rain* and *The Bitter Twins* each winning the Robert Holdstock Award for Best Fantasy Novel. Her debut crime novel *Dog Rose Dirt* was published in 2021, and Jen had two new novels out in 2023: *Talonsister*, a return to fantasy published by Titan, and *Games for Dead Girls*, a true-crime-inspired horror novel, published by HarperVoyager. She's also partly responsible for the creation of the Super Relaxed Fantasy Club and is partial to mead, if you're buying.

Adam L.G. Nevill was born in Birmingham, England, in 1969 and grew up in England and New Zealand. He is an author of horror fiction. Of his novels, *The Ritual*, *Last Days*, *No One Gets Out Alive* and *The Reddening* were all winners of the August Derleth Award for Best Horror Novel. He has also published three collections of short stories, with *Some Will Not Sleep* winning the British Fantasy Award for Best Collection, 2017. Imaginarium adapted *The Ritual* and *No One Gets Out Alive* into feature films and more of his work is currently in development for the screen. The author lives in Devon, England. More information about the author and his books is available at: www.adamlgnevill.com

Lee Murray is a multi-award-winning author-editor, essayist, poet, and screenwriter from Aotearoa-New Zealand. A *USA Today* bestselling author, Shirley Jackson and five-time Bram Stoker Awards® winner, she is an NZSA Honorary Literary Fellow, a Grimshaw Sargeson Fellow, and 2023 NZSA Laura Solomon Cuba Press Prize winner. leemurray.info

Katie Young is a writer of dark fiction and poetry. Her work appears in various anthologies including collections by Shortwave Publishing, Cemetery Gates Media, Brigids Gate Press, Crystal Lake, Haunt Publishing, Dark Dispatch, Scott J. Moses, Nyx Publishing, Ghost Orchid Press, and Fox Spirit Books. Her story, 'Lavender Tea', was selected by Zoe Gilbert for inclusion in the Mechanic Institute Review's Summer Folk Festival 2019. She lives in west London with her partner and an angry cat.

Stephen Volk created BBCTV's notorious 'Halloween hoax' *Ghostwatch,* ITV's paranormal drama series *Afterlife* and the crime/supernatural thriller *Midwinter of the*

Spirit based on the book by Phil Rickman. His other screenplays include *The Awakening* (2011), William Friedkin's *The Guardian* and Ken Russell's *Gothic* starring Natasha Richardson as Mary Shelley. He is a two-time British Fantasy Award winner and the author of four collections of short stories: *Dark Corners*, *Monsters in the Heart*, *The Parts We Play* and *Lies of Tenderness*. His acclaimed *The Dark Masters Trilogy* features Peter Cushing, Alfred Hitchcock and Dennis Wheatley as protagonists, while his latest book, *Under a Raven's Wing*, sees Sherlock Holmes and Poe's master detective Dupin investigating bizarre crimes in 1870s Paris. www.stephenvolk.net

Benjamin Spada is a dedicated taco aficionado, self-described 'Professor of Batmanology', proud Fil-Am and lumpia enthusiast, and the author of the award-winning Black Spear series of military thriller novels. After making a career in the military, he pursued his lifelong passion for writing and spinning of stories by drawing upon his own real-world experience serving alongside larger than life personalities in uniform. Readers interested in following more of Cole West's missions can find his debut in *FNG* and its follow-up *The Warmaker*.

H.R. Laurence grew up in North Yorkshire, and now works in the film industry in London. His weird fiction and sword & sorcery has appeared in multiple magazines and anthologies, including *Old Moon Quarterly*, *Broadswords and Blasters*, and *Heroic Fantasy Quarterly*.

405

Alison Littlewood's first book, *A Cold Season*, was selected for the Richard and Judy Book Club. Other titles include *Mistletoe*, *The Hidden People*, *The Crow Garden* and *The Unquiet House*. She also wrote *The Other Lives of Miss Emily White* and *The Cottingley Cuckoo*, as A.J. Elwood. She has won the Shirley Jackson Award for short fiction and her tales have been published in collections including *A Curious Cartography*, *The Flowering* and *Quieter Paths*. Alison lives in a house of creaking doors and crooked walls in deepest darkest Yorkshire, England.

B. Zelkovich writes Speculative Fiction, anything from dragon hunting and space whales to demon-dealing and ghost tales. She likes to explore human emotions in very inhuman situations. When she isn't escaping through her imagination, she escapes into the wonders of the Pacific Northwest with her spouse and their four-legged son, Simon.

Helen Grant writes Gothic novels and short supernatural stories. Her most recent novels are the Dracula Society's Children of the Night Award-winning *Too Near The Dead* (2021) and *Jump Cut* (2023), about a notorious lost movie, *The Simulacrum*. Some of her recent short fiction includes 'The Professor of Ontography', inspired by an imaginary academic title created by M.R. James, and 'Nábrók', based on an unpleasant piece of Icelandic mythology. Helen lives in rural Scotland, and when not writing, she likes to explore abandoned mansions and swim in freezing lochs.

Kathryn Healy is a horror and fantasy author, as well as a writer for the 'Tale Foundry' Youtube channel. Her work has been featured in *December Tales II* (Curious Blue Press), *Elegant Literature Magazine*, and *Creepy* Podcast. She can be found online at kathrynhealy.com, or in person wherever haunted antiques are sold.

V. Castro is a two-time Bram Stoker Award-nominated Mexican American writer from San Antonio, Texas now residing in the UK. She writes horror, erotic horror, and science fiction. Her books include *The Haunting of Alejandra*, *Alien: Vasquez*, *Rebel Moon* (the film novelisations), *Mestiza Blood*, *The Queen of the Cicadas*, *Out of Aztlan*, *Las Posadas*, and *Goddess of Filth*. Her forthcoming novel is *Immortal Pleasures* from Del Rey.

New York Times Bestseller **Cavan Scott** is the creator of *Shadow Service*, *The Ward*, *Dead Seas* and *Sleep Terrors*. A lead story architect for Lucasfilm's hugely successful multimedia initiative, *Star Wars: The High Republic*, Cavan has written comics for Marvel, DC, Dark Horse, IDW, Legendary, *2000AD* and more. He is currently developing several new properties for television and film and is creative director of Strange Matter, the production company he founded with fellow *Star Wars* writer George Mann in 2019. A former magazine editor, Cavan lives in the UK with his wife and daughters. His lifelong passions include folklore, audio drama, the music of David Bowie and scary movies. He owns far too much LEGO.

Christina Sng is a three-time Bram Stoker Award®-winning poet, writer, editor, essayist, and artist. Her work appears in numerous venues worldwide, including *Interstellar Flight Magazine*, *New Myths*, *Penumbric*, *Southwest Review*, and *The Washington Post*. Christina currently serves as Vice President of the Science Fiction & Fantasy Poetry Association. Visit her at christinasng.com and connect @christinasng.

Linda D. Addison is a five-time recipient of the HWA Bram Stoker Award®, including for *The Place of Broken Things* and *How To Recognize A Demon Has Become Your Friend*, recipient of HWA Lifetime Achievement Award, HWA Mentor of the Year and SFPA Grand Master of Fantastic Poetry. Her site: LindaAddisonWriter.com.

About the Illustrator

Oliver Hurst (Frontispiece and Cover Detail) graduated from Falmouth College of Arts in 2006 with a degree in Illustration. He has produced artwork for various publications, including the *Financial Times*, *Country Life* and The Folio Society. He paints in oils and his work is inspired by nineteenth- and twentieth-century painters. He lives and works in Bath and his website is oliverhurst.com.

About the Editors

Paul Kane is the award-winning (including the British Fantasy Society's Legends of FantasyCon Award 2022), bestselling author and editor of over a hundred books – such as the Arrowhead trilogy (gathered together in the sellout *Hooded Man* omnibus, revolving around a post-apocalyptic version of Robin Hood), *The Butterfly Man and Other Stories*, *Hellbound Hearts*, *Wonderland* (a Shirley Jackson Award finalist) and *Pain Cages* (an Amazon #1 bestseller). His non-fiction books include *The Hellraiser Films and Their Legacy* and *Voices in the Dark*, and his genre journalism has appeared in the likes of *SFX*, *Rue Morgue* and *DeathRay*. He has been a Guest at Alt.Fiction five times, was a Guest at the first SFX Weekender, at Thought Bubble in 2011, Derbyshire Literary Festival and Off the Shelf in 2012, Monster Mash and Event Horizon in 2013, Edge-Lit in 2014 and 2018, HorrorCon, HorrorFest and Grimm Up North in 2015, The Dublin Ghost Story Festival and Sledge-Lit in 2016, IMATS Olympia and Celluloid Screams in 2017, Black Library Live and the UK Ghost Story Festival in 2019 and 2023, plus the WordCrafter virtual event 2021 – where he delivered the keynote speech – as well as being a panellist at FantasyCon and the World Fantasy Convention, and a fiction judge at the Sci-Fi London festival. A former British Fantasy Society Special Publications Editor, he has also served as co-chair for the UK chapter of The Horror Writers Association and co-chaired ChillerCon UK in May 2022.

His work has been optioned and adapted for the big and small screen, including for US network primetime television, and his novelette 'Men of the Cloth' has just been turned into a feature by Loose Canon/Hydra Films, starring Barbara Crampton (*Re-Animator*, *You're Next*): *Sacrifice*, released by Epic Pictures/101 Films. His audio work includes the full cast drama adaptation of *The Hellbound Heart* for Bafflegab, starring Tom Meeten (*The Ghoul*), Neve McIntosh (*Doctor Who*) and Alice Lowe (*Prevenge*), and the *Robin of Sherwood* adventure *The Red Lord* for Spiteful Puppet/ITV narrated by Ian Ogilvy (*Return of the Saint*). He has also contributed to the Warhammer 40k universe for Games Workshop. Paul's latest novels are *Lunar* (set to be turned into a feature film), the YA story *The Rainbow Man* (as P.B. Kane), the sequels to *RED – Blood RED* and *Deep RED*, all collected in an omnibus edition from Hellbound – the award-winning hit *Sherlock Holmes & the Servants of Hell*, *Before* (an Amazon Top 5 dark fantasy bestseller), *Arcana* and *The Storm*. In addition he writes thrillers for HQ/HarperCollins as P.L. Kane, the first of which, *Her Last Secret* and *Her Husband's Grave* (a sellout on both Amazon and Waterstones.com), came out in 2020, with *The Family Lie* released the following year.

Paul lives in Derbyshire, UK, with his wife **Marie O'Regan**. Find out more at his site www.shadow-writer.co.uk which has featured Guest Writers such as Stephen King, Charlaine Harris, Robert Kirkman, Catriona Ward, Dean Koontz, Olivie Blake and Guillermo del Toro. He can also be found @ PaulKaneShadow on X, and paul.kane.376 on Instagram.

Marie O'Regan is a British Fantasy Award and Shirley Jackson Award-nominated author and editor, based in Derbyshire. She was awarded the British Fantasy Society 'Legends of FantasyCon' award in 2022. Her first collection, *Mirror Mere*, was published in 2006 by Rainfall Books; her second, *In Times of Want*, came out in September 2016 from Hersham Horror Books. Her third, *The Last Ghost and Other Stories*, was published by Luna Press early in 2019. Her short fiction has appeared in a number of genre magazines and anthologies in the UK, US, Canada, Italy and Germany, including *Best British Horror 2014*, *Great British Horror: Dark Satanic Mills* (2017), and *The Mammoth Book of Halloween Stories*. Her novella, *Bury Them Deep*, was published by Hersham Horror Books in September 2017. She was shortlisted for the British Fantasy Society Award for Best Short Story in 2006, Best Anthology in 2010 (*Hellbound Hearts*) and 2012 (*The Mammoth Book of Ghost Stories by Women*). She was also shortlisted for the Shirley Jackson Award for Best Anthology in 2020 (*Wonderland*). Her genre journalism has appeared in magazines like *The Dark Side*, *Rue Morgue* and *Fortean Times,* and her interview book with prominent figures from the horror genre, *Voices in the*

Dark, was released in 2011. An essay on *The Changeling* was published in PS Publishing's *Cinema Macabre*, edited by Mark Morris. She is co-editor of the bestselling *Hellbound Hearts*, *The Mammoth Book of Body Horror*, *A Carnivàle of Horror – Dark Tales from the Fairground*, *Exit Wounds*, *Wonderland*, *Cursed*, *Twice Cursed*, *The Other Side of Never* and *In These Hallowed Halls*, as well as the charity anthology *Trickster's Treats #3*, plus editor of the bestselling anthologies *The Mammoth Book of Ghost Stories by Women* and *Phantoms*. Her first novel, the internationally bestselling *Celeste*, was published in February 2022. Marie was Chair of the British Fantasy Society from 2004 to 2008, and Co-Chair of the UK Chapter of the Horror Writers Association from 2015 to 2022. She was also co-chair of ChillerCon UK in 2022. Visit her website at marieoregan.net. She can be found on X @Marie_O_Regan and Instagram @marieoregan8101.

Acknowledgements

And now for the important bit – our opportunity to say thank you. Firstly, to all the authors for their contributions, to Nick, Gillian and all of the team at Flame Tree for getting behind this one and their efforts on our behalf. Finally, thanks to our respective families, without whom, etc.

Beyond & Within

THE FLAME TREE Beyond & Within short story collections bring together tales of myth and imagination by modern and contemporary writers, carefully selected by anthologists, and sometimes featuring short stories and fiction from a single author. Overall, the series presents a wide range of diverse and inclusive voices, often writing folkloric-inflected short fiction, but always with an emphasis on the supernatural, science fiction, the mysterious and the speculative. The books themselves are gorgeous, with foiled covers, printed edges and published only in hardcover editions, offering a lifetime of reading pleasure.

FLAME TREE FICTION

A wide range of new and classic fiction, from myth to
modern stories, with tales from the distant past to the
far future, including short story anthologies, Collector's
Editions, Collectable Classics, Gothic Fantasy collections
and Epic Tales of mythology and folklore.

•

Available at all good bookstores, and online
at flametreepublishing.com